BOULEVARD

BOULEVARD

BILL GUTTENTAG

PEGASUS BOOKS
NEW YORK

BOULEVARD

Pegasus Books LLC
80 Broad Street, 5th Floor
New York, NY 10004

First Pegasus Books edition 2010

Interior design by Maria Fernandez

Library of Congress Cataloging-in-Publication Data is available.

ISBN: 978-1-60598-077-5

10 9 8 7 6 5 4 3 2 1

Printed in the United States of America
Distributed by W. W. Norton & Company

For Marina, Misha, Sasha

1

Casey

Casey jammed her shoulder into a heavy oak door, and a moment later was running down a steep, wide driveway. Her frayed backpack bounced on her shoulder. She was already out of breath. Dawn was breaking. Punching out against the sky were bright red-orange neon letters—*Chateau Marmont*. Casey froze. This wasn't the smartest thing to be doing: she was out in the open, and it was getting light enough for anyone to see her—a fifteen-year-old in a ripped leather jacket running from a hotel for movie stars. She looked around. But nobody was out. Even the Sunset Strip— the Sunset Strip was quiet. Had to be the quietest she had ever seen it. The street kids, the punker kids, the hip hop kids, the college kids, the glam girls, the tourists and the kids who roll the tourists, the whores, the johns, the strippers and the bachelor party assholes who drool over the strippers, the junkies, the hustlers and their dates, the baby transvestites, the do-gooders with their stupid sandwiches, the religious jerks and their pamphlets, the maps-to-the stars-homes Latino guys, the wannabe rock stars, wannabe rappers, wannabe models, wannabe starlets, the pimps, the dealers, crackheads, the LAPD, the LA Sheriff, the CHP cops—even the street cleaner trucks—they were all gone. What time was it? Maybe 4:30 or 5:00. Amazing. For once, something was going right.

She hurried down the hill. Voices. Shit. Voices. She thought it was deserted. Two Mexican guys from room service were sitting on the lawn beside the driveway having a smoke. If they turned, they would see her. Casey looked for a gap in the tall hedge on the other side of the drive. None. She looked ahead and behind. Still none. But she pushed through the hedge anyway, the branches grabbing her hair, scratching her face like a rake. On the other side was a garage with a parked pickup. She huddled next to the truck and could hear the waiters as if they were beside her. God, they got those guys trained well. The whole world is asleep and they still go outside to smoke. How much longer till they finish? She glanced at the sky—still lighter—and then she saw her reflection in the pickup's window. She hadn't looked at her face carefully in a long time—now she examined every pore. Her brown eyes were bloodshot. There were droplets of clear water around them. Across her nose were specks of red—but they were only freckles and what was left of freckles fading away. She pushed back long brown hair that fell past her shoulders, and ran her fingers through it. Her hair was wet in places, but she was pretty sure it was only water and sweat.

She could hear everything the waiters said. It was all in Spanish but somehow she knew they were talking about soccer. Soccer. Her life was crashing and the biggest thing these guys have on their minds is some soccer game. She thought, what about a trade? I'll give you that last couple of hours of my life if you give me the last couple of couple of hours of yours. No way? You have any friends who want to make the deal? Is there anyone in the whole fucking city who would make this deal? Soccer. The sky was getting lighter by the second. How much longer could they talk about soccer? On and on. And the score—uno, uno. Who cares? . . . She looked at her feet and then back at the sky . . . But then, they had said all they had to say about the stupid game and went inside.

She pushed back through the hedge—easier now that she had blazed the trail—and raced down the rest of the driveway towards the Strip. Casey took one last glance back. It wasn't completely deserted after all. There was the Marlboro man, behind the Chateau sign—forty—fifty feet high, holding a rope in one hand and a smoke in the other, his body cut out against the electric blue dawn sky. When she got here almost a year ago, she remembered seeing the Marlboro man for the first time and thinking how great the billboard was. He stood high, way high above the Strip. He *owned* the Strip. How many times had she been on the street, hating the street, hating everything about the street, and then looked up to see the Marlboro man. Calm, enjoying his smoke—*nothing* was gonna get to this dude. The street was *his*. And now with everybody in LA asleep but her and Pelés number one and two, the Marlboro man watched over the city like some kinda cool god.

2

It was the most unbelievable chair. So, *so* comfortable. Made of green velvet that rubbed against her back, the chair felt so good. Big, wide arm rests. The whole thing just wrapped around you. Casey got lucky, and it was hers without a wait. Whoever invented Starbucks ought to get some kind of medal. And this was the best one on the planet. Down on Santa Monica Boulevard, it had two of the green chairs, a couch, and lots of magazines and papers lying around. The place was filled with guys from the Sports Connection across the street who had already finished working out. *Finished*—this early. God, they looked buff. Big muscles, little shirts. All gay. But that's why Paul loved this place so much. And the girls, they were buff too. Tons of people come to Hollywood thinking they got the looks and bods to be movie stars, but watching the girls come here after their workouts, if they weren't on TV or something, they should be, Casey thought. Even the guys at the counter were awesome too. They smiled at her, told her to have a nice day, treated her decently. One kid who worked here, and who she used to see at the bus stop in a UCLA sweatshirt, called her his prettiest customer. Who's gonna complain about that? She called it *Maui* because it was so great here. The other kids didn't buy it, thought she was crazy. But the reason was, you come to Starbucks by yourself, you can disappear into your great green chair and everyone leaves you alone. Come with a pack of street kids, and you get different looks from the cuties at the counter.

Casey sipped her coffee. It was hot, good. She flipped through an *Elle*, but there was no way she could read now. Instead she curled her legs underneath her. She could have stayed in the chair all day, all night, all week. Just looking at the guys and girls going in and out of the gym, stopping for their coffees and going off to school, or their jobs, or wherever real people go. Freeze the clock. Stop time. Just sit here. Here. Forever. But even in Maui, there's a limit on how long you can stay . . .

3

Joey's on Hollywood Boulevard, right in the center of it all, didn't have any great green chairs. It had a bunch of hard plastic booths. When Casey pulled the heavy glass door open, the smell of grease was everywhere. The windows were caked with so much dust and grime that when you wrote your name on one with your finger, it stayed for months. There was always a mile-long line to get some of their excellent fries, the location was cool, and they didn't chase you away—at least not usually. Everyone came here. Right now there were ten kids, maybe more. All hanging out. Slowly sipping coffee, sharing a cup between two, or even three. Later, there might be some money for something better. As Casey stepped through the doorway, she felt herself shaking. They were going to see right through her. Know the real 4-1-1. *Back off, and come back again later*. But behind her, she heard Jumper.

"Hey. Where were you?"

"I couldn't get back."

Jumper was nineteen, with short black hair, and despite all the shit, he smiled more than anyone she ever met. He was tall and quick, a distant echo of the junior high swim team captain he'd been a lifetime ago.

"You okay?" he said.

Casey prayed he wouldn't ask any more. "Yeah."

A second later, Dream flew in the door behind Jumper and dropped her arms over Casey's shoulders.

"Got a buck for fries?"

Casey reached into her pocket. She grabbed whatever was there and pulled it out. A wad of bills.

"Woah!" Dream said.

"Damn, Casey!" Jumper said.

Shit. Nice move.

"Remember your friends, girl!" Dream said with a big smile.

Casey slid her a twenty, and Dream practically skipped for the counter. Then she stopped. Turned around.

"How come you wasn't back?"

"Had a date."

Twirling the bill over and over, Dream said, "I guess so."

Dream had pancakes, and when you ordered the pancakes, Joey let you have the syrup bottle to go with it. The pancakes were floating in syrup. Casey thought, with a pencil and a napkin you could make a sail for them. Dream was also working on a plate of fries. She was thin like Jumper, had long curly hair and caramel-colored skin. Dream was from New Orleans and always talked about how much better the food was back home. But seeing her digging in now, this looked like the gourmet meal of a lifetime. Jumper had the Woodsman's Special: pancakes, eggs, sausage, bacon, toast, home fries, orange juice, coffee. Woodsman's Special—what a joke. There weren't any woods around here for a hundred miles. Someone told Casey the guy who owned the restaurant before Joey used to be a hunter and that's where the name came from. In Seattle, lots of people hunted. On the Boulevard, if you see someone with a gun and he's not a cop, you better run 'cause you can bet your ass it ain't a deer he's looking to shoot.

Casey couldn't eat. She sipped coffee from a styrofoam cup. Watching Jumper eat, made her feel a little better. But then Dog-Face showed up. He was six-three, wiry, and with tatts up one arm and down the other. He grabbed a handful of fries from Jumper, practically ripping them out of his mouth, and slid into the booth beside Dream.

"Assholes. Assholes. Assholes," Dog-Face said.

"You got a real gift for words there," Jumper said.

"Hey. They're assholes. Alright?"

"Who, Doggie?"

"Fucking cops. Giving everyone on the Boulevard shit."

"Sure they're giving shit," Dream said, "it was the mayor's best buddy or something who got taxed."

Casey stared into her coffee, stirring it around with a straw.

"And that gives them the right to fuck with everyone on the street? There's gotta be a million cops out there now. Everywhere you look, there's another fucking cop."

Casey felt it in her stomach. She kept moving the straw . . .

"Doggie, you're the mayor—you gonna let some street scum tax your buddy and not do nothing about it?" Jumper said. "That's really gonna happen."

"Man, it's ten in the morning!"

"It's *appalling*," Jumper said as if mortally offended, "At least wait until lunch before giving us shit."

"I didn't kill the asshole. And I got two cops asking me all this bullshit like I did."

"What planet you on, man? I see you on the Boulevard, you're the *first* one I ask."

Casey stared over at the counter, anything to avoid being sucked in. By the window, Joey was lighting a cigarette and at the same time reading the sports while he filled the coffee maker. Passing right by Joey's window, was a cruiser. A minute later, another one.

"Chill, Doggie," Dream threw in between bites. "They'll get the guy who done it and this shit'll be over."

"Got that right," said Jumper. "One thing I learned in County—crime makes you stupid. Look at O.J. Leaves his glove, his blood, his hat, everything."

"O.J. beat it, man," Dog-Face said.

"O.J. had the million-dollar lawyer. Ninety-nine point nine percent of everyone else don't. He still done it. And they're gonna try him over again, right? You gotta be good to pull off the perfect crime and not get caught. You get pissed off and kill some dude, it don't make you the perfect criminal—it just makes you a killer. Everyone's guaranteed to fuck up. Watch— a week from now—they got the guy who greased the mayor's buddy. And you ain't gonna find no million-dollar lawyer there to get him off."

Casey kept looking ahead. Just look out the window. Better to see the cruisers and cops than the eyes of the kids. She felt something. Dream's hand on her wrist.

"You alright, girl?"

"Yeah." Casey said it strong and tough, but even as she said it, she thought, that's one shitty acting job. She kept telling herself: *just make it till tonight and they'll forget about it. It'll be just another jerk who got taxed in Hollywood. Make it through tonight . . .*

"You sure? 'Cause—"

There was a loud bang on the restaurant's window. Casey spun around . . . It was only Tulip, slapping the glass with the heel of her palm. She was wearing her usual battered leather miniskirt and torn fishnet stockings. Tulip was yelling over the noise of the kids talking inside, and the traffic going by outside. Casey could barely make out what she was saying:

"You gotta do me a favor."

Outside, Tulip leaned against the glass and lit a Marlboro. She had dirty blonde hair, sort of a pretty face, and Casey always thought if she'd been hanging out in some suburban mall instead of on the street, she'd probably actually look seventeen—that was her real age—but nobody here would ever guess it. She offered Casey a smoke which Casey was happy to take.

"You gotta do me a favor. See that girl—"

Tulip pointed down the block to a girl who looked about sixteen or seventeen. She was pretty, wearing clothes that were cool—not LA cool—but cool if you were from someplace else, which everyone was, and unlike all the other kids, she looked clean—her hair was pulled back in a tight ponytail, her jeans were nice, her backpack was just a little ratty. She couldn't have been out too long. The girl looked over at Casey and Tulip. Casey's and her eyes met. She knew they were talking about her and looked away.

"I found her, like an hour ago. By the bus station," Tulip said as Casey stole another glance back at her.

"Another one?"

"She don't know nothing. Like you was when I first seen you."

"Yeah, right," Casey said.

"That *is* right . . . Just take care of her for a coupla hours, okay?"

"I can't."

"I got a date. C'mon."

"Don't do this to me. Not now. Not today."

"You gotta. Date. Money. C'mon—"

"Please—

Before Casey could say anything else, Tulip was off down the street, waving back over her shoulder. As she went, she called back, "Her name's Robin—at least for now."

4
Jimmy

Jimmy McCann always thought the place looked a little sad. He had been coming to the Peking for years, and as much as he liked it, he really didn't *like* it. It was a dive. The place smelled like a window hadn't been cracked in years; it was dark, and when he first started coming, Jimmy thought the darkness was intentional, a mood thing, but later, he came to realize, they just never got around to changing the bulbs. For 20 bucks worth from Thrifty's, you might actually be able to see the food on your table—but on the other hand, maybe that wasn't such a good idea at the Peking. The walls were lined with headshots of actors, almost all of them no one ever heard of, but who might have had a bit part thirty years ago in some long-forgotten television show. Sometimes you found the same actors at the bar, but with a lot more mileage on them. That was a little sad too, because there it was, framed on the wall, proof that once they had their golden smiles, perfect hair and teeth, and dreams unshattered. Now, when Jimmy looked at them, they were nursing Bloody Mary's and watching a basketball game that no sane person gave a shit about. The crowd didn't change much, but every few years the place would get trendy for fifteen minutes, and Jimmy would have to fight a bunch of kids, pierced and inked from head to toe, to get a seat. But for all the regulars bitching about the new arrivals, Jimmy liked the kids, and they often came over to his booth or sat beside him at the bar. The kids never knew quite what to make of him; he had a warm, round face, thick hair that was once dark red but now brown, and looked in his early thirties, but in truth, he was thirty-nine. He wore jeans and flannel shirts like it was a uniform and was cool to knock down beers with and talk about anything from the Dodgers hopes for winning the division, to how the CIA screwed the pooch on everything they touched. But he was also a cop so they never felt completely comfortable around him. That was okay with Jimmy, he already had plenty of friends. Besides, part of Jimmy's theory of life was, everybody needed a place to escape, and his was this shit-hole bar on the corner of Santa Monica and Hibiscus.

In a dark booth, where long tears in the red leather were patched with fraying gray gaffer's tape, Jimmy took a pull on a Rolling Rock. Across from him, was a full bottle, untouched. He glanced up at the game, finished his beer, and wondered whether the time had come to go for the other bottle. A hand dropped down in front of him and lifted the bottle.

"Hard at work?" Christian said, as he slid into the booth.

"Meeting with you, right?"

"Most detectives come to my office, you know."

"That would make far too much sense."

Christian threw his backpack on the table. He was tall enough to have to duck through half the doors in LA, in his early-thirties, and in good enough shape to be the guy to beat in the killer basketball games down on Venice Beach. Jimmy never could figure him out. He was good looking, got the girls, went to medical school, and now spent his days around the stiffs. A couple of months ago Christian confessed to him—and it seemed to Jimmy that everybody was always confessing to him, so much that he sometimes felt like a street-corner priest—that his dream was to become Thomas Noguchi. Noguchi? Yeah, Christian told him, he did the autopsies on Marilyn Monroe, Sharon Tate, Natalie Wood, and every rock or movie star that kicked in LA. If you're gonna be in the autopsy biz, Christian told him, this is ground zero, the greatest place on earth. Some dream, Jimmy thought.

"I've been thinking about this," Christian said, "and I think I got it all figured out . . . The problem with you guys is, you're always behind the goddamn curve. Never ahead. The slime-balls you're after always know what you're up to, because you're always following behind them."

"I'll have to remember to get to the murder *before* it happens next time."

"You know what I'm talking about. If the perps weren't such dolts, you guys would really be screwed out there."

"How's work?"

"We got bodies stacked up like CD's at Virgin. I even got a dog to do."

"An autopsy on a dog?"

"Yeah. Some genius was smuggling dope by putting the shit in balloons, and had his dog swallow them. Bright, huh? Acid in the dog's stomach popped the balloons, and the pooch went toxic and kicked. I said to my boss, why don't you get a vet to do it?"

"Wha'd he say?"

"He said most of our customers are complete low-lifes. A dog's a step up for you."

"Who's gonna argue with that?" Jimmy said.

"Can't. But you know what's weird? Right before I came over here, when I looked at the pooch stretched out on the table—it was this real pretty golden retriever—I felt kinda, you know, bad about it."

"You felt bad?"

"I felt bad."

"I don't believe it."

"Yeah. I got more goddamn feelings for a dead dog, than for the average gangbanger that shows up every night."

Jimmy shrugged his shoulders. "How about my guy. Any feelings for him?"

"Man, it's a hot a case. I can't believe they gave it to you."

"Hey—thanks a lot."

"You know what I mean. Just, you know, I figured they'd give it to some buddy of the chief's."

"I don't make the call. They say do it, I do it."

"What was the vic doing at the Chateau, anyway?" Christian said.

"No crime being there. Right? Maybe he had a squeeze."

"He was a big deal over at city hall."

"The mayor's oldest buddy, or some such shit," Jimmy said.

"He an asshole?"

"Dunno yet." On every other case, Jimmy would be the first to call this guy an asshole. What was he doing at the Chateau, when he had a wife and kid at home? But on this one, even with Christian, he'd better be more careful with what he said. And the reality was, mayor's best buddy, trash collector's best buddy—anyone can be an asshole. Jimmy thought about when he coached little league, back when they were all together. In his first meeting with the parents, he would always say to them, "As parents, you gotta be super careful who you trust your kids with. How do you know I'm not a coach *and* a child abuser?" The parents would say things like, "You're a parent yourself," or "You're a police detective." Jimmy would answer back, "We arrested an officer for child abuse right out of my own stationhouse last year. The guy had been at it for years." As far as Jimmy was concerned, everybody was an asshole—until proven otherwise.

He looked back at Christian, "How's my dead guy? Got anything wonderful for me?"

"Know something, he really must've pissed someone off..."

Christian reached into his backpack and pulled out a large chest x-ray. He held it up to a faded, red Chinese lantern sconce. Jimmy leaned closer to the dim light.

"*That* is one hell of a lot of cuts. Big ones, little ones and lots in between. He was way-dead and the knife kept going in and in and in. Twenty-nine times."

"Nasty shit."

"Way nasty. This was no stick it, and grab the wallet."

"What time did it go down?"

"I got the death between one and four a.m. Knife, of course. Serrated edge, very thin, pretty small. Just under four inches.

"The blood?"

"Tons of the vic's. A-pos'," Christian said. "But they also found some B-pos' which came off the backboard. Have to figure that's the killer's. Probably got sliced with the blade."

"What else on the perp?" Jimmy said.

"Not much. But it's a southpaw, which you get a lot less of. Anything come back on the prints?"

"Nothing in the computer. A virgin."

5

The car was unmarked but if you spent more than five minutes on the street, you'd have to be pretty dense not to know a slow-moving Crown Victoria had to have a cop inside. Jimmy suddenly pulled the car hard to the right, jerking to a stop in front of Tulip. She eyed the car suspiciously, slowly drifting away. Then she recognized Jimmy, slid up to the door, and crouched down beside it as she looked in the window.

"Tulip. Get in."

She pulled open the door, and at the same time, tossed her gum into a garbage-strewn parking lot. He knew her for years, and last winter she gave him the I.D. on a psycho pimp who killed one of his whores over sixty bucks. Tulip saw it all go down, and when the public defender read her statement, the pimp instantly plead out.

"Long time," Jimmy said. "Keeping out of trouble?" As Jimmy talked to her, his head rested on his crossed hands on the top of the steering wheel.

"Trying."

Tulip checked behind her, and then out the window. She reached for Jimmy's fly and tugged the zipper. Jimmy pulled back.

"What are you doing?"

"Whaddya think I'm doing?"

"Not interested."

"Right. Only cop in Hollywood who isn't."

"Come on," Jimmy said.

"Come on? You wanna work, gotta pay."

"That's bullshit."

"No. That's for real."

"Yeah? Who's been asking you for it?"

"Who hasn't? You want the list?"

"Goddamn right I want the list."

"How about Sergeant Cooper, Coop or whatever you call him. Duran, that jerk, gets it all the time. And the new guy with the mustache and real short blond hair and—"

"Stop. I don't wanna know . . . I do, but not right now. Sometime, I promise. What I do want, is something on who greased the mayor's pal."

"Like I got the 4-1-1?"

"You hear shit," Jimmy said.

"Yeah, someone's really walking the Boulevard saying 'I taxed the dude'."

"No, but there's lots of big-mouths out here, who might have dropped something they didn't mean to." He passed Tulip a card. "My beeper. You hear something, you let me know."

"Why should I help you out?"

"'Cause there's a killer out here and you're sharing the street with him."

"There's lots of killers here, you still ain't offering shit."

What a waste, Jimmy thought. She should be out at a movie or on a date—a real date, not this. Jimmy looked at her . . . and through the thick black mascara, the red and blue tattoo of a tulip on her wrist, and the ice-hard pro in torn fishnets act, she was still a kid. Then the pain hit. His daily dose. He thought about Rancher. His kid. Sixteen. Where was he tonight? God only knows.

All day long he worked like a dog trying like hell to stick a finger in the dike against the drugs, killings, hustlers, serial rapists, child-abusing assholes, and all the other horrendous shit that goes down on the street—but he couldn't even save his own kid. He thought about it every day of his life.

"Help me out with this one," Jimmy said, "and I'll give you a get out of jail free card."

"For real?"

"For real. As long as you didn't grease him yourself. But regular shit—dates, drugs—free ride."

Tulip smiled and pushed open the car door. "Okay. Deal."

Before she was gone, Jimmy called after her, "You seen Rancher?"

"Not in a while."

"You see him, ask him to call me. Tell him, no questions, I just wanna talk."

6
Casey

C asey walked the Boulevard with Robin, the new girl, both looking down at the bronze stars imbedded in the sidewalk, watching them silently sweep below their feet: Marilyn Monroe, Stevie Wonder, Walt Disney. Those guys she knew. She also knew the astronauts who were on the corner of Hollywood and Vine. Walk on the moon, get the best spot on the Boulevard, no complaint with that—but all these other guys—Walter Houston, Marlene Dietrich, Vincent Minnelli, Joanne Woodward—who were they? No one she ever heard of. But they came here, probably from someplace else, like she did, and made it. Made it enough that in a hundred years people will still be looking at their stars, knowing they had done something with their lives. As many times as she walked the Boulevard, she always checked out the stars, and now Robin was doing the same.

Robin told Casey she was from Boston. There was a fight with her parents that ended up with her sister going to jail and Robin running away. Robin wasn't offering anything on the details. Which was okay. Who was she to her anyway? But Casey had no trouble filling in the blanks—if the sister was locked up, this wasn't some little family fight over not doing homework. And Robin didn't come 3000 miles because life was so great back there.

Robin seemed sweet—she was also scared, that was obvious. But so's everybody when they first get here.

"You sure you wanna do this?" Casey said.

"Yeah," she said softly.

"'Cause there's people who have this place on Vine where you can call your parents. For free. They'll even give you the money to go back home."

"I just spent four days getting here. No way I'm going back now."

"You just gotta know, you gotta be tough here . . ." Casey looked at Robin and knew what Robin had to be feeling. Robin was cute, with shoulder length black hair and nice blue eyes. So she probably had jerks hitting on her all the time in school. And Casey would bet it wasn't just kids—adults too. Maybe it was somebody in her own family. Probably it was a lot worse than just being hit on. Maybe Robin was strong and got through it okay. But in her heart of hearts, Robin had to know she really wasn't tough at all. She was just a kid from the suburbs who always had a roof over her head and a refrigerator full of food. She was trying to look calm, like she had it all covered, but Casey knew, inside, Robin was shaking like crazy—and however rough she thought it was here, she couldn't imagine the reality.

"See," Casey said, "lots of kids come here saying they're tough enough to make it on the Boulevard, but they find out real fast—"

Before Casey could finish, Robin cut her off: "*Anything's gotta be better than what I left behind.*"

Casey stopped.

"I know," Casey said. "I know."

7

Ten months ago Casey *was* Robin. Everything in her life sucked, and Hollywood was the lighthouse . . .

She pushed her head out from under the rain shelter and searched the darkness for the Seattle city bus. Freezing rain pelted Casey's face. Her jean jacket and flannel shirt were drenched and pressed heavy and cold against the skin of her back. The shelter glass, with an enormous, brightly lit perfume ad of a woman, sun-drenched and laughing in a bridal dress, protected Casey from the rain. Not all the rain—some flew in from the side. Unbelievable. Not only does it never stop raining here, but it rains from the side, too. It pours from the top. It does everything but rain straight up. The bus wouldn't come. She shuffled her feet back and forth. More than anything, she hated being cold—there were days when the only time she felt truly warm was in the shower, the hot water cascading around her. Sometimes she would take two, or even three showers in a day, and for those fifteen minutes she felt happy, like she had somehow escaped. Still no bus. And then—there it was, its headlights pushing through the night, reflecting on the wall of rain. She was the only rider. Sitting half-way back and bathed under the fluorescent lights, she pushed her hair back and looked at her reflection in the glass. Her face was wet. But not from tears. *Just wet.*

On the porch, she rang the bell. Beside the door was a couch resting on two legs; it tilted down sharply into a puddle caused by a busted drain pipe, which spilled a constant rush of water. A flower pot in front of the couch held a shriveled skeleton of something, probably a poinsettia plant from last Christmas or the Christmas before. Ringing the poinsettia remains were crushed cigarette butts and water-logged matchbooks. A light came on inside. God, she was glad to be here. The door opened. She would understand. She *had* to understand.

"Casey. Baby."

"Mommy."

Casey fell into her, laying her chin on her mother's shoulder, pushing her face into her hair.

Casey sat across from Deidre at a faded yellow Formica kitchen table. Deidre was wearing a long silk robe that Casey had bought her two years ago in Chinatown. She pushed a strand of straight blonde hair off her face. Casey noticed her mom's roots were dark. Her face was developing lines, especially across her forehead, but considering she was putting in eight to ten hours a day standing on a fish processing line, she still looked pretty good. Casey had on a big Irish wool sweater Deidre had given her. The dryer rattled in the nook off the kitchen, and on the wall, a black kitty-cat clock ticked, the cat's eyes swinging back and forth with each passing second, and loud enough for Casey to never forget it was there.

"He's an animal," Deidre said. "We should call the cops on him."

"Like something would really happen."

"We'd make it stick."

"Like it did last time?"

Casey stared at her mom, and she looked away.

"I'm sorry, honey," Deidre said. "I'm so sorry."

"I fell asleep watching TV, and then . . . it's just like it was before."

"Baby . . ."

Deidre circled around the table and gently stroked Casey's hair. She liked that. Deidre pulled her hair into a ponytail and kept running her hands through it. Casey shut her eyes. Since she was a little girl, she had *always* liked having her hair stroked. Life could be crashing all around her, but her mother's fingers, moving smoothly and gently through her hair made her feel protected and loved.

"I can stay here, right?"

Deidre paused a moment. And in that moment, Casey knew things were going south. *Here it comes* . . . Don't let it come . . . Please. Count to three and she won't say it. One . . . two . . . three . . . She didn't say it—out of the woods! But Deidre gripped Casey's hand.

"Honey, you can't. You know what Tom thinks."

"But you got some say in this, too, don't you?"

"Sure. But so does he. We're together."

"I'll be at school all day. He'll hardly ever see me."

"You remember what happened last time? You two just don't—"

"That was before—"

"Baby—"

"*He* was the one cheating on you. If I had to do it again, I'd still tell you I saw him with Mrs. Magnuson."

"That's over."

"Yeah. Thanks to me."

"Casey honey, look at me. I'm no kid no more. I gotta make it go with Tom."

Casey got it. She pulled off her mom's sweater and laid it on the back of her chair. She got it.

"I can at least spend the night, right?"

"Sure. I'll call my sister in the morning. She'll take care of you. I'll *make* her take care of you."

Casey lay on the couch, her legs tucked into a sleeping bag. She pulled the zipper the rest of the way up, sealing the bag up to her chin. Her mom was *making* her sister take her. Great offer—live on a tiny, freezing houseboat, an hour and a half from school with a sixties burnout who was in and out of rehab, and wanted a kid around like she wanted a hole in her head.

The room was dark except for the light of the TV, where silent videos threw back soft, ever-changing colors, that danced over her face. Through the living room wall she heard her mother and her shithead boyfriend, Tom.

"I don't care," the shithead said.

"One night!"

"One night? Bullshit, one night. You expect me to believe that?"

"Yeah. I do," Deidre said. "One night. That's all. Tomorrow she'll go. What's the matter with you?"

"What's the matter with me? I'm not the one messing around with my father."

"That's *molested* by her father! Jesus, Tom, this is my little girl!"

Silence.

Casey hated him. She hated herself.

"We're talking one night, okay?"

"Okay. Okay . . . Jesus fucking Christ!"

They went on. Casey pulled her head still deeper into the bag and pulled the cord tight, making it quiet and warm.

At five to eight the next morning, Casey was on a bus leaving for LA. Later, whenever she remembered sitting there, she thought how crazy it was—kids come to LA from all over the country, for all kinds of reasons—some think it's gonna be something right out of *Pretty Woman*—they'll be working Sunset as a beautiful hooker and a Richard Gere type in a mile-long limo will pull up, they'll fall in love and she'll be taken care of forever by the hottest, richest guy in the city. Other kids spend their last ten bucks to get to Hollywood, thinking that if they can get a gig at the Whiskey, instead of buying CDs, they'll be *on* the CDs. There's also the kids who are the only gay boys in some fucked-up little town, and they figure LA will be full of gay boys just like them, sort of a queer paradise where you can fuck your buddies all you want, and no one says boo. Plus there are the girls who are the hottest thing in their high school class, the cutest faces, buffest bodies, who *know* there are movie roles and modeling contacts just waiting for them. And there's kids who all their lives see LA in the movies and on TV and say things like, "everyone in my town talks about coming to LA, but they didn't have the balls, like I did, to just do it." But, Casey, she didn't have any of those things. All she knew, was she *had* to get out of there, and she wanted to go where it never rained and was always warm.

As the bus pulled onto the street, waves of rain swept across the window. Casey tore open the Velcro on her wallet and carefully counted her money: after the bus ticket, bagels, and the orange juice, she had $79 left. It wasn't a fortune. She didn't care. She didn't look back at the city. She never wanted to see Seattle again.

8

T he Hollywood bus station was tiny. Casey couldn't believe it. *This* was Hollywood? When the bus pulled in, she asked the driver if it was the right place. The main depot was downtown he said, but if you wanted Hollywood, this was it. She walked through the station, her backpack slung across her shoulder expecting something cool . . . something *Hollywood*. She went up to a newsstand. The woman behind the counter was in her sixties, with a big, juicy mole on the right side of her chin, and long white hairs growing out of it. She was watching a fuzzy black and white TV and Casey had to almost yell to be heard over the news. Some guy had just shot someone and was speeding down a freeway as the cops chased after him. You could see it all from a camera they had up in a helicopter. The anchorwoman, who looked like some kind of grown-up beauty queen, was talking about how whenever these things happened, it usually ended with the guy being shot by the police. No wonder the lady was so into it. Casey called over the TV to her.

"Miss, can you tell me how to get to Santa Monica?"

Santa Monica. Casey loved the name. On the bus, someone had left behind a *San Francisco Chronicle*, and Casey read about Michelle Pfeiffer, and that's where she lived. It was on the beach, and there was a pier there where Michelle would take her kids that had all sorts of rides, including the most beautiful merry-go-round Casey had ever seen. Someone had to work at the rides. Why couldn't she? If Santa Monica was good enough for Michelle Pfeiffer, it was good enough for her.

"Boulevard or city?" the lady said. She didn't turn an inch from the TV.

"What?"

"You want Santa Monica Boulevard, or Santa Monica City?"

"The city. Where the beach is, right?"

"You got another hour on the RTD bus."

"Do you know what number bus?"

"I told you, it's outside."

"What number?

"Outside."

Casey leaned into the heavy glass door, but unexpectedly, it opened with ease. Above her head, was a hand with a gold bracelet, pushing on the glass for her.

"I heard you asking directions. You need some help finding something?"

Casey turned towards him. The guy was in his late twenties, had an okay looking face and expensive blue sunglasses hanging from a leather strap around his neck. Still, there was something a little creepy about him.

"You look like you need some help."

She did, but she wasn't going to tell him. "I'm okay."

"Hey. I know what you're thinking," he said. "'Who's this

29

guy talking to me in a bus station? Do I really want to have a conversation with some guy I don't know who comes up to me in a bus station?' Well, I'm not a mugger. I promise. I'm just here to pick up my sister and her little girl who are coming to visit me. But typical bus company shit, they're two hours late. Yours on time?"

"We were like half-an-hour late."

"It's all messed up, isn't it? California has the best freeway system in the world and they still can't get you from point A to point B on time. I heard you asking Madam Personality over there for directions."

As soon as he said it, the lady at the newsstand shot over a nasty look. Casey thought all she cared about was her stupid TV. Guess not. The guy saw her glare, and smiled. Casey grinned a little too—Madam Personality—she liked that.

"I can show you how to get anywhere you want."

"I'm fine. Really."

She pushed past him, not rudely, she thought, but like she knew the score.

Casey looked down the street and saw a bunch of low buildings which were just like the streets in Seattle, lined with mini-malls. *This* was the Hollywood people dreamed of? She didn't get it. Half a block from the station she stared at a pole topped with a triangle-shaped RTD sign. There were four separate bus route maps in chrome and glass frames, all of them covered in graffiti. Casey tried to read through the tags, but they were impenetrable. She'd wait for the next bus to show up, and then ask the driver.

"Messed up, huh?" It was the guy again. He shook his head and said, "The whole reason you have maps, is so people can use them. Then some jerk sprays his tag on it, and you can't.

Now is that some kinda rebellion, or is it a screw-you to the rest of us? You ask me, it's like a dog pissing on a pole, telling everyone he's here. But does he care that he's leaving piss all over the place? These guys are just flat-out disrespectful to normal people like you and me who just want to ride the bus in peace. Am I right?"

"It's okay, I'll ask a driver."

"Ask me. I live here."

"It's okay. I think I know where I'm going."

"Then don't ask me. But I'll tell you, anyway. Take these buses, and you're heading straight to Pasadena. But next block up, on Sunset, that's your bus. I'll walk you over. Look. I'm not some scum, I'm just a guy waiting for his sister with two hours to kill."

"Thanks. But I'll find it."

Casey headed up towards Sunset and he was still beside her. He *was* being kind of helpful; she began to think maybe she'd been too quick to put him into the creep category.

"Let me guess something," he said. "You're from Minneapolis?"

"Wrong. What is this?"

"Just a game I play, okay? Let me guess again. Dallas?"

"Beep. You only get one more."

"Only one, huh? . . . Then it better be a good one . . . Seattle?"

Casey stopped.

"How'd you know?"

"Because I live around here. I meet lots of kids . . . and you know something, ten years ago, I ran away to come here myself."

"I didn't run away."

"Never said you did. But lots of kids do. You gotta know that. It can be hard at first. I know, I been there. C'mon, I'll buy you something to eat."

"I can't. I'm visiting a friend in Santa Monica, and he's gonna be worried if I don't get there by seven."

"Take twenty minutes. When I came here, nobody did nothing nice for me, so I says to myself, some day, when I got some money, I'll share it a little. Now I got some money. Look, you get a free meal, and I get to pick up my kid sister and her little girl, knowing that while I was waiting, I got to do a little good in this world. Coming?"

Casey nodded. Dinner, that's it, she thought. The reality was, she *didn't* know anything. There wasn't exactly a guide book for people like her. And one way or another she had to start figuring out the place . . . Dinner, *that's it*, and then down to Santa Monica. For real.

"My name's Dennis. What's yours?"

They turned onto Cahuenga. It was just after six, but the street was nearly deserted. She pulled her jacket tight around her.

"That jacket don't seem so warm, I'll lend you my coat."

"I'm okay," she said.

"I got a long sleeve shirt on. It's no big deal."

"I'm fine."

She *was* cold. But she wasn't about to let him know. She had to be tough. She had to *stay* tough.

"You're gonna love this place. Chao Prya—Thai food. You ever have Thai food before?"

"Nah."

"It's the best. Hot, spicy. Try it once and you're never gonna go back to McDonald's again."

"I hate McDonald's."

"You do? Only kid in the city."

"It's terrible for your body, you know. And on top of that, McDonald's is destroying the rain forest in Brazil. I'm a vegetarian."

"No shit. That's great. Me too."

"You are?"

"Five years."

"Longer than me," Casey said.

"I been around longer. This place's got it all, lots of great veggie stuff. You know, I got an idea. We're right near my apartment. We can run up and get you a sweater or something."

"I'm okay. Really."

"I'm telling ya, it gets fucking cold here at night. It'll take a second to grab it."

"I'm from Seattle, I'm used to the cold."

Casey felt weird. The guy was strange. Time to bail.

She slowed down as they walked, and as she slowed, a space opened up between her and Dennis. A couple of feet . . . and then a few more. But Dennis turned back around.

"You don't want a sweater, you don't want it. We'll just eat."

He was checking out the street. Casey *knew* he was bad news. She had seen it before, but not like she saw it now. She quickly glanced up and down the block for someplace to run. Up ahead, nothing. Just closed-up stores. Behind her, a Shell station. Near the gas station, she saw a cool, punked-out couple throwing duffel bags into the back of a new, red Beetle. Casey slowed her walk to a crawl. Don't reveal anything . . . Just let him get a few more feet ahead, and then make a run for the gas station and the couple. It wasn't that far, it would take thirty seconds, less even . . . Just let him get a tiny bit more ahead. Then he lunged for

33

her. His hand wrapped around her throat and he jerked her towards him.

Casey screamed. She screamed loud, she screamed with everything she had. But no one heard her. The Beetle pulled into the street. *They* would hear her. They *had* to hear her. She yelled again, but Dennis' other hand, big and cold, slammed around her mouth. Casey fought to break free, but he was stronger than she ever would've guessed, and he dragged her into an apartment doorway. But even with his hands around her face, Casey managed to scream again—her loudest yet. She had timed it perfectly—the Beetle was just passing by.

But it drove on.

9

ennis had her arms tied up to the bed frame. A rag was stuffed in her mouth and another was tied tight around her face, stopping her from screaming or even talking. The street outside was quiet; it had to be the middle of the night. Her eyes were open, but she knew they should be shut. What did she want to see for? She watched in frozen terror as Dennis sat on the bed, and without a word pulled off his boots. She tried to yell, but with the rags stifling her, all that came was a groan, full of pain, like a dying animal. The next thing she felt was Dennis' hands tearing down her jeans. She tried to squirm free, but there was no place to go. Dennis was on top of her and she was ripping apart with pain. Suddenly she thought of being in fifth grade and staying the weekend with her father and his latest girlfriend. She was at the kitchen table doing homework while his girlfriend was cooking spaghetti. The girlfriend and her father, who were both crazy-drunk, got into a killer-fight, and the girlfriend threw the pot of boiling spaghetti water at him. Only it missed him, and landed all over Casey's back. She fell to the floor screaming. The pain was unbearable—unending—the whole ride to the hospital she felt like she was burning up—a roaring fire—shooting right down to her bones. She wanted to live the rest of her life without ever feeling that kind of pain again. But this was worse. A thousand times worse. Dennis was on top of her and she was ripping apart. She tried to scream again. Still nothing. So she screamed silently to God. But he didn't hear her. Where was he? If he wasn't here for her now, when would he be? The pain never stopped. Blood was streaking down her legs. The fire was back, tearing into her flesh. Where was God? Where was anyone?

Morning came. She never thought it would, but it did. Her hands were still bound and the only thing she had on was her T-shirt. There was wet blood on the mattress. Dennis wasn't there. She *had* to get out. How? This was the most horrible place she had ever been. It was the most pain she ever felt.

She shut her eyes and tried to think of something—anything—that would chase away the pain. Come up with a good memory—the greatest thing she ever did . . . when she was seven, in the first month when she and her mom were on their own, her mother would blast Van Morrison singing *Brown-Eyed Girl*. She'd sweep Casey up in her arms and dance her around the room, while they would both be singing along with the CD—*Hiding behind a rainbow's wall, Slipping and sliding all along the waterfall, With you, my brown-eyed girl*. She'd be so happy—she *was* the brown-eyed girl. And with her tongue pushing through a space where she just lost a tooth, she would lean way back and then bounce forward, wrapping her arms around her mother's head, all the while singing, *You—you're my brown-eyed girl—*

The door swung open and Dennis came in holding a Burger King bag.

"Woken up?" He pulled out a burger, took a bite, and twisted it around. "Want some?"

She wasn't going to answer him. He came closer. She thought, *Stay away from me! Stay away!* He came up to the bed and held out the grease-stained bag.

"Good fries."

Casey shook her head.

"Okay."

Then he pushed his disgusting hand under her T-shirt and grabbed her breast. God she hated it; she had only let two boys in her whole life put their hands there, and now this ass-hole, with his cold, greasy hand, was doing it. She started to pull away, but then she stopped. She stayed still. She let him have his feel. She stayed still as a rock. He smiled a little.

"Good. Gonna be my good girl now?"

Casey nodded.

"Can start trusting each other?"

Casey nodded again.

He reached behind her to untie the rag which went around her head. He pulled the other rag out of her mouth. Casey coughed . . . then screamed out as loud as she could—

"Help me! Help me! Help!"

Dennis jumped on top of her and quickly retied the rags. She was done—she knew it. He had rage in his eyes. But for the moment, he was deadly still, not moving . . . just listening.

But again, no help. Not one person in Hollywood heard her. Dennis' fist flew right at her face.

That afternoon, or maybe it was the next afternoon, she was alone in the room, the same bed, the same hell. She had no plan. She had no hope. When Dennis returned, he came in with two guys. Two assholes who should be dead. They were laughing. As they took turns raping her, through all the pain, she kept thinking, what had she done? First her father, then Dennis, and now this. She was only fourteen-years-old. What had she done? And when they finished, even if she could've yelled, she wouldn't.

They were gone, and it was just her and Dennis. Never, ever, did she want that again. Never, ever. Dennis sipped a bottle of Coke.

"Mind if I sit down?"

Casey stared blankly ahead.

"Good."

She had nothing to say.

"Look. I'm sorry about what happened. Real sorry. But, you know, all that yelling and everything, things just got out of control. And we can't have that happen, right?"

As he talked, he pulled the blanket up to cover her.

"See, there's a hell of a lot of assholes in Hollywood—and hey, you may think I'm one of them. You may *know* I'm one of them. But one thing I do know, if you're gonna survive here, you gotta have someone looking after you. And you don't got no one. But you do got me. Now . . . how about this, if I take that thing off your mouth, you think we can behave decently?"

Casey nodded. Dennis took the rags off. She could yell as loud as she wanted. But she didn't.

"Better?"

She nodded again.

"You want some Coke?"

"Sure," she said weakly.

He put the bottle to her lips.

Casey felt hope. The tiniest bit, but hope all the same.

Dennis crossed his hands and leaned over his knees. "Let's get rid of the games, huh? You're a big girl, I'm a big boy. What do we need them for? You don't got no friends in town, do you?"

"I do. In Santa Monica."

"Come on. Games. I thought we ain't doing that no more. I'm gonna ask you again. You don't got no friend in town, do you?"

"No."

"Good. So it looks like I'm your only friend in town. And as your only friend we have to figure out how you're gonna make it here. I mean, what are you gonna do, live on the street, begging for dimes? You don't want that. Who would? But what about this? You do a little something for me, and then I'll make sure you have all the money you need, all the clothes you need, and a roof over your head. Everybody needs money, right?"

Barely audibly, she whispered, "Yeah."

"Well, your number one friend in Hollywood is gonna keep you safe and in all the money you need."

"Untie me? . . . Please . . ."

He did. For the first time in days she wasn't tied up, she didn't have anything in her mouth. She brushed the hair back from her eyes.

10

Standing on Sunset Strip, Casey was wearing a miniskirt, black stockings, a tight, tiny top, and stupid heels she could barely walk in, which she hated even more than the rest of the stuff. Makeup covered the purple bruises on her face. Beside Casey was a girl named Christina, who was a little older than her and didn't seem so bad. She was wearing pretty much the same thing. Down the block, at the corner of Vista, Dennis sat in a black jeep sipping a Coors. Casey shivered in the cold—and at that moment, she knew she was the loneliest person on the planet.

She looked back at Dennis.

"As long as we're here, he's here," Christina said. "And as long as dates know he's there, they don't do shit."

Casey kept going over in her mind how she would do this. She *couldn't* do this. *She couldn't.* But what choice did she have? A BMW pulled to the curb in front of her. Casey glanced towards Dennis. He lifted up his bottle and tilted it towards her, like he was saluting her with it. She turned back to the car.

Inside was a guy in his thirties in a suit. He looked like the kind of person who worked at a bank or something. He could be a junior high principal, or the guy in charge of the movie theaters in the mall. It was too weird. Too sick.

"How much?"

He could be a doctor. A lawyer.

"How much?" he asked again.

"Forty," she managed to get out.

"How much?" He sounded kinda mad. But Casey realized she had spoken so softly, that it really wasn't his fault. Nobody could've heard her.

"Forty."

"Okay."

She slid into his car. He didn't even look at her. Good . . . But how could he not even look at her?

"I'm going to go over to Genessee. That's okay with you?"

The guy reached his hand over and touched her thigh. She pulled back. *Get away!*, she thought. He was surprised. She caught herself, and moved back over. Let him put his hand on my thigh. She saw a garage clicker attached to the visor. Then she looked in the back seat. There was a child's car seat. An open box of Animal Crackers and a Barbie was lying beside it.

The car turned the corner and drove half a block down Genessee. He parked in front of a nice house; the street was quiet with no other traffic. He turned off his engine. Without looking at her, he unzipped his pants and pulled his dick out. Casey looked at the gross dick, then up at him, waiting for her to start—and she threw the car door open. She jumped out and raced down the street. The guy was probably pissed, but *fuck him!* She kept moving on the dark street. The further away she got, the faster she ran, gasping for air, but never slowing. Her right heel broke off, so she kicked off the shoe, plus the other one. She didn't look back. In her stockings, she ran—and she knew she'd run as fast and far as she'd have to. Past De Longpre, past Fountain, past Lexington. Out of breath and her lungs burning with exhaustion, she reached Santa Monica Boulevard—and entered a world she never knew existed.

Lining both sides of Santa Monica Boulevard were boys— all kinds of boys—white boys, black boys, Asian and Latino boys. Tall muscular boys in jeans and cowboy boots, others who wore tiny shorts and were almost delicate looking. Some were punked-out in studded leather jackets, but a lot more looked like they stashed their surfboards before hitting the street. Some looked like they were in their late teens or early twenties, but most were younger and some, much younger. Half were shirtless, not caring about the cold, and all were eyeing the street, as cars slowed to a crawl as the drivers looked over the boys, like they were in a drive-through sex supermarket. Casey walked slowly down the block, taking it in—when shooting over the curb, and heading straight for her, were three surfer-looking boys, on mountain bikes, laughing as they raced down the sidewalk. Casey scrambled to get out of their way, and as they flew by, she realized they were triplets. Two of them jumped into the open door of a Land Rover and the third stayed behind and held his brothers' bikes. He threw Casey a smile, and when she looked back, she saw Dennis' jeep behind him. He was stuck in traffic, but moving down Santa Monica towards her. She didn't know what to do, where to go. *Do something.* She looked all around. *Do something. Do Something.* Then she saw it—a 7-11, with a narrow passageway separating the store from the next building.

The passage was dark and grimy, smelled of piss, and there was shattered glass all over. As she ran, she prayed it wouldn't cut up her feet. But piss—no piss, glass—no glass—if it got her away from Dennis, it was the most beautiful street in the world. It led to an alley which as soon as she reached, Casey heard something slamming hard against metal. Just ahead, she saw a shirtless boy, sixteen or so, throwing a guy twice his age into a garage door screaming, "Fucker!"

The guy hit the garage door and dropped to the ground. He landed beside a two-by-four board, which he picked up and swung right back at the kid, hitting him across his shoulders. The kid didn't scream like Casey knew she would have. Instead, he leapt up and shook off the pain. The old guy saw his chance, and started running away. He was heading in her direction, while the kid, running like a track star, followed just behind, and was catching up fast. Casey hurried behind a dumpster— the kid was wacko. The last thing she needed was him to see her. She ran a few feet further and found a tiny alcove in the brick wall of a building where she silently slipped down to the asphalt and pulled her knees up to her chest. Through a thin opening between the dumpster and a telephone pole, Casey could see the kid catch up to the guy and tackle him. The kid's bare back was covered with sweat, dirt, and cuts. He scrambled on top of the guy, his knees pinned the guy's arms to the ground and he smashed his fist into his face.

Casey crouched lower still, trying to become invisible. Blood was all over the guy's face. The kid reached into the old guy's jacket and pulled out his wallet. He took out all the money, threw the wallet on the ground and walked away.

Grabbing onto a rusty chain link fence for support, the old guy pulled himself up, and ran off down the alley.

Casey pushed her head between her knees. She felt like she was going to explode—her life was shit—there was no place to escape, not one tiny pocket where she could see normal people doing normal things—*everything* was fucked up. A shadow fell over her. She screamed. She was found. *It was all over*. She looked up. It wasn't Dennis—it was the kid. He had a flannel shirt tied around his waist and the old guy's money was proudly tucked into the front of his jeans.

"Get away from me!"

She could feel her body shaking. *Stupid!* Why was *she* yelling at him? *He* beat the shit out of people. The kid took a step towards her.

"I got no money. I got nothing!"

She had to get out of there. He was in front of her, but if she sprang up and moved fast enough, maybe she could make it past his left side . . . but then what? She didn't even have shoes, and he was way fast—she just saw it. She froze. The kid untied his shirt and tossed it to her. She caught it—but threw it right back.

"Take it," he said, "it'll help hide you from whoever you're hiding from."

He held the shirt out to her.

"Take it."

She dropped her head to her knees and again wrapped her arms tight around them, pulling her legs so close it hurt.

"C'mon—" he said.

"Why are you helping me?"

"'Cause you need it. No one hides behind a dumpster in Hollywood 'cause they like it. If you want, I can set you up for the night."

For what? He wanted to be her pimp too? *"You'll* set me up? How do you know I need to be set up?"

"You just got here, right?"

Casey didn't say anything. She looked up at him as he brushed the dirt off his bare shoulders.

"It's that easy to tell?"

He took a step back. "C'mon—"

"A minute ago, I see you beating the shit outta someone, and now you're saying follow me."

"The john didn't pay. John don't pay—john gets taxed. I gotta eat."

He looked straight at her. She couldn't look in his eyes. She thought about her father, her mother, the shithead boyfriend, the jerk with the Barbie. And then, it seemed like the wave that held her under had washed over. She could finally lift her head an inch above the water.

"And he hit you," Casey said.

"Fucking right, he hit me. You saw that? He hit me hard. For an old guy, he was tough."

"Hurt?"

"Nah . . . Yeah . . . A little. Probably'll hurt more tomorrow."

Casey looked at him and their eyes met. This was it—if she guessed wrong on him, she knew she'd never make it—he could do what he wanted with her and no one would ever know—she had no money, no strength. She knew no one. She had no place to go.

11
Jimmy

"What do you have?"

What do I have?—Jimmy couldn't stand the question, or closer to the truth, he couldn't stand the guy doing the asking. It was, after all, a reasonable request. The guy talking, John Miller, looked like he just popped out of Brooks Brothers. This was LA—Captain Charles Brooks' office in the Hollywood police station, and Miller in a gray suit and yellow tie, was dressed like he traded bonds on Wall Street. Jimmy knew the look too well from all his years in New York—half the joy of leaving the city was saying *sayonara* to guys like that. Miller was also wearing a college ring, and Jimmy clocked him as being one of those guys whose four years of college were the highlight of their lives and they never shut up about it. Probably still jogged in the college sweatshirt. "What do I have?" Jimmy said. "What should I have? The body's still warm."

"You should have something," Miller said. "Evidence, maybe. Witnesses. You want me to write out a list for you?"

"Thanks. That would be a big help. Can't believe I didn't think of that myself."

"Jimmy, hold on." Charles shot him a look. Jimmy knew it was time to shut up.

Miller continued, "No progress, but awfully defensive. That's a winning combination."

"I'm defensive?"

"He's right," Charles said.

"What, I'm defensive?"

"No, not that—I mean, yeah, that is right too, but so's Jimmy."

Charles leaned back at his desk and looked towards Miller. He was sitting in the office's only nice chair, which the guys chipped in to buy after the last one shattered into half a dozen pieces while some sleazebag lawyer was pontificating in it. The lawyer got a nail jammed in his back and a huge rip in his Armani suit. But as a result, his scumbag client probably chopped five years off what he deserved.

"Look, it's still early," Charles said. "Give us some time, huh?"

"No. You look. Mark Lodge was the mayor's former chief of staff, and an extremely close friend of his. You understand what that means?"

I'm starting to, Jimmy thought.

"So detective, I'm asking you one more time—what do you have?"

"The same as thirty seconds ago. But can I ask you a question?

"Shoot."

"Lodge, and don't take this the wrong way—was he having a fling?

"What?"

"A fling. Maybe even with a kid?"

"You're joking. What kind of question is that?"

"I'm just asking. You want me to do my job?—That's part of my job."

"Mark had a wife and a small child. He was in the public eye. You really think he would do something that stupid?"

"I don't know. That's why I'm asking."

"He was a devoted family man. There was no fling. I have to tell you something—both of you. This mayor has increased the police budget nine percent a year for the past three years. And you know who sold him on that proposal, fought the do-nothing, cop-hating, city council to get it implemented?—Mark Lodge. The same Mark Lodge who you're now pointing a finger at."

"I'm not pointing a finger at anyone—if he was fighting for us, then I was his number one fan. No one likes a pay raise more than a cop. You say he was on the level, that's good enough for me. It's just business."

"The *business* of the police is making arrests."

"Then help me out. What was he doing at the Chateau?"

"Christ, between the restaurant and the Bar Marmont, there's hundreds of meetings a day at the Chateau."

"So he had a meeting there?"

"I don't know."

"You're his law partner, right?"

"Yes."

"And you don't know what he was doing there?"

"I'm his partner, not his secretary."

"Fair enough. Say he did have a meeting there, would it be the sort of meeting he might not want people to know about?"

"I don't believe this. Instead of solving the crime, you're looking to blame the victim, not the scum who did it."

"Scum is exactly what we're looking for. Your friend was stabbed twenty-nine times. That defines scum. I promise you we're gonna nail the guy who did it."

"I didn't give this case to you because of your stroking skills," Charles said when they were finally alone, "I gave it to you because I think you can deliver. You *can* deliver, right?"

Jimmy wanted to deliver. If for nothing else, he wanted to for Charles. Wherever Jimmy went, people hated their bosses. But he liked his. Charles was in his mid-forties, had chestnut-colored skin and a shaved, almost polished head. He grew up in Culver City, and when the Vietnam war came along he was the sort of poor black kid that went in without bitching and had their lives changed forever. He was nineteen, and walking just behind point, when the kid ahead of him hit a mine, and in a flash had his insides ripped out. Charles held the kid until the medic chopper came—thirty-five horrendous minutes. The guy died, of course. In all the years he had known him, Charles only spoke about it once, but Jimmy figured it was always there in him. After he came back, and joined the force, Charles and his partner, who by some weird coincidence was also named Charles, were bringing in some punk kid. His partner patted the perp down and threw him in the back seat. But the perp had a gun concealed in his boot which the partner hadn't found. The perp pulled the gun and squeezed off three shots. The partner fell onto the steering wheel, and before Charles knew what was happening, he felt blood trickling down the back of his neck. His partner was dead before the paramedics got there, and the surgeons worked all night on Charles at Cedars-Sinai. They pulled out one bullet, but the other one was too far in to reach without doing more damage, and they left it in. Most of the time Charles had no idea the bullet was in there, but sometimes he got these headaches that made him crazy. On nights like that he knew if he went out on the street and saw all the usual shit that always pissed him off—a baby abandoned by her mother to whore for crack, a nurse raped in the hospital parking lot—he knew he would go off on someone. On those nights he asked to stay in the stationhouse and do paperwork. The other cops called him "bullet-head", like "Hey bullet-head, what shift you pulling, man?" But Charles kept getting promoted and by the time he made captain, you never heard 'bullet-head' again.

"I think I can deliver, "Jimmy said.

"Better. For both of us. This case is a monster. You nail it, I go to major and you, man, make captain—which you deserve. So don't fuck it up."

Jimmy smiled. It didn't sound so bad. He hadn't spent his cop life grubbing for the next spot on the totem pole, but he'd been around enough clueless brass to think he could run a precinct and fix a ton of the bullshit that he was forced to slog thorough.

"Hey, we're not dealing with some unsolvable Russian mob hit," Jimmy said. "We'll get it. What do you think about the vic?"

"He may not have been an asshole," Charles said. "We had nothing on him. There's ten thousand nutty kids in Hollywood. Not to mention the adults. He could've been legit like his prick buddy said. Wrong place, wrong time."

Jimmy took a nibble on his thumbnail.

"I don't think so," Jimmy said.

"Yeah? . . ." Charles said, "neither do I. The hotel room."

"Absolutely. Miller's right—every day hundreds of people go to the Bar Marmont or eat in the restaurant there. But how many of them end up in a room upstairs afterward?"

"You see the paper today?" Charles asked.

"Not yet."

"Lodge was the mayor's roommate at UCLA. And Miller was a couple of years behind them. Same frat house. Be nice to him. Or at least try."

Jimmy looked up, to see something hurling right at him. He snapped up his arm and snagged some kind of ball out of the air. It was blue, about the size of a large egg, and had a Chinese dragon painted on it.

"What's this?"

"Chinese stress reliever. Next time you feel like the shit's getting to you, shake this thing instead."

Jimmy shook it. There was something springy inside that vibrated wildly. It gave him a smile.

"I got a message from Erin Sullivan," Jimmy said. "You know what it's about?"

"I told her to call. You know her?"

"I played ball a couple of times with her husband—best third base in the league. I thought she was out."

"She's back. She'd just made detective and the Chateau used to be on her beat. I asked her to help you out on this one."

"Charles—"

"Stop right there . . ."

Jimmy hadn't worked with a partner since Manhattan South. Better that way.

"Done deal," Charles said.

"I don't get a say?"

"Yeah. You say 'yes'. Shake the ball, man."

He did. It worked. For three seconds.

12

It was pushing ten when Jimmy was cutting through West Hollywood heading for the Chateau. He had Erin with him. She was in her late twenties, with dark blonde hair that fell just past her shoulders, and had what Jimmy always thought was a sweet smile. Most cops seem angry—a lot angry, or a little angry—but angry all the same. Not Erin. He thought she was cute, but so did every guy in the precinct, and they all knew she had the husband, Rick, who was not only a tough, in-your-face cop, but good guy, too. She had been through a rough time.

She pulled a Marlboro Lights pack out of her jacket.

"You mind?"

"Go ahead."

She cracked the window a little and blew the smoke out. Jimmy stole a look over and saw the reflection of Erin's face in the dirty glass—pretty, but uneasy—floating silently over the streets of LA. She brushed a thin strand of hair off her eyes and looked out into the city—brightly lit stores selling 50's furniture; valet parkers in their red vests standing at attention in front of one trendoid restaurant after another; two ancient homeless guys, one black, one white, shuffling along with shopping carts overflowing with cans; three ultra-real, ultra-sexy mannequins on the curb outside *Trashy Lingerie* leaning over into traffic, their perfect but plastic breasts barely covered in tiny green bras. All of it drifting under the reflection of Erin's soft, sad face.

The Chateau's lobby was nearly empty. A guy dancing an unlit cigarette in his mouth hurried past them with a pony-sized Great Dane. Behind the desk was a clerk in a Nehru jacket—so far out of fashion Jimmy figured that it must be the cutting edge of fashion. He had very short bleached blonde hair and blue-tinted, tiny, round John Lennon glasses. But what the Beatle had for them was worthless. He searched the computer and came up with the earth-shattering news that the room was charged on the Mark Lodge's Amex card.

"He ever stay here before?" Jimmy said.

"No."

"He make any impression on you?"

"Impression?"

"Yeah. Was the guy happy? Sad? Pissed off? Anything?"

"In truth—I can't remember him at all." He looked at Jimmy with a barely perceptible sneer. The kid was pissing him off. The pecking order around here was pretty obvious. Jimmy was only a lowly cop—a cop who'd taken two bullets, arrested a battalion of child abusers, pimps, and murdering assholes, and on the other side of the desk was coolness incarnate—an actor, model, singer, whatever, wannabe. He may be a twelve-buck an hour desk clerk, but *he* got to print the hotel bills for the stars. And that gave him the right to look down on bottom-crawling cops.

"He *was* here, right?" Erin said.

"Sure. There were about a hundred cops taking out his body."

"But he checked in here. At the desk. With you?"

"He's registered. But you have to understand, with our clientele, no one is going to remember someone like that."

"Like what?" Erin said.

"Vanilla."

"Print me a copy of his bill," Jimmy said.

They went into the huge, nearly-deserted kitchen—and the instant they came in, the back screen door bounced shut as two waiters in white jackets ran out. Jimmy followed fast after them—scooting around tables and room service carts, racing for the door, passing a rail-thin chef at the grill who barked "Fuck!" and stared at him with venom. Jimmy made it to the doorway to see the two guys disappear down the hill and into the night. Uncatchable.

Jimmy turned back around. The kitchen was something out of the thirties, with glass cabinets and beautiful floral-pattern tiles everywhere. On a long, pale-yellow tile counter, a small TV was playing a soccer game with an announcer screaming in Spanish. The chef, a tall scraggy guy with a blonde goatee that hung past his chin, and a barbed wire wrap tattoo on his upper arm, paced by the grill.

"Fuck a duck!," he said, throwing his spatula onto the counter. "Now who's gonna take this shit upstairs. You, buddy?"

"Sorry, man," Jimmy said.

"Bet you are."

"Hey. We're LAPD, okay?

"Oh. Thanks for telling me. Why do you think they ran like dogs?"

"You tell me."

"Fucking obvious."

"People with nothing to hide don't bolt like that," Jimmy said.

"What do they gotta hide? They're making five ninety-five an hour bringing trays to rooms that rent for seven hundred and fifty a night. That's what they gotta hide. Fuck a duck."

He slammed a plate on the table in front of him. Jimmy could feel himself getting pissed, but Erin jumped in.

"It's not green card stuff," she said. "All we want is to ask them about the night the guy was killed. His last supper came from room service."

"That's all?"

"All. After that, they can work here forever as far as we're concerned."

"Yeah?"

"Yeah."

"Then stick around. They need the bucks. They'll be back."

Nice job, Jimmy thought.

The Chateau pool was lit by half-a-dozen flood lights below the surface turning the water a cool, pale blue. It was too cold for anyone to swim, and Jimmy and Erin sat at the edge on green iron chairs. Over a tall hedge, there was a model photo shoot in the hotel driveway and one flash after another heated up the night sky, like they were next to a war—too far to hear the exploding bombs, but close enough to see the flashes. Every so often faint voices of drunken laughter could be heard going into cottages on the hill behind them—but mostly it was quiet. In front of them, past the pool, was the Sunset Strip and the lights of the city.

Jimmy glanced over at Erin and wondered what to say. He

had to say something—or did he? He could avoid it altogether. That's what most of the guys were doing, and he was tempted to do it himself—but he thought it would be crummy, and it was exactly what the guys who knew, did to him about Rancher. On the other hand, what if she didn't want to talk about it?

"I heard you were off for awhile?" he said.

"You know what happened?"

"Kind of. I'm sorry."

This was tough for him. Then he got mad at himself. Tough for him? How about her?

"How long? . . . Sorry, bad question."

"It's okay. He lived four months."

"Sorry."

"They were a good four months. I tried to make them good anyway. You want to see a picture?"

"Sure."

Erin passed him a small photo of her baby from her date book. He was beautiful, with a sweet round face and wisps of light blonde hair. Erin was cradling him in her arms as she sat in a rocking chair in the infant ICU. As Jimmy held the picture he could sense Erin's sad eyes looking over at the photo too.

"He looks just like you."

"Yeah. I always thought so. His name was Timmy." She smiled a little.

"You got any more pictures?"

"Really?"

She reached into her date book and seemed to freeze up for a moment.

"You okay?" Jimmy said.

"It's nothing."

"Sure?" He noticed a bit of white paint on her right thumb which she was subtly rubbing off with the other hand.

"No. Not really. But you don't wanna hear it, right?"

"No. Tell me."

"It's just . . . you know . . . It's with you all the time . . . He was the most wanted baby ever. And before he was born, I painted his room with pictures of farm animals—friendly faces of sheep, ducks and cows to wake up and go to sleep to. But he was born with these big problems. And instead of us taking him home, we were meeting with heart surgeons, a lung expert, kidney doctors. Two days after he was born he was operated on, for six hours. And three weeks later they did it again. For even longer. It's the worst feeling in the world, waiting while your child is in the operating room. He was a tough guy and he hung in there until he couldn't hang on any longer. I just about lived at the hospital, holding him all day while he slept, as I fed him, as the nurses changed his IV's. He didn't have a long life, but it was filled with love, and in his own way I think he loved us back. Well, today, since I was coming back on, I went into my baby's room, which he never saw, and I took down the crib and painted over the pictures of the animals."

They sat in silence for a moment. She turned back to him, her face lit by a gently moving blue light, reflected from the pool.

"You have kids?"

"A boy. Sixteen."

He looked back down at the baby's picture. Jimmy didn't know why—he never knew the baby, and this was his first conversation with Erin longer than two minutes in the stationhouse hallway—but he felt his eyes becoming moist, and he was glad it was too dark out here for her to tell.

She took out her pack of smokes, but then put it away. "Trying to stop," she said.

"Been there."

"But you did it. Not like me. How long did you smoke?"

"Only fifteen years-plus. I started when I was a kid."

"You miss it?"

"I miss the way it sorta punctuates the day. No matter what happened at work or anything else, before I'd go to bed, I'd go outside and have a smoke. Every night. It was great."

"I do the same thing. But Rick thinks I should be able to stop."

"He never smoked?"

"No. He's this serious athlete and all. He thinks you should have enough control over your body to quit. When I was pregnant I stopped. It was actually pretty easy. But at the hospital, when the baby was sleeping, I'd go to this nice little courtyard they had there, and smoke and think about the baby. Sometimes I'd try to get Rick to come outside and talk. But it never happened."

"Know how that is."

"The person wanting to talk? Or the one not saying a word?"

"Both. But mostly the one who should've been talking, but wasn't."

She turned towards him. Their eyes met for a moment, as though she didn't know whether or not to go on. It was quiet. Only the distant rumble of traffic from the Strip. Erin smoked. Jimmy wanted to say more. He wanted to talk about Rancher. It was different, he knew. But pain is pain. He wondered if Erin was the person to talk to about him. No one else was. Jimmy turned to her—then heard a noise by the kitchen. The screen door swung open, and both waiters were back, each with a can of Tecate.

Seconds later, Jimmy, with Erin just behind, came into the kitchen. The waiters looked over in a panic, but then held still, seeing they had no place to run. One was about twenty. The other was a couple of years younger.

"Okay. Okay. I go with you," the older one said.

"Hold on," Jimmy said. "We're not *migra*, we're LAPD."

"It's about the man who was killed," Erin said.

"The governor friend?"

"Close enough," Jimmy said. "You brought an order up to him the night he died, right?"

"I no give it to him, sir."

"You went to room 310?"

"Si. But I no give it to him."

"Yeah? Who'd you give it to?"

"The girl."

"Girl? What girl?" This was news.

"She took the tray. Gave me good tip."

"What did she look like?"

"Brown hair. Long. She pretty."

"How old was she?"

"Dunno, sir."

"Take a guess."

"Sixteen—fifteen?"

"How tall?"

"Dunno. Not big. Not tiny."

"Anything else you can remember about her?"

"No, sir."

"How about you," Jimmy said to the other waiter, "You see her?"

"No, señor."

"Sir, there was something," the older waiter said.

"What?"

"I do remember something about her. She was wearing two earrings in both ear."

Jimmy laughed. The waiter looked at him.

"Señor?"

"No. You just gave me a description which only fits two thousand girls in Hollywood.

"No señor. She was *muis* pretty. No like every girl."

Jimmy looked at Erin. She gave him a shrug.

"Thanks, guys." Jimmy and Erin went for the door. The waiters followed him. Jimmy stopped by the door and turned back around.

"Help you?"

The waiters got it. They were happy. Jimmy had next to zero. On the other hand, all that garbage about working alone, it was just that—garbage. As they walked through the Chateau courtyard, Jimmy looked at Erin and thought, she was beautiful, she was sweet. He liked talking with her, and she had a heart the size of the Chateau. He wondered, if there was any chance? He had Dani, and things were okay there. And after what she had just been through, Erin was a definite no. Any chance?—no chance.

13

Casey

C asey followed the boy from the alley up the narrow path beside Laurel Canyon Boulevard. There was no sidewalk, and the road which twisted through the Hollywood Hills was so steep her thighs throbbed. She was nearly out of breath. The boy's name was Paul. He barely knew her, but thanks to him, she was wearing red high-tops, too big, but it was the best they could come up with at the 24-hour Thrifty's. He also bought her a pink sweatshirt with *Hollywood* written in swirling multi-colored glitter. It was about as far from cool as you could get. She didn't care, it was cheap and a million times warmer than the stupid tube top Dennis had forced her to wear. Best of all, her stomach was full from a banana-strawberry smoothie.

When they were in the smoothie place, Casey looked right at him and said, "Why are you being so nice to me?"

"Look, you're driving down the street and see a dog wandering around without a collar—"

"Thanks."

"Okay, a cute Labrador Retriever puppy," he said with a smile. "You stop. Try and find the owner, give him some food and water. Anyone would do it."

"Anyone like you."

"You'd do it, too."

And as she pushed through the high weeds which lined the canyon road, she thought Paul had done more for her in the last hour than all of the other people in her life who claimed they loved her but really didn't give a shit at all, had ever done. The path widened a bit, and Casey walked beside him.

"How'd you end up here?" she said.

"Same as everyone. Stupid shit."

Casey looked at Paul, wanting him to tell her. He turned away and kept moving up the hill. "It's boring," he said.

"But you wanna be here, right?"

"Sure. Where else am I gonna go?"

They turned off Laurel Canyon and went up a smaller road, deep into the canyon. It was even steeper, with huge trees alongside it. The trees had a nice smell, eucalyptus, and the noise of the main road faded away. They passed houses jammed into the hillside. A lot of them had picture windows and the lights still on. In one house, with a smoking chimney, five or six women in their twenties sat around a table crowded with wine glasses and bottles, laughing. Next door, in a house that looked like it was made of glass, she saw two girls a little older than her, playing pool and listening to the old Rolling Stones song *Ruby Tuesday* which slipped through the glass walls. At the corner, they passed an elementary school surrounded by the hills of the canyon. Casey read the school's name, and thought, they sure got that right—*Wonderland*.

Just past the school was a weed-covered piece of hill

surrounded by a chain-link fence. There was a sign with some construction company's name, but there wasn't any building going on that she could see. Paul went to the corner of the fence and by taking off a couple of rusty rings, opened a space wide enough for them to slip through.

"It's not a suite at the Chateau Marmont . . . ," he said with a smile.

"But it's perfect," Casey said.

It was. There was no Dennis, no anybody, ruling over her life, forcing her do what *they* wanted—not what *she* wanted. Paul led her to the top of the hill, and when she looked back, she was in awe. Below her were millions and millions of glistening lights that went on forever. Towards the ocean, there were actually searchlights crisscrossing the sky, like for the premiere of a movie that you see in the movies. In the far distance, an endless line of tiny planes slipped lower in the sky and turned their landing lights on as they descended into the airport. For the first time, Casey thought LA was beautiful.

"Los Angeles—you know the name means?" Paul asked.

"Something about angels?"

"Yeah. It means City of Angels—but if you ask me it's more like the gates of hell." Casey nodded. She just met him, but everything he said was right.

Casey slept on the cold, wet, grass with one of Paul's blankets wrapped tight around her. It was freezing and every fifteen minutes—sometimes less—she would wake up shivering. Each time she did, she caught another glimpse of the city and heard Paul's words echoing in her head—*the gates of hell.* Finally, she fell asleep for good.

Something soft and fuzzy tickled her nose, waking her. It

also smelled good. Casey opened her eyes and had to smile. Paul was giving her a sugar mustache with powdered doughnut. He also had two enormous cups of coffee.

"You asked for room service?"

"Awesome! Where'd you get it?"

"They're building a house a couple of blocks away. A food truck comes for the construction guys."

She sat up and scarfed down the doughnut. A fog hung over the canyon, and through the mist she could hear faint voices of children as they were being dropped off at Wonderland. She sipped her coffee and knew she had survived. She'd been beaten, she'd been raped. She was sore all over. But she *had* survived. Yesterday, she never felt so weak, now she was stronger. *A lot* stronger. She was ready to put all of this behind her.

As she laced her high-tops, she said, "If I just keep going downhill, I'll end up in Hollywood, right?"

"Sure. But where are you going?"

"Home."

"Home?"

"I'm gonna find a phone and beg my mom to give me enough money for a ticket back."

"And you're really gonna go back?"

"I'm not staying here," she said.

"You really sound like you mean it."

What was he saying?—she *did* mean it. "I'm gone," she said.

"Sure you are."

"I am."

"See ya."

Paul turned away and rolled up his blanket.

"Hey . . . thanks," she said, "without you . . . I don't

know what would've happened to me. I way owe you. But I gotta go."

Casey started down the hill. Fast. Three huge steps, nearly running. Hollywood was close. A bus out of here had her name on it. *By tomorrow this was all going to be just a fucked-up memory . . .*

She took another step, but this one was smaller. And the next step was still smaller. *Back to Seattle?—that's where she was so hot to get back to? . . .*

And instead of bolting down the hill, like she knew she would, she was standing still . . . *What was back home?* Her father who should be in jail? Her mother who would freak when she showed up again? Her mother's shithead boyfriend who thought she was Satan? And even if someone—anyone— took her back, what was she gonna say to them?—I really proved how much I could take care of myself by running away to LA and getting beaten and raped.

They wouldn't understand. How could they?

Casey dropped onto the wet grass. Paul came down the hill and sat beside her.

They sat in silence. Children's' voices floated up from Won- derland. Casey stared ahead—stupidly she knew—as if a plane was going to fly by with a banner telling her what to do with her life.

"I feel the same way," he said.

"You do?"

"Less than a year ago, I was living in a farm town outside of St. Paul."

"What happened?"

"What happened was, in my tiny, little town—population, two thousand, one hundred and twenty to be exact—I did everything right. *Everything.* In my sophomore year I was president of the student council, I was the starting end on the football team, and by far the leading scorer on our basketball team, which made my parents, especially my dad, who was this super jock himself, super-fucking-proud. And one day I came home from basketball practice and saw everything I owned thrown out onto the front lawn. My dad had found my journal—I guess I hadn't hidden it very well—and he was upstairs in my bedroom window throwing my all stuff out the window and screaming 'Get off my lawn you faggot. You're not my son, you're a goddamn faggot!' And that was that. Nobody, cared what I had done before that—I was just a goddamn faggot. Two days later, I was here."

He leaned over and ran his hand down Casey's hair. She shuddered a little.

"I like that."

He did it again. And again.

She didn't know where to go, or what to do, but she loved the feel of his hand on her hair.

Walking the Boulevard with Paul, Casey knew like she never knew anything else, that if she was going to survive here, she *had* to be strong. As strong as Paul.

"One way or another, you gotta make money," Paul said. "There's really only three things you can do. You can sit on the street begging tourist jerks for loose change—which is shit. I can tell you that from personal experience. But if you don't look too much like you got the scabies, it works pretty good. Or—"

"What's the scabies?"

"Disgusting little bugs. You don't wanna know, trust me. Another thing is doing bump-and-runs."

"Which is?"

66

"Find a tourist, run up, grab their pocketbooks, cameras, whatever you can, and bust away as fast as you can. It used to be pretty easy, but now they got these undercover cops all over the place, and even worse than that, lots of regular-looking tourists got guns on them now. So, way I see it, that's not the greatest choice either. Or last thing, you can play the dating game, like I do."

No way, Casey thought. *Not now. Not ever.*

"Hey, Saint Paul!" someone yelled down the Boulevard.

Casey turned around to see a girl in a miniskirt and fishnet stockings coming towards them. When she reached Paul, she planted a wet, sloppy kiss on his lips.

"Hey, Tulip. This is Casey—first girl in history you didn't find first."

"Who did?"

"Dennis," Paul said.

"Pervert," Tulip said. "You're not still—"

"No. Thanks to Paul."

"The Saint."

"She ran away from him," Paul said.

"Man, that's great!" Tulip said. "I hope that asshole gets shot. Deserves it."

"Tulip's the best," Paul told Casey. "You're hungry, she'll get you something to eat. You wanna call someone back home— she's got a way to score you a calling card. You're sick of sleeping under some freeway overpass, she'll get you a squat. The best." He leaned over and kissed the top of her head.

Casey liked her. Casey had to *pretend* to be tough. But Tulip, even though she was pretty and not big at all—she *was* tough. Casey thought if she could just be like Tulip, that was all she would ever want.

They reached the end of the Boulevard and were surrounded

by tourists at a huge, wild-looking theater. It might not mean anything to Paul and Tulip, but to Casey, this was the Chinese Theater! Footprint and handprints of the biggest stars in the world—Bruce Willis, Sean Connery, Tom Cruise, Whoopi Goldberg. She snaked through mobs of tourists, where in two minutes, she heard ten different languages, and slipped her red high-tops into the same cement to where Marilyn Monroe and Sofia Loren had carved out their tiny footprints in high heels.

Casey found Paul by the ticket booth watching a line of people file through the doorway handing their tickets to the ushers. "This is great," she said.

"I guess."

"You don't like it?"

"Sure. When I first got here is was my favorite place in Hollywood. I came here every day for three weeks."

"Every day?" Casey said.

"Yeah. But it wasn't for the movies, believe me."

"What was it?"

"Something better—where I was from, being queer was the biggest secret you could ever have. But my first day in LA, I came to a movie here and the ticket taker was this super cute guy who might as well have had *gay* written in big gold letters across his forehead. We started talking. His name was Ted. He had been in college and dropped out to come here to be an actor. He was incredibly smart. I mean, I did pretty good in school, but Ted was a thousand times smarter than I ever was. One thing follows another, I hang out for one show, and then another one. We just connected. And he had this deal worked out with the projectionist, who was this fat, lazy fuck, who would start the movies and then go to a bar on Orange, and pay Ted ten bucks to hang out in the booth and page him if the film broke or something. The booth was small and hot, but it had this old yellow couch which would get covered with the reflection of the movies off the booth's glass. Pretty cool. That first day me and Ted hit the yellow couch and completely went at it. And then we did it every day."

"Really?"

"Man, it was intense. I never knew anything like that before. He had an apartment up on Franklin which we sometimes went to even after doing it down here. But he shared it with a USC film student, who was this stone cold bitch who treated me like I was a piece of shit he stepped in. On top of that Ted was always on the phone with his parents back in Connecticut who never stopped harassing him. And like a month after we hooked up, he just moves to Westwood, starts classes at UCLA, and biggest joke of all, decides he's not really gay. Could've fooled me. I go out to Westwood to find him. Spent two whole days looking for him there. And when I finally find him, he's got some girl hanging all over him. I run up to him. He introduces me to her—Stacy, like we're old friends from back home—not the guy he spent the last three weeks fucking day and night. He says he and Stacy have a playwriting class, and gotta go. Part of me says follow him, follow him, you ass-hole . . . . But I just watched him go. I walked all the way home from Westwood. That night was the first time I fucked for money.

"Sucks."

"Yeah . . . Sorta. Everyone else walks by the Chinese and looks at the footprints. I think about having my heart broken. 'Course I also think about that yellow couch and even with all the shit, it was still the greatest time with the greatest guy."

He smiled, shrugged. Along with Tulip, they walked away from the Chinese, heading back to where they started. Casey understood that this was a big part of life on the street—up one side of the Boulevard to La Brea, cross over and walk the other side back to Western. And when you're finished, do it all over again. There were places to stop and kids to see, but it was all an endless loop. Hurrying straight towards them was a tall boy Casey's age with thick, long blonde hair. With him was a Hispanic girl, a little older.

"Tulip, Tulip, pretty, pretty Tulip," the boy said, speaking a mile a minute.

"No way," Tulip said.

"Saint Paul, Saint Paul. Saint Paul!" the kid continued, never slowing. "Man, am I happy to see you!"

"No, man, I don't have any money," Paul said.

"What do you do with it? I see you out there all the time."

"Yeah. A bunch of millionaires for dates."

"Something's wrong then, buddy."

"No shit, Rancher."

"No, I mean it—look at it, if you're out there sucking cock for all those jerks, and you're still crashing at that same fucked construction site, the numbers don't add up, do they now? Do they—"

"Ranch'—"

"They don't. No way! But listen, I got something. *We* got something. Something big! Mary—she's got this modeling gig tomorrow and we need a few bucks so she can get some makeup and shit."

"That true?" Paul asked.

"Yeah," Mary said. "It's for a magazine. This guy's gonna take a bunch of pictures of me. He's got a studio over on Gower."

"If this thing goes," Rancher said, "they told us it's gonna lead to real acting gigs for the same people."

"They said that?"

"That's the way it works, man. You know that."

"If you're, like, unbelievable lucky," Tulip said.

"It ain't luck, guys. Mary's *got* the looks. Anyone can see that."

Casey turned to her, and he was right. She had amber eyes, high cheekbones, and very long black hair. She *was* beautiful. As beautiful as any of the girls you saw in magazines.

"Just one good break and you're on your way—*one*. It's all it takes," Mary said. She leaned into Paul and whispered loud enough for the rest to hear, "Some day, all you guys are gonna see me putting *my* hands into the cement at the Chinese."

"No one wants it more than me," Paul said.

"So whaddya say, Saint Paul, a few bucks for Mar'?" Rancher said.

"Not for rock."

"No way. Not this time."

Paul looked over at Mary.

"Makeup," she said. "That's all. Promise."

Paul reached into his pocket, pulled out a couple of crinkled one-dollar bills and gave them to Mary. She threw her arms around him and said, "You're the greatest!"

"Greatest idiot."

As they hurried off, Mary sipped her arms around Rancher's waist. There wasn't a feather's distance between them.

"Our very own Boulevard Romeo and Juliet," Paul said. "One more girl who came here thinking she's gonna be a movie star. Look around—you see any stars here?"

"On the sidewalk," Tulip said.

"The only place."

"But she's so pretty, she could be," Casey said.

"Right . . . star of the Boulevard crackheads," Paul said.

Down the block, Rancher stopped, gently pushed Mary

against a streetlight and they kissed. A long, sweet kiss, like they were they only ones on the street. Maybe they were crackheads, Casey thought, but at least they had each other, and that was something.

With his flannel shirt tied around his waist, bare-chested and defying the cold, Paul sat on a concrete trash can on Santa Monica, showing his stuff to an endless line of cars that moved at a mile an hour, as the drivers slowed to check him and the other boys out. On a low wall in front of the 7-11, across the sidewalk from Paul, Casey was having a Marlboro with the triplets, who were fooling around with their bikes. The three of them had come down from Winnipeg together and Casey thought nobody must be seriously looking for them—how hard could it be to find three identical fifteen-year-old hustlers? Tracy, the triplet who had been supplying Casey with the smokes all night, picked up his bike and offered it to her.

"The frame's what makes it happen. Try it."

Casey lifted it up easily.

"Weighs like nothing, right?" Tracy said.

"It better, for eight hundred and fifty," his brother Timmy, said. He was nice, with a broad, toothy smile. Casey liked hanging out with him—all of them.

He leapt onto his bike and raced off, disappearing down Santa Monica, then up a side street. Casey heard a strange combination of laughter and retching behind her. She turned and saw a pack of six or seven skinhead kids, all wearing torn, studded leather jackets covered with weird, white handwriting. She couldn't make out most of the words, but saw enough *fucks* and anarchy-A's in circles to get the idea. The two oldest, rough-looking kids, were laughing hard at the youngest of the gang, who couldn't have been more than twelve, as he leaned over the curb and was throwing up into the street. Beside him, rubbing him on the back was a girl who wasn't a skinhead but running with them. One of the older skinheads, with a fat ring through his nose, held a nearly empty quart of Colt, leaned over the kid and the girl, taunting them.

"Can't take it, huh, baby?"

"I can take it," the little kid said in a voice that had yet to crack. "I can take it—"

And he threw up again. The pack took off down the street, but the girl wrapped her arm around his shoulder and stayed next to him.

"I'm sorry June Bug," he said.

"Don't worry about it. Just get the shit outta your body and you'll be okay."

Casey looked from the skinheads to Terry, another of the triplets.

"Poor kid," she said.

"Yeah?" Terry said, "you won't be saying that in a year, when he has a knife shoved up against your throat."

Casey suddenly jumped back. Scared. Timmy had silently flown back behind Casey and pulled to a tight stop behind her—so tight his handlebars lightly bumped into her ass.

"He got ya," Terry laughed.

He did. But then, she leaped backwards—up onto his handlebars. Timmy didn't seem to mind, and rolled her back and forth. Casey liked that.

"Nice jump," Timmy said.

"Gymnastics classes—four years."

"Really?" Paul called over.

"Really and truly. I wanted to be a cheerleader. Can you

believe it? Hey, I could've done it for your games. We could've gone out."

"Right."

"You didn't go after cheerleaders? Not once?"

"Once."

"See."

"I was faking. Whole thing was a joke."

"You were probably a good faker though?"

"Wanna see?" Paul said with a smile.

"Yeah."

Casey waved for him to come over. Every minute he was with her was a great minute—she may have been, grimy, cold, and living on the street—but Paul somehow made it better. He hopped off the trash can heading to her—but a Camry pulled to a stop. Paul looked at Casey, then ran over to the car.

The little skinhead made it to his feet, and along with the girl, scrambled after the rest of their gang. Timmy, leaned forward on his bike to where his face was beside Casey's.

"Where to, madam?"

"Where to? . . . Hollywood!"

14

The street whipped past Casey. Perched on Timmy's handlebars, she stretched her arms out in front of her, like she was reaching for something, and watched the Boulevard fly by—the Chinese Theater with its tall spires bathed in red light; the El Capitan Theater with families pouring out after a show; the hot lights of L. Ron Hubbard's place, its doors wide open to the cold; street kids grinding their skateboards on the curb in front of Joey's; an endless row of shiny Harleys parked outside a bar next to the Egyptian Theater; a linebacker-sized guy painted entirely in silver—his clothes, a top hat, face, everything—standing dead-still as tourists dropped money into a silver top box by his feet; a tattoo parlor at Vine with a bunch of kids barely in their teens staring in the window; a guy with movie star-looks playing a piano on wheels, and miles and miles of blue, red, pink, and purple neon. Busses were chugging; low-riders cruising; cars honking; drunk kids leaning out a jeep yelling; and a little kid, maybe ten or eleven, in a pure white suit, playing the most beautiful song on a trumpet she had ever heard. Racing beside Casey and Timmy, were the other two triplets. They took turns taking the lead, and whenever Timmy fell behind, Casey called out to him speed back into first place, which he always did. She felt the wind blowing back her hair, her eyes were sweetly moist from the cool air rushing by, and a smile came to her face. Even the Boulevard *itself* was happening—the street had glass buried in it, so it literally glittered. *This* was the Hollywood she came for—and if the ride never ended, that would be okay with her.

15

L ater, at a much slower speed, Casey and the triplets were back riding down Santa Monica Boulevard, heading for the 7-11. She had tired Timmy out, and now was sitting on Tracy's handle bars. For once, Hollywood was fine with her. More than fine—no one telling you to go to sleep, to go home—do anything you didn't want to do. Tracy was happy for the passenger and lead the way with Casey leaning forward like a masthead. As she silently blew down the road, lit by orange-tinted streetlight lights, she saw her shadow passing like a flying ghost over one hustler after another. When they breezed by Carl's Jr. at the corner of La Brea, Casey saw Paul.

"Hey. Stop."

"You bet," Tracy said. "I love this place."

Casey thought it was pretty much like the rest—and then she saw it wasn't. She jumped off and went over to Paul, who was surrounded by half-a dozen girls—all cute—the oldest of whom couldn't have been more than seventeen. Paul took a smoke from a girl who looked fourteen and was wearing a super-tight yellow miniskirt. Beside her, was a girl a year or two younger and the cutest of all, wearing tiny shorts, a skimpy black bra and black leather boots which rose past her knees to the middle of her thighs.

"Meet my favorite girls," Paul said.

He slipped his hand around the waist of the girl in the miniskirt, "This is Barbara . . . ." Then he put his other arm around the younger girl. ". . . And this is Gina."

Gina sweetly said, hi. A second later, Timmy leapt off his bike, and suddenly planted a kiss on Gina's lips while at the same time grabbing her crotch.

"Get outta here," Gina said, pushing Timmy away.

Casey couldn't stop looking at her. She had olive-colored skin and long beautiful jet-black hair. There was something cool and mysterious about Gina.

"What? You don't like my bra?" Gina asked Casey.

"No. It's great," Casey said.

"It don't really fill out like it should. Does it?"

"Gina's a fucking idiot," Paul said.

"Why you say that?"

"Because you're paying seven bucks a shot."

"What's the matter with that? Cheap."

"Yeah? What do you expect for seven bucks?"

"The guy who sold 'em to me said they was okay."

"Where'd he get them?"

"Mexico."

"And you expect them to be good," Paul said. "Think about it—seven bucks. They gotta be poison. Don't keep putting that shit in your body."

"Can't stop, honey," Gina said, pushing her breasts up with her hands, "Some of us gotta help Mother Nature out a little."

Casey laughed. She got it. Finally.

"Why you laughing?"

"I'm sorry . . . Wow. Sorry," Casey said. What an idiot, she thought—two inches from her and she still didn't click.

Timmy again grabbed Gina's crotch. "What? You didn't know we're talking chicks with dicks?"

Casey looked all around. Gina, Barbara, the rest of them—they were all boys. Pretty boys.

"I do now." LA was like the world's biggest sex store, Casey thought. Sunset Boulevard was for the girls and their pimps; Paul's end of Santa Monica was for boys, and this part of Santa Monica was for the baby transvestites.

Gina arched her back, thrust her chest out, and looked at her profile in the reflection of a dusty Land Rover window.

"They're perfect," Paul said. "Just lay off the shots, huh?"

"Alright. Alright."

"Now say it like you mean it."

"Sweetie, for you, I'll go pay double to the Russian doc down on Fairfax."

"Right."

"No. I will! But Paul, honey, I got something for you," Gina said.

"What about me?" Timmy put in.

"And me," Tracy added.

"Forget you and your stupid bikes. For Saint Paul."

"What?" Paul asked.

"Last night, I do this judge up in the hills," Gina said.

"How do you know he was a judge?" Paul said.

"He was, believe me."

"What—while you were doing him, he told you all about his day in court?"

"No. I saw his I.D. card while I was getting paid."

"While you were getting paid?!" Tracy yelled. "How about you saw the I.D. while you were ripping him off."

Gina looked at Tracy like he was a cockroach, and then turned back to Paul.

"Well, he didn't know nothing about ripped off . . . He was in the bathroom and I only took an extra two twenties. I could've taken a lot more. But when I was getting out of there, he wanted to know if I knew any blond, GQ-looking boys. So I tells him about you."

"Yeah?"

"Oh yeah."

16
Jimmy

J immy stood just outside the dressing room door checking out the girls as they passed by. He knew he probably shouldn't—but try to stop. They were wearing little more than bikinis when they came out, and going back in, they held their tops in one hand and a wad of crinkled bills in the other. A Chinese girl in a leather bikini, singing *Hey Jude* to herself as she headed towards the stage, told him Dani wasn't inside, so he scanned the room for her. The place was packed; four days a week, this was a dance club, but every Wednesday, Thursday, and Friday, it became the SR club, with three small stages around the room, each featuring a girl swinging around a pole. Jimmy recognized some faces in the pumped crowd. In one jammed booth was a kid in his twenties, who was starring in a shoot-'em-up movie that Jimmy thought was pretty good. His girlfriend, throwing down tequila shots, was an actress whose huge picture was on half the bus stops in Hollywood. On the poster, she was wearing a ruby necklace and a long white dress from the turn of the century—the picture of sophistication. Not tonight. She and the boyfriend were screaming with the rest. Just about everybody here was young and hip, and a lot were in the movie and music business. Jimmy had been a cop long enough to know this was a pretty unusual strip bar—no postmen and hardhats pawing skanky druggies here—the guys who came to the SR *could* get girls—this was a laugh for them.

One of Dani's acting class friends, Andrea, stepped out of the dressing room wearing a glittery white bikini and came up beside Jimmy. She was small and cute, nineteen at most.

"Hi, Jimmy. I'm nearly blind without my glasses. That table by the corner of the stage—is the guy with the Cubs shirt back?"

"Sure—who is he?"

"Who is he?—only like the biggest agent in town. He's here for a bachelor party or something."

"Opportunity."

"You got it. My girlfriend saw him two weeks ago at the Strip Sunset. Can you believe it? Look at the girls we got— we're twice as good as them. I figure, I'll lap dance him, and that'll be it."

"It?"

"Shit, Jimmy. He gets girls in the movies all the time. What do they have that I don't?"

"Nothing. They got nothing that you don't have."

"Thanks. You're nice. You looking for Dani?"

"Not doing such a good job."

At that moment another girl came by, slipping on a thin pale pink tank top and looking like she could be a sophomore in high school. "I just saw her in the back room," she said. "I'm Tara. Dani told me to keep an eye out for you."

"Thanks."

"No problem. She's about to go on."

As Jimmy watched her go into the dressing room, he thought, once they got their perp on the Chateau case, he was going to come back—and find out how many girls Tara's age the scumbag that ran the place had working here.

By the time he pushed through the mob at the bar, Dani had taken the stage and had the crowd exactly where she wanted them. She was tall, twenty-four, with light blond hair and as she danced, Jimmy felt a little sad. He was sick of the feeling, but it was happening all the time now. As Dani whipped around the pole, thrusting her leg as high as any ballet dancer, he wondered what he'd be thinking if he was seeing her for the first time. He'd probably be like every other jerk in the room, where the only thing on his mind would be, when-oh-when was she going to unsnap that top and give him a taste of the eye candy he was dying to see.

But Jimmy knew too much. A year and a half ago, Dani was a kindergarten teacher in a pissy little town outside of Charleston. Since she was a little girl, she had always dreamed of coming to Hollywood and becoming an actress. When she finally got the courage to drive out in her VW convertible, a girlfriend from her junior college, who had arrived a couple of months earlier, told her the drill—cute girls with crazy fantasies of seeing their faces next on the screen next to Mel Gibson's were a dime a dozen. If she wanted to get someplace, she'd better get some sort of competitive edge. Her girlfriend introduced her to a guy named Kevin, who worked for some of the biggest names in Hollywood, most of them studio execs, and some were big-time stars. Dani wanted to know what 'worked for' meant. This crowd would throw parties, which were usually in huge places in the canyons and Kevin supplied the girls. Amazing looking girls, he trolled all over town for. No one told the girls they *had* to fuck the creeps at the parties, but the reality was, these were the guys who could hand out acting gigs.

Dani hated the parties—she came to Hollywood to be an actress, not a whore. And even if the girls didn't go home with the guys that night, more often than not, there'd be a call from an assistant in a few days, and an invitation to the producer's house to read for a microscopic role in some huge movie. The part required a nude scene, and, naturally, the producer would have to see in advance what the audience would see—after all you couldn't have a hundred and fifty crew members, costing tens of thousands of dollars an hour, discover on the set the girl had scars on her tits. Dani played the game for a while, and it led to a Budweiser commercial, and after that she did an episode on a late-night Cinemax series, which, of course, called for lots of nudity. Her first night on the set had her reeling—in a way she was living a dream, she *was* acting, in fact, starring in an actual show. But in the first scene they filmed she was in a tiny tank top and panties turning on a shower. A guy walked in, she said a few incredibly stupid lines, pulled off her tank top and was fondled by someone who enjoyed it too much. At the end of the night, she was in tears. No one was making her do this, but still, she never felt so bad. She did a couple more shows in the series, and at the same time Kevin began to take more than a professional interest in her. Dani finally clicked to what bad news he was, and wanted nothing more to do with him. When she wouldn't fuck him, he started threatening her.

At first it was just a couple of nasty phone calls but then, things got worse. Ten or twenty times a day she'd get paged the number 187. She had no idea what it meant, until her girl- friend told her it was the California penal code number for murder. She was freaked by it. Then it wasn't just 187's, it became full-out stalking, where she'd see him in her rear-view mirror or in the bushes outside her apartment. That's where Jimmy came in. He was the detective assigned to deal with it. Jimmy put cops in shifts around Dani, so that for the first time in months, she felt safe. She told Jimmy he was the only truly decent person she had met since coming to LA. They never got enough on Kevin to send him to jail, but he backed off—at least for now. The checks from the Bud commercial stopped coming, and so did any other acting gigs. Dani ended up here, at the SR club. As the Kevin mess was going down, Jimmy would speak to her every day, and sometimes a couple of times. They started going out. She was pretty and fun, and despite everything that had happened to her in Hollywood, the kindergarten teacher from South Carolina sweetness, never left her.

Now, she was swinging around pole about to take off her top as a room full of drunken assholes cheered and stuffed her bikini bottom with bills.

Jimmy looked at her, and for the tiniest instant, their eyes met—and in that moment, he knew she was glad he was here—that there was at least one person in the room who understood what she was feeling. He went to the bar, and as he ordered a Sam Adams, he was grabbed by Josh, a writer in his late twenties, who he knew from the Peking. When Jimmy first met Josh, he was eating Cheerios three meals a day—the only thing he could afford. He lived in some shit-hole apartment in Hollywood, blasting unlistenable soundtracks of horror films, and writing screenplays that were re-hashes of old horror movies. He'd find a long-forgotten movie with a plot hook he loved, move the setting to LA, or some suburban high school, and hip it up. But unlike a lot of the pretentious phonies in the movie business that Jimmy met all the time, Josh was completely sincere. He knew he wasn't writing *Chinatown*—he loved horror movies. The scarier the better. Jimmy must've spent a small fortune buying the kid drinks. His film ideas were all pretty lousy, but hearing him talk about movies with such passion was worth the price of admission. One day Josh came into the Peking and offered to buy. Jimmy almost fell off his stool. The kid had sold one of his bad ideas for two hundred and seventy-five G's. The Bad Idea went on to make a gillion dollars and after that they made two sequels of The Bad Idea. He hardly saw the kid anymore—Josh was spending his time at the poker tables down at the Bicycle Club in Gardena, which he had the good sense to avoid in his Cheerios–diet days.

"Man, great to see you," Josh said, giving Jimmy a hug "but cheating on the Peking?"

"Don't tell them. Who's warming your seat at the Bicycle Club?"

"Don't ask."

"I won't."

They both glanced at the stage. A small blonde was doing flips like she was going for the gold.

"Okay, ask," Josh said.

"What am I asking?"

"Why I'm here, and not down at the Bicycle Club?

"Okay, Josh, why are you here, and not get getting your clock cleaned at the Bicycle?"

"Because I'd been spending a bunch of time there. And when I say a bunch, I mean *a bunch*."

"What's a bunch?"

"Let me put it this way. Last week, I went down after dinner. I played Texas hold-'em all night. Before I go, I tell my girlfriend

I'm gonna leave at twelve, no matter if I'm up or down. Twelve o'clock—I'm a pumpkin. No matter what."

"Right. What happens at twelve?"

"Twelve comes, twelve goes. I'm still there. One comes, and one goes, and I'm still there. But shit, if I'm gonna stay again until the sun comes up. I finally drag my ass out around two-thirty and drive back home—I got a house in Laurel Canyon now, you know that?"

"Nah. Not bad."

"Cool place. Blue Jay Way. I'll get you over sometime. Anyway, I get home. Completely beat. My girlfriend's asleep. I crawl into bed next to her, and a minute later, know what I'm thinking?"

"What a schmuck you were for leaving her in your bed all night, while you lost your money to the low-lifes?"

"Nah. I was up a couple of hundred, anyway. So I'm staring up at the ceiling. Can't sleep. All I can think about is the Bicycle Club—all the hands I'm missing. I can't get it out of my mind. Finally, I can't take it any more. I get out of bed, get dressed, and spend an hour driving down again. I didn't get back home till eleven the next morning."

"With your shirt or without?

"I ended up losing a few hundred. I can take it. But when I got back, my girlfriend was all pissed, which given what happened, isn't so crazy, right? She wants to talk about our relationship. Our *fucking* relationship—and how I'm spending more time with the jerks at the Bicycle than with her, and is it worth ruining what we got over the stupid card tables? But I'm not hearing her at all. Which only makes things worse. All I can think about is crashing. But when she finally lets me alone and I drop down to sleep, I can't sleep. She was right. That was the bottom. Now I'm trying to kick it."

"Any luck?"

"Sorta. That's why I'm here. Watching the girls. And they're fucking cute, right? I figure as long as my dick's hard, I don't want to leave. And as long as I don't want leave, I'm not at the Bicycle."

"I hate to tell you, but sooner or later you're gonna get bored with it."

"So far, so good. I can't believe I never went to the strip bars before. I mean, you can do all this shit to the girls, have them lap dance you, rub their tits in your face, say hot stuff to them—everything—and still go home and face the old lady. It's great."

Good luck, Jimmy thought. Anybody who comes home from the tables in Gardena only to drive all the way back down again, has bigger problems than the girls here were going to solve.

Josh jerked his head to the side, riveted on a girl just lowering her top. Reflexively, he drifted towards her. Jimmy watched him go, not saying anything. How could he? Josh was in therapy, after all.

Through an archway, Jimmy looked into a smaller room without a stage for the girls, so it was nearly empty. In a back booth, pulling a smoke from a box of Dunhills, and talking on his cell, was the sleazebag who owned the club, Sean. He was half-a-foot smaller than Jimmy, but had tough, broad shoulders and a nose that had been broken more than once during his days as a London street thug. He had been a bass player in a punk band who came to LA a decade ago to cut a CD. But the lead singer OD'd, and once Sean lived LA, there was no way he was shipping back to the Old World. As Jimmy looked at Sean, it frothed him that the guy was getting over. For all the shit Sean did, he never spent a day in jail. There were girls in here like Tara who were guaranteed to be underage, more than one sicko Saudi prince had paid tens of thousands for Sean to provide the entertainment with his jail-bait, LA's drug flavor of the month was guaranteed to be available here, and the club was laundering drug money for the Russian mob. Sean always managed to be around for the money, but never to do the time. Jimmy thought if there was a drug connection to the killing of the mayor's buddy, Sean might know something about it. He played with the idea of grilling the guy, but figured Sean would never give up anything real, and it would only depress him.

Dani found Jimmy by the payphones, the one place in the club where he knew he wouldn't have to deal with anyone. Dani gave him a kiss. She was wearing a blue satin Yankees jacket and smelled sweetly of sweat.

"It's so nice of you to get me," she said in a soft South Carolina accent.

"Come on."

"Wasn't a hassle, was it? With work?"

"Kidding? You're the one page I don't dread getting."

"Thanks, baby. I just needed to see you."

She moved close behind him, slipped her arms around his waist and rested her chin on his shoulder. She wrapped her arms tighter and he felt her pressing into his back. He was going home with her. He was happy to be going home with her . . . but then he wondered if there was a way out. *He was crazy.* She had a body that ninety-nine percent of this room would kill to crawl into bed with—hell, ninety-nine percent of LA for that matter. She was sweet, she was good to him. What the fuck was wrong with him?

"Smile, baby," she said.

He tried.

At four a.m., Jimmy wasn't sleeping. He was staring at the ceiling—just like Josh. At least he wasn't lying awake because of the poker tables in Gardena. And it wasn't because Dani was anything but a sweetheart. It was Erin. And it drove him nuts that he was pushing forty, she had a husband, he had a girlfriend, and here he was thinking about her like he was kid. . . .

In the morning, when he came back from his jog to Venice Beach, he found Dani sitting in the kitchen nook resting her chin in her palms. She wasn't looking so good.

"What is it?" he said.

"I don't know. I just don't like seeing you in the club."

"But you asked me to come. You paged me."

"I know. I needed to see you."

"You gotta get out of there."

"It's sick. I didn't used to think it was, but it is. Guys think they can say whatever they want to you—stuff they wouldn't be caught dead saying to their wives or girlfriends."

"They're jerks—what do you think?"

"I hate every guy I've ever lap danced. They're disgusting. I came to Hollywood to act, and my best performance is not showing those guys how much I hate them."

"You gotta get out, sweetie."

"And do what?"

"What do you want to do?"

There was a long pause. Jimmy didn't say anything. He was tempted to fill in the gap. But this was her question. He knew what the answer would be—back to acting.

"Maybe I should go back to being a teacher."

He couldn't believe it. "That's great. I think you should."

"You'll help me, baby?"

"Sure. Anything."

As he headed to the precinct, Jimmy thought, absolutely, he would help her. It would be giant leap up from what she was doing now—who wants to have assholes pawing you all night? But she wanted to be a kindergarten teacher again, and what the hell did he know about that?

17
Casey

Casey was still with Robin on the Boulevard. She hadn't left her side, which was good for both of them—it was Robin's first day on the street, the day more than any other when you need someone, and for Casey, by hanging out with Robin, she was sometimes able to push away where she was when the day began.

The sun was dropping over the hills above the Boulevard and anyone with a real life was going home to it, leaving the rest of them. The girls crossed Western and cut through a narrow alley overgrown with weeds, between a supermarket and a strip-club, which led to Fountain. A block later, they were in front of a large house with half its windows boarded up and most of the rest smashed away. The side porch had separated off the house and sloped to the dirt. The chimney was broken midway and chunks of its bricks were strewn around the yard. Casey always thought it must have been a great place once, a doctor could've lived in it. Now it was covered up with sheets of graffiti-sprayed plywood and surrounded by a rusted-out cyclone fence. She pulled up the bottom of the fence; Robin slipped below it, and Casey did the same. Casey quickly headed across the yard, stepping over blowing newspaper sheets, junk-food boxes, and a sea of broken glass. Robin was right behind her. They reached the broken porch, sealed up with boards. Casey pulled on a large sheet of plywood. There were nails hammered all over it, but it easily pulled loose and the girls slipped inside. Casey took a single step then jumped down into a hole that led to the foundation of the house.

It was dusty and nearly dark. Thin shafts of orange sunset light shooting through cracks in the boards above them let Casey find her way through a maze of pillars, low overhead beams, wires and pipes. She led Robin by the hand until they came to an overturned milk crate below a hole in the floorboards of the house.

"The Fountain—" Casey said, as she leaned down and helped Robin up through the hole and into the room. "Best place on earth."

Robin looked around.

"Then, the best squat," Casey added.

They were standing in what Casey guessed had been a nice, big living room. Now the walls were cratered with chunks of crumbling plaster, and nearly every inch was sprayed with graffiti. Sleeping bags were tossed on the floor, along with backpacks and loose pieces of clothing. Bottles, cans, and fast-food wrappers were scattered all over.

"What do you think?"

"It's okay," Robin said weakly.

"The smell, right?"

It was pretty bad. The first time Casey came here the smell

reminded her of a disgusting bathroom in a park—times a hundred. But that's a squat. The bathroom is just a room with a bunch of big tin cans, and when things got really unbearable, they held their noses and ran with the cans to the nearest dumpster.

"You get used to it," Casey said. "Here's where Jumper and Tulip stay. I'm upstairs."

She led Robin up a crumbling staircase. "Be careful of the steps."

Even in the half-light, Robin could see a bunch of them had boards missing. The banister and wooden spindles were in just as bad shape.

"Hug the wall—you'll be okay."

Robin followed Casey, staying within a few inches of her. They reached the top landing and walked down a hallway, also strewn with trash.

"Till you figure out what you're doing," Casey said, "you can stay in here with me and Dream. If you want."

"Yeah?"

Casey pushed open the door—and screamed. Robin jumped back. Standing before them, in the dark, was a very thin, very tall guy in his twenties, rifling through a backpack. Crackhead.

"Hey! Yo!" Casey screamed out.

The thief shot back, "Fuck are you?"

"Fuck am I? That's *my* jacket you got on!"

"Too fucking bad."

That leather bomber jacket was the one piece of clothing she owned that had good memories attached to it.

"My coat, man—give it back!" she yelled.

"Was your coat."

"Come on. I'll give you twenty bucks. Give it back. Twenty bucks."

"Lemme see it."

Casey reached into her pocket and found a crinkled bill. The thief looked at it. An instant later he grabbed her, pulling out a knife and jamming it against the side of Casey's neck. She felt the point pressing against her skin. She was shaking all over, but she kept telling herself: *Stay calm. Tough it out. It's just a crackhead.*

He snatched the twenty from her hand.

"Any more? You got more?"

She gave him the rest of what she had—a couple more bills.

"That's it?"

The blade tightened against her neck. It was sharp. Its point was digging in, and she knew the crackhead would push it home and not think twice about doing it.

"That's it, man. All I got."

This is it? This is how I die—a crackhead. Over a jacket?

Casey felt the knife push in still harder, like it was going to break straight through her skin—any second . . . when Robin yelled, "I got sixty!"

The thief looked over. The knife point lifted off her skin.

"Lemme see it."

Robin quickly opened her backpack and pulled out a bunch of bills.

"Here."

Robin held out the money. The thief let go of Casey, and grabbed the money—when Robin kicked him fast and hard— right into his balls. The crackhead screamed and dropped to the floor, holding his balls in pain. The second he did, Casey bolted past him, and together the girls raced for the stairs. They could hear the guy following after them.

They made it to the bottom of the steps, and the thief was just behind. Casey looked back over her shoulder as she ran, and saw he was pissed and getting closer fast. She turned back around—and saw Jumper and Dream.

The thief saw them too. And froze.

"Fucker tried to rip us off!" Casey yelled to Jumper.

Jumper got a crazy look in his eyes. He lunged towards the banister and pulled off one of the loose spindles. The thief tried to run off, but Jumper instantly caught up and went psycho on him, beating the thief with the spindle—across his back, his stomach, and into his head.

"Give it up, man—now motherfucker!" Jumper yelled.

The thief tried to cover his face, but Jumper kept swinging the spindle until there was blood all over it. Finally, the jerk pulled off the jacket, threw back the money and scrambled out through the hole in the floor.

Jumper triumphantly tossed the spindle across the room and said, "All those years in little league finally paid off!"

Casey dropped down on the steps, trembling, but feeling an amazing rush.

"You know what she did, Jump?" Casey said, pointing at Robin, "know what she did? She saved my ass by giving that asshole the biggest kick to the balls you ever saw! She's all quiet-like, but, when that fucker had a knife right on me, man, did she come through. *Yesssss!*"

"Steel-toed Doc Martens—the best," Robin said. She smiled. Maybe for the first time since she had been here. Casey knew Robin for less than a day, but loved the idea that this girl who seemed so scared and quiet, was so cool when they needed it the most. Robin had the stuff. She'd make it here fine.

They were all feasting on the family-sized El Polo Loco Chicken. Dog-Face and Tulip were back, and so were June Bug and Casper, the baby skinhead. There hadn't been this much food around in a long time. It felt like a celebration. They almost lost everything. As Casey ate, she looked at Jumper's hands. They still had blood on them. She thought, for what Jumper had done to get blood on his hands, no one would give a shit. Going postal on a crackhead—who cares? But what about her?

She watched Robin sucking the food down. Probably her first real meal in days. Casey was glad Tulip found her. Robin reached for another piece, but stopped.

"It's okay if I take this?" she said.

"Okay?" Dog-Face said, "Okay? If it wasn't for you and Jump, all our shit'd be way gone." He hiked up his right jeans leg and pulled out a long knife that that was jammed into his Doc Martens. Twirling it, he said, "Anyone sees that motherfucker on the Boulevard, you lemme know."

"He means it—" Dream said looking over at Robin.

"Don't go there," Dog-Face said.

There was a strange silence for a moment . . . Casey broke it.

"You were so great," she said to Robin, "like you knew what you were going to do all along."

"I did. Sorta."

"You rehearsed it? Smooth." Jumper said.

"Twice a week . . . Nah, it's just, my sister back home started taking this self-defense class. She was like, women-rule, and she made me go with her. Said she always wanted me to know that no guy could do what he wanted to me just 'cause he was a guy."

"I could've used that class," Dream said.

Casey thought, *so could I.* She figured ninety-nine percent of the girls in Hollywood could've.

"You done good," June Bug said

"Wasn't only me," Robin said, "We would've been meat without Jumper."

"Hey, just another superhero, protecting the great life of Hollywood," Jumper said.

"There's nothing here to protect," Dream said. "Nothing good anyway."

"Nothing good? You're crazy," Jumper said.

"*I'm* crazy? No *you're* crazy." Dream said. "I seen all the Hollywood I need. The sooner I get outta here the better."

"You really think it's gonna be different any place else?"

"Might be."

"No way. I done the whole tour."

"You have?" Robin said.

"Absolutely, Jumper said. "After my old man killed himself, I came to Hollywood straight. Did the Boulevard 24-7. But after a while, I start thinking, maybe there is someplace better. It sure ain't paradise here. I go to Portland, Seattle, San Francisco. Shit, I even go to New York. They ripped my sorry-ass off good there. It's all the same. I came back to where my friends are. I ain't never going nowhere else again."

"I am, man," June Bug said. "I'm gonna get out of this."

"And do what?" Jumper said.

"I wanna write about things. I got, like seven notebooks full of poems. I met a guy yesterday who said if they were good, he was interested in publishing them."

"Right. He's interested in publishing pictures of your tits," Dog-Face said.

"Fuck you. What am I gonna do—just give up? Say, hey, I'm gonna be living on the street or fucked-up squats for the rest of my life? Fuck that."

"She's right," Casey said, "you gotta have *something* to hope for."

"Like what?" Dream said.

Casey didn't answer for a second. Then she saw Dream and June Bug were looking at her.

"What?" Robin said gently.

"It's stupid . . . really stupid . . . but I want to have my own preschool place. In the mountains. In Montana or something. It'll have swings and stuff, and a place for the kids to run around. Maybe a big field. And all the people working there will really love the kids." Casey smiled inside. It was only a stupid dream but sometimes it seemed *so* real. Just thinking about it made her feel good.

"I got something I want too," Robin said.

"Yeah?" Casey said.

"I want to have a real talk with my stepfather. Five minutes of truth—no bullshit. Just truth."

"You wanna have the talk. How 'bout him?" Casey said.

"Doubt it."

"Always that way," Dream said. "What happened?"

"I dunno . . ." Robin stopped. But then she went on. "Actually I know real well. My dad was a cop in Boston. Great cop. Won all these awards and shit. He was even officer of the year when I was a baby. But later, some jerk shot him. For no reason. Just 'cause he was a cop. I was fifteen, my big sister was sixteen. My mom was a mess after he died. We all were. But me and my sister got tight. We were tight before, but now we were really tight. And like a year later, my mom married some fucked-up asshole who was a captain in the same division. Only thing was, the asshole was more interested in my sister than my mom. He kept hitting on her, and she was always telling him to get away. But he keeps doing it. One night my mom's asleep and he goes into my sister's bedroom and tries to get over. But she's waiting for him. As soon as he gets on the bed, she takes out a broken bottle and rips his whole face up. It was nasty, but man, he deserved it. My sister—and I still can't believe this—she gets sent to juvie—thanks to the captain's buddies. And of course, he gets nothing at all. My mom did the right thing—threw him out. But a couple of months later, the asshole comes crawling back, and says he's been in therapy, and he's a changed man. My mom, she lets him back. Says it's the most Christian thing to do. Christian? My sister's still in juvie! What about her? He gets away with everything. Me—no way I wanna to be there any more."

That night, Robin slept beside Casey. Every couple of hours, maybe less, Casey would wake up and look over to see if Robin was sleeping. She never was. The last time she checked, it was nearly dawn, and when she glanced over, Robin looked back at Casey with almost a smile. In the morning, when Casey woke up for real, Robin was sound asleep.

18

J ust down from the Chinese Theatre, Casey and Robin sat on the sidewalk beneath a huge movie poster with a girl in a long white gown with a ruby necklace, locked in the hottest kiss Casey ever saw. It was a good spot. As the tourists came past, the girls held out their palms and called out, "Got some change for food?" or "Can you help us out, please. Anything at all. We're trying get back home."

The line of people never ended: Japanese tour groups who always followed some peppy woman with a flag; tired-looking parents dragging their kids on the way back from Universal Studios; cool couples from places like Italy or France—they were easy to tell, even without hearing them speak—their clothes gave them away every time; and busloads and busloads of people who were taking the Hollywood tour, who Casey thought had no idea at all of what Hollywood really was like. But they all had one thing in common—everyone walked past them like they weren't even there. They acted like they couldn't hear, or pretended to suddenly be so interested in what the person next to them was saying, that they looked intently at their faces as they walked. Anything to avoid looking down at them. Every now and then, a quarter—or less—would drop down.

A guy with a pretty girl of nine or so gave Casey a buck. She was wearing a purple AYSO soccer uniform. Casey's mom had signed her up to play soccer when she was the same age. She had never played before, and was never really good in sports, but her coach, Stephen, didn't mind. He played her as much as everyone else, and in positions all over the field, even center-forward for two games. The first game of the season she was so scared—scared she would make some stupid mistake—lose the ball as she dribbled it, or miss some super easy shot, and Stephen and the other girls would hate her. But Stephen didn't care when she messed up. Instead, he'd call over, *Nice try, Casey! That was great!* And the other girls didn't care either. It was so strange, Stephen never yelled at them, and all the time would say things like, *Fantastic! Good try! You're doing fabulously!* So unlike her father. She missed Stephen. Stupid. But she did. It seemed like so long ago, but really, what was it? Six years? Six years ago she was wearing a purple AYSO uniform, just like the little girl.

After a couple of hours, Robin stood up. "I can't do this any more," she said, "I know I don't got a lot of choice, but I can't."

"You get used to it," Casey said.

"I feel like screaming."

"I know, I know. You feel like yelling at them, 'I used to live in a nice house like you do, have nice clothes and money in my pocket. I'm not some piece of shit that's not even here.' Everyone hates it. But unless you wanna do dates, this is what you do."

They took a walk around the block and went back to begging. At the end of the day, when they counted out their change, there was four dollars and twenty-three cents.

"Don't worry about it," Casey said, "There's always Mickey D's."

A little before ten, Casey brought Robin to the parking lot in back of the McDonald's on Highland. Everyone was under a light by a cinderblock wall, and when Rancher saw Robin he yelled, "Nice fucking job!"

Robin smiled. "I guess."

"No guess—you did it—you're the Fountain dragon slayer!"

"Dragon slayer," Casey said to Robin, "man, that's *exactly* what you did!"

She looked at Jumper. "Know what I'm thinking, Jump?"

Jumper turned to Robin. "It's perfect if you want it—Dragon Slayer."

"Or Dragon," Casey said.

"*Dragon.*" Robin rolled the word slowly off her tongue. And then again, "Dragon . . . Dragon." She smiled.

From then on, nobody ever called Robin anything but Dragon.

Casey looked at the clock on the Asahi beer billboard down on Wilshire: eleven on the nose. The back door of the McDonald's swung open, right on time. The manager, a young, fat guy with slicked back hair, and a black tie that lay on a white shirt stretched out over his paunch, came out holding a big, open cardboard box. The kids watched him as he quickly walked across the lot. He threw a fast look at them, and then tossed the box into the dumpster. And knowing twenty pairs of eyes were on him, he hurried back. As soon as he slipped inside, the kids raced across the lot and pulled out the box. In it was the night's unsold food—Big Macs, quarter-pounders, fries, fruit pies. Everything.

It was a great haul. Some nights there wasn't enough for everyone, and fights would break out. Casey had seen more than one nose broken or tooth knocked out over the shit in that box. But tonight, there was plenty for everybody.

Casey and Dragon sat with Jumper and Tulip on a small grass hill at the side of the McDonalds. The grass was wet and cold, but Casey didn't mind—the food was what counted. Just below them, Rancher and Mary were sharing a Big Mac. Jumper finished his burger, crumpled the paper into ball and said, "Mickey D's—it's the greatest."

"What do you think?" Casey said to Dragon.

"It's great . . . but . . ." Dragon said.

"But?"

"It sucks . . ." June Bug said rolling a stick between her palms, "when you first get here you say—hey, I'm on my own—awesome! All the freedom in the world, and no parent ruling over you . . . but then, you see the shit—live the shit—and you say, I *should* have a parent looking out for me. I got—we all got—the greatest friends a person could ever want, but still, sometimes it's hard to acknowledge I'm even here."

After she escaped from Dennis, Casey told herself she was tough, really tough, and no matter what shit was thrown at her, she would make it. But, what was she doing? Eating out of a dumpster on Highland. She missed Paul. Missed his hand slowly running through her hair, sleeping beside him and feeling his breath on the back of her neck. Every time she thought of him, she ached more.

19
Jimmy

It was getting harder and harder for Jimmy to get out of bed in the morning. He'd open his eyes, and the first four words into his head were *I hate my life.* As the morning went on—a cup of coffee, reading about a Dodgers win in the *Times*, a joke from Charles—and the feeling would gradually go away. Until tomorrow morning. But the thought of working with Erin these nights actually made him want to go in.

He looked over at her, the lights of the police radio casting a faint orange glow up at her as they slipped down Sunset. They rode in silence. Erin pulled out a Marlboro Light, then put it back in the pack. A minute later she pulled it out again, cracked her window and lit it.

"Everything okay?" Jimmy said.

She nodded. But not like she meant it.

"You know Rick?" Erin said.

"Sure."

"He's a great guy. No one would argue with that, right?"

In truth, Jimmy didn't know anyone who would.

"When we had the baby, Rick never wanted any pictures of him around. But you saw the pictures. He was a beautiful boy. After he died, I took two of my favorite pictures to get framed. They did a great job, and last night I hung them in our bedroom. I sat on the bed and looked up at them and thought about what a great boy he was. When Rick came home from his shift, as soon as he saw the pictures he took them down. He said that every picture reminded him of the pain he went through. But for me, it was something sweet to remember him by."

"Sounds rough."

"Yeah . . ."

The car slipped past the Chateau where an enormous line of kids stood behind a velvet rope waiting to get into Bar Marmont. Over the radio, the dispatcher was putting out a call on a domestic violence in progress. A cruiser on Fountain took it and Jimmy could hear the distant siren.

"Taking you away from all that," Jimmy said. "Hate me for it?"

"A weekend without seeing some woman with her face pummeled? It's a vacation."

"What percent of guys out here think it's their God-given right to smack around their wives or girlfriends?"

"Some nights it feels like a hundred." Erin said.

"I never got it," Jimmy said. "I grew up in a rough neighborhood. Guys who worked hard. Putting up iron, working the docks, that sort of thing. And they beat the shit out of their wives like it was nothing. My old man—no saint, believe me—he always said 'never, ever, hit a woman'. He was obsessed with it. 'Never hit a woman'. He said it to me and my brother constantly. His father used to pound on his mother whenever he got drunk, which was basically all the time. He never did it once to my mother, and he wanted to make damn sure we didn't either."

"Worked."

"It did. And on the job—he was a New York City cop—woe to the wife-beater who was collared by my old man. It's not like I got a million good memories of him—but he trained us right on that."

"It makes me crazy. Guys going off on girls half their size. My Lamaze helps."

"Lamaze?"

"It's the breathing training they give you before you give birth."

"Oh yeah, my wife did it."

"Most people do. They teach you how to breathe deeply, stay in control. Be real focused and stay calm. Before I went on leave, we got an abuse call at this motorcycle guy's place on Stanley. He'd taken his girlfriend and her sister, drugged both of them up, and tied them to the bed with clothesline. They try to get away and he beats them up bad, and then rapes them. But, while he's sleeping the sister somehow got out of the rope and made it to a neighbor's. I get there, and she was hard to look at. She only twenty, twenty-one. I'm sure she was real pretty, and now she had three or four teeth knocked out, and her whole face is covered in blood. I call for the paramedics, do her report, and now me and Cooper gotta go into the house and take this guy. We get in there and he's acting like the girls somehow deserved it, and who the hell are we to get involved in his personal business. I tell him put his arms on the wall while Coop's gonna frisk and cuff him. Of course that pisses him off even more. Now he's screaming, and I'm trying to talk him down. I can't stand him. He's an animal, there's no other way to describe him. And that's where the Lamaze kicks in . . . I tell myself, stay calm . . . all I have to do is just get him to the car without him going crazy. He's screaming away—cunt cop, you fucking assholes, that sort of thing, and Coop's starting to give it back. And you know how Coop is. He's an inch away from going off on him, and then it's really gonna be a mess. But I just breathe deep and calm, talk soft and nice to everybody. Just get him calm enough for Coop to cuff him . . . breathe deep . . . talk nice . . . Coop cuffs him. I get him to the car. It works out fine."

"How about later?" Jimmy said, "With her face beaten like that, I'll bet you thought about it."

Jimmy knew he was entering a place most cops don't want to go. His buddies would say what they saw on the streets didn't bother them at all. Show up at a horrendous car accident, and a cop will be eating a sandwich while the paramedics are removing the body. There was a huge effort put into acting like whatever it was, *they were cops* and nothing was going to get to them. But it does. He knew it as well as anyone.

"I thought about her a lot," Erin said. "All the way home. When I got into bed. I had dreams about her. It went on for weeks. I couldn't shake her. You know what I mean?"

Here it was, his call—play the usual cop game, and say, part of being a cop is not letting the stuff get to you, you just gotta push it aside and move on. Or he could tell her the truth.

"Yeah," he said, "I do. My very first month on the force, in Brooklyn, I get a call where a little kid's been raped. Six years old, by her cousin who was nineteen. He confessed to me right there. She was this adorable little girl and he's big an asshole who ever walked. And while I'm making the arrest, the asshole's mother, who was also the little girl's aunt, tells me the perp had gonorrhea. So he's not only raped her, but he's given her that too. I was twenty-three, and I don't think any-thing had ever bothered me like that. I couldn't stop thinking about it. When I get home, my wife's asleep. I wake her up. I didn't mean to wake her up, but I kinda had to. I tell her about the little girl and what happened to her, and she looks at me like I'm from Mars—she doesn't want to hear about it. And she's not wrong—I mean, what reasonable person wants to hear about a child rape at two-thirty in the morning. Or anytime for that matter. After that, all the things I would see in the streets, I would never tell her."

"What would you do?"

"One guess."

"Choir practice," Erin said.

"Yeah. Every night." Jimmy thought about what a waste it was—night in and night out, finishing up the shift and going to the bar with the guys from the precinct. But he needed it. Who else can you talk to about the shit you see? No one else but a cop knows what's out there. And even at choir practice, the amount of time they talked about real stuff was small. Most of the time it was other things—the union contract, the Giants, bitching about the brass, fishing at the shore. But knocking down the beers chased away the street for a couple of hours and made it easier going home. For a few years it worked, but then he got sick of it—too many nights drinking, too many hangovers. What good did it do? Rolling Rock against the street?—the street always wins.

"I saw that little girl for a long time," Jimmy said. "I still see her."

Erin looked over at him. He wanted to say more, but all he could feel were his ghosts. The faces, the dead bodies, the screaming—the things he saw, that would never leave him.

Jimmy hit the brakes. Ahead of them, on La Cienega was a

flatbed truck ringed by orange cones which closed off the right-hand lane; the bottleneck reduced the other lane to a crawl. On the truck's bed, a crane lifted a huge yellow board that twirled slowly in the wind, high above the street. Three hardhats stood on an enormous steel frame and positioned the board next to four other pieces, already in place. It completed the billboard, which read, *Yes On 120—We Need It.*

"What exactly do we need?" Jimmy asked as they crept past the crane truck.

"I think it's the prop' for legalizing card tables and slots in West Hollywood."

"That's gonna make a buddy of mine very happy."

"Big gambler?" Erin asked.

"Trying to stop. Now he'll be able to lose in the comfort of his very own neighborhood."

"But we need it?"

"Hey. What do I know. Maybe we do need it. It's not like we're in paradise now."

A couple of blocks later, they were driving through the heart of Boys Town. Definitely not paradise. The hustlers were out in full. So were the johns. Near La Brea, a Land Rover in front of them pulled to the curb and dropped off Gina, the baby transvestite, who was wearing a fluorescent green miniskirt. She skipped over to a pack of other baby trannys hanging out in the Carl's Jr. lot.

Erin watched the Land Rover's driver, a young guy, pull back into traffic. "Where you think that guy told his family he was going?" she said.

In that moment, Jimmy realized something else was different about Erin—to ninety-nine percent of the cops he knew, a guy in a Rover dropping off a thirteen-year-old boy-playing-girl at one a.m., wouldn't be a guy—he'd be an asshole. Stone asshole at that. Most cops divided the world between assholes and everyone else. When you first come on the force, the people you think are okay are the public, other cops, your family, friends, and really, just about everyone; only the perps were the assholes. As time goes on, you start crossing people off the okay category and put them into the asshole category. It doesn't take long before the public slides onto the asshole side, and then your captain goes in there too, and soon the only people who aren't assholes are you, your partner, and other street cops. Then, even other cops become assholes, and the only ones who aren't, are you and your partner. And here was Erin, looking at this guy in the Rover, who was clearly as big an asshole as anyone in Hollywood, and to her, he was still just a guy. He had to admire that.

Jimmy glanced back at Gina through the rear-view mirror. She was lighting a smoke and getting back in position for her next date. When he looked forward again, he saw a scuffle in the 7-11 parking lot. A couple of kids and an older asshole were going at it—no guns or knives that he could see—but he knew the way these things went.

"You mind?"

"We should," Erin said.

20
Casey

C asey, Dragon, and the triplets were throwing a small blue, plastic Gap bag back and forth, around the parked cars in the 7-11 lot as a john was trying like crazy to grab it away. He was probably fifty, but he was strong and tough, and had a full head of thick black hair. He was pissed, and charged after them for his bag.

"Give it back," the john yelled, "or you're gonna regret it!"

"Regret this, man!" Tracy said laughing and throwing it to Timmy.

"I'd give him what he wants, if I were you," Casey half-yelled, half-razzed.

Timmy tossed the bag to Casey, and she passed it to Dragon, who threw it to Terry, who gave it back to her. But the next second, the john grabbed Timmy and pushed him hard against the wall. He pulled Timmy's arm behind him and twisted it up high behind his back. Timmy yelled in pain.

"Okay. Game's over. Lemme have it," the john said, glaring at Casey, who was the last kid with the bag. Timmy screamed again. The john looked like he was ready to break his arm and enjoy it.

"Here!" Casey said.

She extended her arm with the bag—when a car's headlights blasted the john and Timmy, showing them bright against the cinderblock wall. The car doors jerked open. Casey didn't know what was going on.

"Shit," the john said.

It took Casey a second to catch up.

Oh, God, she thought. *Oh, fuck.*

The cop driving was out in a flash with a girl cop right behind him. Casey felt her heart pounding against her skin. This was it. Jumper was right—everybody fucks up. She couldn't run. Not now, anyway. Could she fake her way through? *No way.* She *had* to run—it was the only thing to do. But the cop moved past her, towards the john. Like she wasn't there.

"What's going on?" he said.

"You're a cop, right?" Timmy said.

"It's Jimmy. We know him," Tracy said.

"You busted us?" Timmy said.

"I bust everybody sooner or later."

Casey wondered if this was a cop trick, before they got to the real business. She watched the cop carefully. He was a good-looking guy. Not too old. He was calm and not doing the attitude stuff. The girl cop—Casey was sure she had seen her before, in a uniform, cruising the Boulevard. When she was in the uniform, with her hair tucked under her hat, she was like every other woman cop: tough, like they had to prove something. But now, she looked different. She had long blonde hair pulled back with a tortoiseshell clip. She was wearing jeans, cool-looking black boots, and a white button-down shirt. She was pretty, and without the uniform, she seemed friendly, like someone's older sister.

Jimmy turned to Casey. The pounding in her heart came back. Stronger than before.

"Who are you?" he asked.

"Casey." She could barely get it out.

"And you?"

"Dragon."

"Nice company girls."

Casey stole a glance at Dragon. She looked as if she was shaking inside. If they called her stepfather back in Boston, it was game over.

The girl cop walked up to the john. He was looking away.

"Who's the date?" she asked Timmy.

"Jerkoff took a bunch of pictures, and then wanted to pay us like it was only head."

"Too bad."

She turned to Casey. Casey thought, *play it right—they go. Play it right—they go* . . .

"I think I've talked with you before. Right? I'm Erin."

"I don't remember," Casey said. "Sorry."

"What do you have that everyone wants so badly?"

Casey passed Erin the bag. She took out a small, yellow, disposable camera.

"This yours?" she asked the john.

He was silent. But Timmy jumped in. "Fucking right it's his."

"They say it's yours. They lying?"

The john still wasn't talking. Erin shook her head and passed the camera to Jimmy.

"What's the big deal?" Jimmy said. "Just a camera. Anything here you wouldn't wanna show at a family reunion?"

The john stayed silent.

"Hey, asshole," Jimmy said, "you were real talky before we arrived. You know how old these boys are? . . . Tell him Timmy, or are you Tracy?"

"You got it right first time," Timmy said.

"Tell him."

"Fifteen."

"Fifteen. Hey. Look at me, john."

He looked away.

"I said look at me! . . . Shy? Weren't shy before we came. Which car's yours?"

"The Suburban," Tracy said with a grin.

Jimmy went to the car. Out of the back seat he pulled out a magazine. A naked boy was on the cover.

"Nice," Jimmy said. "You are one sick fuck."

He scooped out more magazines. He turned to Casey and passed them to her.

"Here, make yourself useful, and put these in our car."

As she walked over, she looked at the magazines. The cop was right, he was a sick fuck.

"Let me see your I.D.," Jimmy said.

The john passed over his wallet. Jimmy shook his head.

"You still a teacher?"

"Yeah."

"Ah. He speaks. What grade?"

"Sixth."

"Jesus fucking Christ."

Later, while two uniform cops took the report on the john, Timmy called after Jimmy and Erin as they were about to leave.

"What about our money? He still owes us."

Jimmy threw him a *you're kidding* glance. He then looked at the john, now in cuffs, and turned to Casey and Dragon. "Try to get off the street girls. Pieces of shit like this are all over it."

When the cops drove off, Casey thought she'd feel like celebrating. Instead, she felt like collapsing.

21
Jimmy

It was hardly news that the crowd who picked up boys to screw on Santa Monica had the sort of jobs that you'd trust your kids with—he'd busted his share of boy scout leaders, Big Brothers, priests, plenty of teachers—but still, it ate at him. It always ate at him.

"A teacher," Jimmy said. "How'd you like your kid to be in that asshole's class?"

Erin shook her head and said, "Sometimes . . ."

She stopped.

"Sometimes what?" Jimmy said.

"Sometimes it seems like no matter what we do, or how hard we try, we don't get anywhere. We could have twice as many of us, but there's always going to be a hundred times more of them. We can try to stop them, but in the end, it's like they're winning. Know what I mean?"

"Yeah."

Jimmy thought, *I know it. God do I know it.*

22
Casey

C asey and Robin each held the corners of a ratty blanket as Casey watched the entrance to the alley. It was way into the night, and the streets were empty, but still, she was worried. She looked up, just as a cardboard box dropped down from a second story window. It was falling fast and they were way out of position. Casey jerked the blanket to the side, and they just managed to just snag it. A Sony laptop.

"Good grab, dudes!"

Casey looked up to see Jumper leaning out the back window of Amos' Electronics. "Couple more," he said, "and we're outta here." A second later, Dog-Face appeared in the window and tossed down another one. But this time they grabbed it like they'd been doing it all their lives.

Dream took the box from the blanket and piled it against the alley wall. They already had six and couldn't really handle much more. Casey prayed they would toss just a final one and get out. After dodging the bullet earlier with those detectives the last thing she needed was to get popped for this.

She bit her nails. There was hardly anything left of them. "Come on. Come on. Come on," she whispered. She was a complete mess, but Dragon, who had been on the street for no time, looked like it was hardly bugging her at all. You can never tell who's gonna be the one to lose it in a second, and who's gonna be the one to tough it out.

Come on. Come on.

Suddenly, the lights went on inside. Shit. What was going on?

"Hold it right there, kid!" Casey heard someone yell from in the store. Her stomach snapped tight.

She and Dragon quickly pulled in the blanket and huddled against the brick wall . . . Listening . . . .

"Don't shoot me, man!" she heard Jumper yell. Security guard. Had to be.

"Okay, kid, come to me slow . . . real slow," the guard said.

"Shit," Dragon whispered. *"Shit."*

"Even slower, kid."

Casey waited. Was the guard going to nail them too? Call for backup?

"Good boy," the guard said. Then, Casey heard an enormous crash of what sounded like a ton of boxes and metal shelves. Jumper raced to the open window and leaped down to the ground. Just behind him was Dog-Face.

"Let's go!" Jumper said as soon as he landed. He scooped up a box, and Dog-Face grabbed two boxes. Casey and Robin grabbed a box each and they ran through the store's parking lot, heading for another alley. As she ran, Casey saw Dog-Face's T-shirt was splattered with blood.

"What happened?"

"Guy was a dick." Dog-Face said.

"Talk later," Jumper yelled.

They made it to the park off Lexington and collapsed onto the grass. Casey was heaving for breath when Dog-Face, lying on his back, took out his knife and started twirling it.

"That guy was lucky he only got a fucking fist. Next time he gets this."

"You proved that, Doggie," Dream said.

"Not again, man."

"Why, you got regrets now?" Dream said.

"Fuck regrets," Dog-Face said.

"Yeah? Most people would at least feel bad about it."

"I ain't most people."

"No shit." Dream turned to Dragon. "Doggie buys some dope from this guy and—"

"Hey, tell it right, at least—I got a rich kid at Hollywood High who wants to buy a quarter-z of crack. Were not taking grams—this is *ounces*. So I go to this shaved head dude, who looks like some kinda a pro wrestler, who thinks he's so fucking cool 'cause he works the door at the X Club, who says he can get me the dope. I kill myself to get the bucks and two days later, me and Dream take the shit over to the Hollywood High kid. We're talking monster profit. The kid's got the cash all ready, but first he tests the dope. And it's fucking soap or something! . . . Yo, Dream, I need to feel bad so far?—I got anything wrong yet?"

"Your story, man—"

"I go back to this bouncer fucker and we wait for him to come out after the club closes. Me and Dream follow him to his pickup. He's about to get in when he sees us there. I say, 'What the fuck's going on, man—you sold me shit soap and I want my fucking money back'. He just gives this shrug and says 'That's the breaks, dude.' Oh, yeah? That's what he thinks. I'm ready with my blade, but before I can do anything, he whips open his jacket and shows me a .38 tucked into his pants. Like I'm now supposed to back the fuck off. Right. I go tackle that motherfucker and the last thing he ever saw was that little .38 going into his stomach."

"You killed someone over some dope," Dream said, shaking her head. "That's so lame, Dog. They'll put your ass in jail forever for that."

"Fuck that. They got half the cops in LA looking for the guy who smoked the mayor's buddy. How many did you see for my motherfucker?—zero."

"I still can't believe you did it."

Neither could Casey. *Kill somebody and not feel anything?* Suddenly, they heard sirens, two or three of them. Everybody was back on their feet. They'd better make it back to the Fountain. And again they were running. Casey ran with all she had. And as she ran she was overtaken by a wave of sadness. Running. It was all she had done since she got here. Run, run, and run some more.

23

Back in February, it was freezing on Wonderland—back before the Chateau, before Dragon came, and back when Paul found her. It never snows in LA—that's what Paul told her, and she supposed it was true—but, man, it gets really, really close. She had only been in Hollywood a couple of weeks and as warm as it got during the day, the nights were something out of back home.

She could see her breath dart out in front of her. Casey had four layers of clothes on and she still danced her feet back and forth to keep warm. So fucking cold she couldn't stand it. She rolled up a page of a blueprint she found blown against the fence and tucked it under a piece of plywood. She put a match to it, hoping it would catch fast. Paul was stomping his foot on some scraps of wood, breaking them so they'd fit inside their small fire pit. Casey blew on the little flame. It burned blue, but wasn't catching. She blew some more . . . gently, but steadily. The flame danced . . . and then went out. Casey lit another page of the blueprint. She never stopped blowing. She needed to get warm. She *had* to get warm.

The fire was catching and she held her hands just above the flame. She wanted to somehow sanitize them against the grubby coins that people dropped in. She hated begging. Hated the way the jerks looked at her like she was a piece of shit. And the worst part of all—they were right. She *was* a piece of shit. She was, after all, sitting on Marilyn Monroe's star begging for loose change. Most of the time it seemed like no one would ever, ever give her any money. But then someone would. And then a couple more people. After a while, she would go to the Korean market at Sycamore and buy an apple. They had the most beautiful apples. Mountains of them, all different kinds. The Fuji's were her favorite. The lady always washed the apple for Casey. It was funny—she was living on the street, never taking a shower, never washing her clothes, always feeling disgusting—but the apples she ate were clean— the only thing in her life that was. There were days when Casey was striking out, no one giving anything, and she would walk by the fruit market just to look at the apples, and imagine how they would taste—the first bite, when the juices would ooze into her mouth. Crisp and sweet. How she would slowly eat the rest, going right down to the tiniest of part of the core. She could literally *taste* it—and it gave her the stuff to go back and beg some more.

When it rained, the apples seemed really far away. Tourists were in museums, or shopping, or doing whatever tourists do—they sure weren't here. As the rain would sweep the Boulevard, she would slowly walk past the Korean market looking at the fruit. The lady would be working the cash register and her husband would be in front cutting vegetables. She would see him cutting vegetables at six in the morning, cutting them at midnight, at two a.m., five a.m. She never saw anybody who worked as hard. Lots of times their kids would help, too. There was a girl who was twelve or thirteen who wore a school uniform, and a boy who had to be in high school. The boy was cute. When he worked the register, he always had a pile of books next to him which he would dive into as soon as there weren't any customers. He was super shy, and would never look directly at her. She wished he would. Yeah, right.

So many times, Casey thought how great it must be never to worry about being hungry. She'd get tired of waiting out the rain, standing under the awnings of the Roosevelt Hotel, her sneakers heavy and wet, and then she would slosh though the lake that covered the Boulevard's stars and walk to the fruit market. Her stomach was twisted in pain, her head was pounding. Sometimes the lady would call Casey over and give her an apple for free. It was heaven. For a few minutes. And then she'd go back out in the rain again.

Paul brought over the wood scraps and pushed them into the flame. Casey stared into the fire, watching as his wet boards fought it out with her little flame. She was so cold, and so down. Her eyes were locked on the fire—it was the only thing in her life that mattered.

"Hey . . . you alright?" Paul said.

Casey nodded. She was anything but alright.

She stared into the fire . . . She was beginning to feel the heat. When the board caught, she threw another one on. Now it was really going, and she felt like she was beginning to defrost. The chill was slipping away from her bones. Finally.

She picked up the rest of the wood.

"Don't," Paul said.

"Don't what?"

"Put any more on the fire. It'll get too big and someone will see us."

"Come on—"

"They will. Then we're really fucked."

"I don't care," Casey said.

"It's fine. We'll be plenty warm."

"Then let's get warmer!" She threw a board on anyway. Who cares about getting caught?

"What are you doing?" Paul said.

"What's the matter with you?"

"Matter with *me*?" He looked at her, and Casey could tell he was pissed. But she was pissed at him . . . A second later, she wasn't anymore. She was only pissed at herself. Was there any other way for her to fuck up? No life. No food. No house. And now, no friend.

"Hey," Paul said softly. He slid next to her and put his arm around her shoulder, pulling her close. She could feel herself shaking.

"I don't know how much longer I can take this," she said.

"Know."

"I mean, I'm sleeping in a construction site—"

Casey felt a tear roll down her cheek. Paul took his finger and gently lifted it off.

"Look," he said, "we'll do better. I'll pull some more dates and we can motel."

She looked at him and felt more tears. Paul caught them all.

"Casey, we're gonna be okay."

The flames danced higher, swallowing up the wood. She looked in Paul's eyes.

"Today's my birthday. I'm fifteen years old, and I'm living under a bush." She put her arms around Paul and pulled him close with all she had. "Happy birthday, Casey," she said, her face pushing into his shoulder, "Happy birthday."

24

asey walked down towards Sunset moving quickly, as though to hesitate would mean to change her mind and retreat. She wasn't going to retreat. She was wearing a tight black miniskirt made out of some kind of stretchy fabric that she picked up at a thrift store on La Brea. It barely covered her ass. She had on black stockings and tiny top she got at the same place. Casey also had the shitty heels and the makeup. She hated dressing like this and hated what she was going to do. But she knew one thing, like she knew nothing else—she wasn't going to freeze anymore.

When she reached Sunset, she stood on the far side of the sidewalk, a few feet away from the curb—like a swimmer not quite ready to jump in the pool. It was less than a month since Dennis tried to make her do this, and shitty as it was, at least he was nowhere to be seen. She started counting down from ten. At *one*, that's when she would go . . . *One* came—and she stayed. She was scared. So scared. Okay. Try it over. She counted down again, this time from twenty. And at *one*, she lifted up her head and took the few steps to the curb.

She stood on a corner looking at the passing the cars. No takers. But no other girls either. One car after another went by without stopping. It was okay. She knew she had to do this, but the longer it took, the better. She heard a laugh—a kind of sick laugh. She followed the laugh and then saw the stare, which was worse. Across Sunset was a pimp standing next to his Vette. A black guy way over six feet tall, wearing a red Clippers jacket and talking on his cell. He gave Casey a gold-tooth grin. Casey turned away. Dennis was way-scary, but this guy was even nastier. Shit. She was doing this for two seconds and she was already max-freaked. The pimp kept staring at her—he wasn't letting it go. She didn't know what to do, when she somehow felt a second stare burning into her. She turned around and saw another pimp, just up the street behind her. This one was in a black Lexus. He was checking her out too. He scared her even more than the Clippers jacket guy—and Sunset's four lanes of traffic weren't separating them. She stared down the strip, trying to ignore them both. She wondered why there were no other girls around, and realized they must be on dates. Casey heard the Lexus pimp's door open. *Shit.* Her body stiffened. She stole a look back. He was tall like the other guy, and he was wearing a pink World Gym muscle shirt showing huge shoulders and arms. He also had the gold-capped teeth, and with diamonds imbedded in the gold. He was coming closer, and now the Clippers pimp had left his car and was also heading for her. Casey looked out into the street—hoping, praying for someone to stop. But no luck. The Lexus pimp was almost down to Sunset, when a new, silver Infiniti pulled to the curb. Inside was a guy in his fifties with a McDonald's bag on the passenger seat. He was scum. But he was here.

"How much?" the guy said.

"Forty"

"Okay."

Casey got in and as the car pulled away and she looked back to the pimps who were watching her go. The car smelled of McDonalds and cigarettes—great combo. The john had long gray hair pulled back into a ponytail. He was wearing faded black jeans and had a big belly which hung over a huge silver and turquoise rodeo belt buckle. He was finishing the last of a burger. A thin line of pink Russian dressing was dribbling down the side of his face and there was a greasy mustache over his lips. How was she going to do this? He was a pig. Disgusting.

"Where do you go?" he said.

"Take a left on Orange Grove."

It was only a few blocks, but it felt like it took an hour. He made the turn off Sunset and went down a narrow street, lined with nice houses.

"Right here is good," Casey said. The guy parked the car by a chain-link fence which surrounded an elementary school yard. The street was dark, and when the guy turned off the engine, it was quiet.

He pushed the automatic seat button and with a low whir, his seat moved backwards, sliding his fat belly away from the steering wheel. He pulled his dick out. Casey could hardly look at it. It was the most foul thing she ever saw. This jerk leaning back with his dick that she was expected to suck. She'd rather die. She thought about blasting out of there—it worked once. And then she thought about freezing and starving last night. And the night before. And the night before that. She went right for it.

"Careful," he said.

She let up. But the faster she could get him to come, the better. When he finally did, she cracked open the car door and spit the cum out on the street.

As she lifted her head, she looked over at the school yard and thought, what would she give to start all over again.

When he dropped her off, Casey stood by the corner and gazed at her reflection in the glass of a parked Explorer. She thought, kids shouldn't have to do this. *Nobody* should have to do this.

She didn't look for the pimps. Fuck them. This wasn't their street. *Fuck them.* A minute later, a jeep pulled right up to her. Another customer. Bring it on. She leaned in the window— and saw Dennis.

She jerked away.

"Nice," Dennis said.

Casey took a couple of steps back and started moving up the street. She was shaking with fear, but she wasn't going to let him see it. She hated him. She hated everything about him. As she walked, he drove alongside her. She heard the awful voice.

"This is how you treat me?"

"You should be in jail. Or killed."

"I ain't either, am I now?"

Casey walked faster. There had to be a way out. Dennis stayed right beside her. Traffic behind him was moving at a crawl behind him. Cars were honking. He didn't care. She kept her eyes straight ahead, but she could feel him alongside her.

"How long you think you gonna last out here on your own?"

Just ignore him, she thought. Fairfax was up ahead. There was a Blockbuster there. Safety. *Keep walking . . . don't look over.*

"Bitch, on my street, you do what I tell you to do," he yelled over. "You hear me?"

The jeep raced forward and jerked into a bus zone. Dennis jumped out. She started to run. But he was much faster. He grabbed her arm so tight it hurt. He jerked her out into the street in front of his jeep. They were bathed in the headlights, like a spotlight was on them—but if was a spotlight, why wasn't anyone stopping? Feeling his hand grabbing her tight around her thin arm, brought back everything he did to her, and how much she hated him.

"Now," he said, "you and me gotta work this out—"

But then a miracle—a police cruiser. Dennis saw it, Casey saw it. And with everything she had—she pulled free and bolted into the street, waving her hands for the cruiser. A cop saw her and pointed just up the street at the Blockbuster parking lot, where he could pull in. Dennis went back to his jeep. But he gave her a look that said, 'your life is mine.'

Out of breath, she made it to the Blockbuster where the cruiser had parked. The cop, a buff young guy with a short blond hair was writing up something. She leaned in the car. She'd tell him what a fucking asshole Dennis was, and what he did to her.

But the cop said, "Hold on a sec." He kept writing. Casey stood outside the car, breathing hard from her run. She looked down. All the parking spaces had the names of movie stars stenciled on them. The cruiser was in Harrison Ford's spot. She could use Indy right now. The cop wrote some more. Then he got a call on his cell. He raised a finger for her to wait another moment. The call went on forever, all about who was bringing the beer, who was bringing the steaks, and where was the best place for everybody to meet. The cop had lots of things to take care of—only she wasn't one of them. He must have finished his party planning at some point, but by then, she was gone.

She lay curled up under the covers in the Starlight Motel, her wet hair splayed out on the pillow. Traffic whizzed by on Sunset. Next to Casey, a dim bulb burned in a ancient yellow lamp shade. For once she wasn't freezing. She was clean. But she kept thinking, *I'm a whore*. No one forced her to do it. Just her. She hated herself.

The bathroom door opened, and Paul came out, just showered, and wearing a towel around his waist.

"Man, that felt good," he said.

She couldn't say anything back. She pulled tighter into a ball, like a baby in the fetal position. Paul sat down on the bed beside her.

"Everything is shit," he said. "But some things aren't. Right? This isn't . . . It's warm. And it's a bed . . ."

"And sheets," Casey said.

"A great blanket."

"Pillows"

"TV."

"And no Dennis," Casey said.

"And no Dennis."

"And you," she said. She meant it. He was the only person in the world she wanted to sleep next to.

Paul lay on the covers beside her. His hand glided slowly down her hair. Over and over, and over again. It felt *so good* . . . And as he stroked her hair, she floated to sleep.

25

At the 7-11 on Santa Monica, Casey sat on the ground with her back against the low cinderblock wall, flipping through a week-old *People* tossed by the clerks inside. Two of the triplets were with her. The third was doing a date. Smoke from a Marlboro filled her lungs. The cement was cold—the miniskirt didn't help—but it was a thousand times better sitting on the ground here, than standing on Sunset. She knew she should be up there, but it wasn't like anyone was going to be pissed if she showed up late. Some kind of classical music floated from speakers mounted above the 7-11's sliding door. One of the Indian guys at the counter told her the company did this study that said playing classical music was a surefire way of getting kids to stop hanging out. Right. Casey wasn't crazy about the screechy violins, but once they started cranking along with the trumpets, drums and everything else, it was actually sort of cool. It sure wasn't chasing her away, or Paul, who was sitting shirtless on an *LA Times* box, his flannel shirt tied around his waist. Casey flipped through the magazine. One girl after another leading the good life. TV stars, models, movie stars. They were thin as spaghetti, but so was she. All through junior high, she tried to look like them—starving herself. It never worked, but on the streets, she pulled it off. Now she was every bit as skinny as America's hottest girls. But so what? One of the girls in the *People*, who played an alien on some TV show Casey had never seen, was shown her sitting inside a shiny white Porsche convertible in her driveway in Pacific Palisades. She wasn't even old enough to drive, but the car would be waiting for her as soon as she was.

"You know how to drive?" Casey called over to Paul.

"Sure"

"Was it hard to learn?"

"Not really," Paul said. "I started when I was around thirteen. My dad would take me out in our pickup and give me lessons."

"Breaking the law."

"I was the sports star, baby—remember? Other people's rules didn't apply to me."

"You think I'd be able to do it?"

"You'd suck."

"Hey!"

"You'd be great!" He jogged over and kissed the top of her head. On the Boulevard a Porsche had pulled to a stop. The guy was talking on a cell and lighting a cigar. He gunned the motor. Paul went to him and they drove off. And when she finished her smoke, she headed off too.

Sunset. Same tiny skirt and fucked-up high heels. She was a couple blocks from where Dennis found her the last time. She scanned the street for him and the other two pimps. Behind

Casey was a Moroccan restaurant with two huge wooden doors with Arabic writing on them. Guys in funny pants worked the doors for nicely dressed couples, and when the doors opened she could hear Middle-Eastern music. Casey stared out into the street. Nobody was stopping. Fine. Then she heard a car door slam, and the pimp in the Clippers jacket was coming towards her. She thought about finding another spot—but where? He came closer. The street lights reflected off his gold-rimmed glasses. She couldn't see his eyes, but just knew they were evil. She looked down the street at the never-ending line of cars. Now things were a lot different—now Casey desperately wanted someone to stop. *Come on. Come on. Stop for me . . .* But no one did. The pimp was right in front of her.

"Now what's a sweet thing like you doing out here all by yourself?"

"Doing just fine." *Don't show him fear*, Casey thought. *Don't show it.*

"Yeah—now you doing fine. But you look like you might need some protection. There be some real motherfuckers out here."

"Like you?" *Shit!* She shouldn't have said it. Stupid.

He was glaring at her. Cold . . . but then, he smiled.

"Not like me. I be your protection. Long as I'm around, ain't nobody gonna fuck with you. And you *know* that's something you need."

He stepped closer to her. "Now what you say, girl? This something we can work out?"

"I'm by myself."

He reached for Casey's arm. She jerked back.

"Get away."

"You know you need me—"

"Get away from me!" Casey screamed.

"No one talk to Roger like that."

He was so close she could see fire in his eyes through the sunglasses.

"You hear me—ain't nobody talk like that to me!"

"Get away!! I don't need anybody!" She yelled it with everything her lungs would deliver. He was a killer pimp—but she could yell loud enough for them to hear her at Venice Beach. The door to the Moroccan restaurant pushed open, and the maitre d', a tall Arab-looking guy in a brown suit, came outside to look around. Casey grabbed her chance, and bolted away from the pimp. But he wasn't bothered by the restaurant guy and followed after her.

She turned and screamed again, "Get away from me!!"

The maitre d' waved his hand, and along with two doormen in the funny pants, he came out to the sidewalk.

"Everything okay, miss?" he asked with an accent. He seemed decent.

The pimp glared at the maitre d', then flashed a gold-tooth grin at Casey and went across the street. The maitre d' and his doormen slipped back inside. Into the music and their paradise.

Casey had beaten the jerk. For now. She leaned against a newspaper box. A Ford pick-up stopped. A guy in a jeans jacket, asking how much. Man, was she glad to see him.

Something was in the air tonight. She'd get dropped off and five minutes later get picked up. This many guys needed blow jobs at one in the morning? A sixteen-year-old who looked like half the boys in her ninth-grade; a seventy-year-old geezer with clacking false teeth; the Good Humor man who she did in the back of his freezing truck; three USC kids in their daddy's Beemer, who she did one at a time, while the others waited outside watching through the car window, and

135

cheering like it was a stage show; a nervous paramedic in a starched white shirt; two cousins, smelling of beer, going home to Malibu after striking out at the X Club; a fat obnoxious rapper with music blasting so loud it rang in her ears for an hour; a dude good-looking enough to be a model—what was he doing here? Tall guys, short guys. Fat jerks. Nice looking. Creeps. Fast comers, never comers. Hard dicks, dicks trying to get hard, ugly dicks, uglier dicks, dicks springing up in her face. White dicks, black dicks, Mexican dicks, a Japanese tourist dick. How many dicks can you suck? Fuck this. Fuck Dennis. Fuck Roger the pimp. Fuck it all. Just keep sucking and you'll stay warm. What do you care? Fuck them! Fuck them all.

Things finally slowed down. Who knew what time? Late. The Moroccan place had closed hours ago. Casey was ready to go and find Paul. A shadow came over her. Roger. After what she did tonight—no fucking way!

"Get away from me," she yelled, "you got your girls. Leave me alone!"

"Hey, girl," Roger said, "I just wanna—"

"I'm by myself. I don't *want* anyone. I don't *need* anyone!" she screamed.

"Girl!—"

Casey's heart was pounding.

"Girl . . . peace."

"What?"

"Peace." He nodded coolly and went away, back to his car.

Casey exhaled. Escape. But her heart was still going a mile a minute. She looked down the Strip and saw the Marlboro man. High above it all. He protected her. She needed him—and he came through. She heard someone clapping. Down the street, she saw a bunch of kids sitting on a low wall, a couple of them smoking. One of them, a tall kid, yelled over "Way to go!" He thrust his fist into the air and gave her a smile. She always liked that smile—it was Jumper. She didn't know his name then, but she had seen him a bunch doing the Boulevard. Beside him was a tough-looking kid and two girls, one white and one black, who she had also seen before.

Casey smiled back. But when she turned around, the Lexus muscle man pimp was coming towards her. Another nightmare. They had all the girls in the world and they still needed her? But she didn't give in to the first jerk, so she sure wasn't going to give in to the next one. If he gave her any shit, she'd yell till every person in Hollywood could hear her. She'd yell help!, she'd yell rape!—she'd yell whatever it took. What gave these assholes the right to think that they could own her? It wasn't gonna happen anymore. No one owned her.

Before the pimp could say a single word, she screamed at him, "You didn't hear me before?—I don't need no one! I don't want no one!"

The creep stopped, stretched up tall in his coolest I'm-in-control pimp stance, and started formulating his clever response. But he didn't have time—a minivan pulled up right in front of her. Thank God. Casey swung the door open and hopped in.

Later, there was almost no traffic. The pimps were leaving her alone—she wasn't worth the hassle, she guessed. She sat down on a bus bench, exhausted. She lowered her face in her palms. Then she felt someone over her shoulder. They were back! Shit! She whipped around. And saw the tall kid. Beside him was the black girl.

"Hey," Casey said softly. They looked nice.

"Hey," the boy said, "you wanna come to Mickey D.'s for breakfast with us?"

26

The McDonalds coffee slid down her throat, washing away the disgusting cum. The place was nearly empty: a homeless woman in the corner with two little kids, a city worker in a bright orange jumpsuit, and a couple of paramedics in white shirts, with squawking walkie-talkies on their belts—probably buddies of the john from earlier. Casey sat in a booth with the boy—Jumper—and the others. She looked into her coffee cup as she swirled a Half and Half into it. Jumper was putting one sugar pack after another into his coffee, seven or eight in all. Dog-Face was dragging fries through a sea of catsup. June Bug, her head on Dream's shoulder was half-asleep. A weird silence hung over the table.

"You—" Casey said.

"You—" Jumper said at the same time.

They smiled.

"Go ahead," he said.

"Nothing . . ." she said.

She took a sip of the coffee. What she wished she had said

was—You're so lucky running with a bunch of friends . . . Is it so great? Is it easier? How do you survive without having sex with jerks? But instead, she just said "Nothing."

A pack of skinheads came in and headed for the counter. They were pushing, laughing, yelling. Probably tripping. After them came two girls who were also doing dates on Sunset. They were followed by a huge shaved-head Mexican guy with prison tatts all over his log-sized neck, and his girlfriend who was half his size but also with the tatts. Suddenly the place was buzzing.

Jumper checked out the crowd and turned to Casey. "Welcome to Mr. Rogers' neighborhood."

She smiled, still looking into her coffee.

"What? You don't think so?" Jumper said.

"No, it's exactly like it," Casey said.

"Actually, I think it's more like Sesame Street," June Bug said, waking up.

"Why, 'cause of the fags?" Jumper said.

"Wait," Dream said, "there's no fags on Sesame Street."

"Right," Jumper said.

"Who?"

"Who? Bert and Ernie. Who else?"

"Bert and Ernie are homos?" Dream said.

"Shut up!" June Bug said, giving Jumper a shove.

"Abso-fucking-lutely," Jumper said, "Burt and Ernie are def' butt-boys."

"Come on," Dream said.

"What? They just sleep in the same bedroom, take baths together and sing to each other while they wash each other off—and they're not queer?"

Casey jumped in. "They could just be friends."

"Sure, friends who shower dick to butt."

"Then, close friends," Casey added, starting to enjoy herself. *"Very close* friends."

"And look at the other freaks they got there, too, "Jumper said. "You got Kermit who's after Miss Piggy's ass. He's gotta be some kinda chubby-chasing fat-chick freak. Right?"

"And Cookie Monster," Dream said getting into it, "the dude eats and eats and eats and eats, and never gains any weight. They got a word for that—"

"Bulimic," June Bug said.

"Right, bulimic. We just never get to see him toss the cookies."

"And Oscar the grouch," Casey said, "he's *always* going off crazy on something."

"Guys going off—that describes half the Boulevard," June Bug said.

"See," Jumper said, "Sesame Street—the Boulevard. It's all the same thing. Every place is fucked-up."

"Every place but the Fountain," June Bug said.

"Got that right," Dream said. She reached her hand high over the table and June Bug slapped it.

Casey wondered what the Fountain was, when out the window, she saw Dennis. Beside him was a new girl. Not dressed like she was doing dates, but wearing jeans and a red Land's End down jacket. Dennis was talking a mile a minute to her. Casey slid low in the booth—the last thing she needed was for him to see her now, ruin the one break she finally got. She could see the other kids looking at her. She wanted them to keep talking—ignore her somehow. But they didn't. Dennis walked past. Casey pulled herself up and stared down into what was left of her coffee. She didn't want to talk about it. She rolled the last thin pool of liquid around and around again.

"Who's that?" June Bug said.

"Long story," Casey said, not looking up.

"That's Dennis, right?" Jumper said.

"Yeah."

"He's slime," Dream said.

"You know him?" Casey asked.

"Lot's of people know him," Dream answered. For a second their eyes met. Casey wasn't sure, but Dream's eyes seemed the tiniest bit shiny. Same thing?

Dream broke the look and stared out the window. Then she turned back.

"When I first came onto the streets," Dream said, "I was thirteen years old. I was very scared. My first night out, I slept on a bench on La Brea. That first night, you don't know whether you're gonna wake up. You don't know if you're gonna die. You don't know what's gonna happen. It's bad for any kid, but it's a lot worse for girls. The street guys all come up to you. 'Cause you got virginity written all over you and they all want it. When I first got here, my friend and me, we go down to Sunset. And like fifteen minutes later, that dude Dennis is all over us. Buying us food, a jacket, Starbucks. But it ain't free. And by the end of the next night he's our pimp. I'm getting dressed up and getting into a car. After the first one, I tell myself, I don't want to do this. So what if I'm hungry, I'd still got my pride. I'd rather be dead. I told Dennis, I ain't gonna be doing this no more. Dennis tells me he wants to talk about it. We go back to his place, and bam—he ties me up. I was raped for a whole week. No food. Couple of sodas a day to drink, that's all. I got lucky and when he was gone, I twisted my wrist over and over until it slipped out and I busted outta there. I told the police what happened. They said they knew all about him and that he was also selling the drugs and they was gonna bust him for that too. That was two years ago. Think anything happened to him? Fuck no. Nobody cares."

Casey looked across the table. She felt like there was a bungee cord connecting her to Dream. She leaned forward, and softly touched her hand.

Jumper turned to Casey, "He treat you like that too?"

"Yeah. But she's right. Nobody cares."

"No. I care. We care."

27

The lights from inside Wing's 24-hour liquor store burned against the first hints of daylight. Through the plate glass window of the store, just off the Boulevard, Casey saw an old guy, who must have been Wing, watching the Weather Channel from behind a counter-to-ceiling wall of bulletproof Plexiglas. Slipping money through the cash slot and receiving for a pack of Salem's, was Dennis. Behind him, his new girl was holding a bag of Fritos and drifting back and forth in front of a long refrigerator, trying to pick a soda. She looked sixteen, maybe a little younger. Casey felt sorry for her. The girl took a Mountain Dew to the counter, Dennis paid for her things, and they came outside into the parking lot. Dennis stopped short, seeing Casey standing by his jeep in the otherwise empty lot.

"Look at that," Dennis said.

Casey didn't say a thing. She just stared at him, thinking about what he did to her and Dream, and what he'd do to the new girl.

"Your timing's not the greatest here, but we can hook up later on. How's that?"

"That's what you think? I'm here to hook up?"

"It's okay. So it took a little to realize what you got." He stripped the cellophane off the cigarette pack. The girl looked at Casey, not sure of what was going on.

"Really," Casey said.

"It's okay. I'll let it slide."

"*You'll* let it slide?"

She turned and walked towards the street. Dennis followed.

"Hey. Hey! Man, where you going?" he called after her.

Casey glanced over her shoulder at him and kept on walking. Dennis crushed the wrapper up into a ball and threw it to the ground. He jogged after her—when springing out from between two parked cars were Dog-Face and Jumper. Dog-Face thrust his arms around Dennis' waist, as Jumper threw a paint-splattered blue plastic tarp over his head. Dennis swung his fists up, trying to break free, but Dog-Face— toughest kid on the Boulevard—instantly pinned Dennis' arms down to his side.

"What the fuck!" he screamed, flailing trying to break free. The tarp started sliding off, and fell so far down Casey could see Dennis' face—covered with dirt from the tarp, and twisted with fury. Dream raced over to help. She swiftly jerked the tarp back down to Dennis' waist.

Dennis fought like a monster to get away, but Dog-Face and Jumper were in control now. They dragged Dennis down the alley that ran alongside the liquor store.

Casey looked around for trouble. Wing was still stuck on the Weather Channel, not seeing, or not wanting to see. The only person on the street was the new girl who stood frozen in place, silent and stunned.

"Go! Get outta here!" Casey yelled. The girl stared at Casey, confused.

"Do it! Go. Go!"

She took off, and Casey raced after the others. Dog-Face and Jumper had dragged Dennis to the end of the alley. He was still fighting, still trying to get away.

Casey ran up to them, and Dog-Face jerked the ratty tarp off Dennis' face.

"Who the fuck are you?" Dennis yelled at Dog-Face.

"I'm the taxman, motherfucker," Doggy shot back. And with that he drove his huge fist straight into Dennis' left eye. Dennis dropped to the ground and Jumper scrambled on top of him, trying to pin him down. Dennis managed to throw Jumper off and came up, swinging. But Jumper smashed his cheek below the other eye, instantly followed by Dog-Face sending another fist into Dennis' stomach, dropping him again. As he hit the ground, Dog-Face muscled Dennis onto his back and Jumper stood over him, his boots pressing Dennis' forearms to the concrete.

Jumper turned to Dream and yelled, "He's all yours."

Dream ran over and screamed, "Remember me?"

Dennis glared at her.

"Come on. You don't remember?"

Dennis turned his head and spit on the ground. And Dream drove a kick straight into his balls. Dennis yelled out, and curled up on his side. Dream circled around and sent another kick between his legs and then kicked him even harder in the stomach.

"Don't hear your rap now. Where is it?" Dream said, kicking him again. She was possessed, almost dancing, taking one kick after another. And every time Dream connected, Casey felt a jolt of satisfaction. She could watch Dream kick him all day.

"Hey—don't hear no sweet talk no more . . ." Dream said, trembling, "I'm such a pretty girl. I need a friend here. You gonna be that friend. Come on. Give it to me. Give it to me! Gimme that sweet talk." And she landed another kick straight into his balls. Dennis screamed.

Dream turned around, and Casey could see she was shaking with rage . . . and crying.

"Your turn," Dog-Face called over.

Casey stepped up to his head. This was going to feel so good. She looked at Dennis on the ground and thought, for once in her life, the tables had turned, and she was going to give Dennis back some of his own—make him taste the pain like she did. She could never make him know what it was like to be raped by him and his disgusting buddies, but she could drive her foot straight into his face. There was blood all over it, and she pulled back her foot back to make some more . . . And she stopped. She couldn't.

"Come on. Feels good," Dream said.

"Let me," Jumper said. And he did, driving two more kicks into Dennis' stomach. Dennis groaned in pain. Casey went to kick him in the same place. Again she couldn't. She stood over his face and screamed, "Fuck you! Fuck you! Fuck you for everything you did to me."

She stomped the ground beside his head, causing him to jerk away, and then she leaned down and spit in his face. She stared at his fucked-up face—that took so much joy in raping her—then turned away, never wanting to see it again.

They were back on the Boulevard. The sun was coming up and Hollywood was bathed in a crisp, lush blue light. Jumper and Dog-Face were walking ahead of Casey and Dream. Jumper raised his hand up and Dog-Face slapped it a high-five. The guys laughed. Casey smiled a little. She felt something good inside. Dream reached over and held her hand.

28

Casey didn't make it to Joey's until almost eleven. Paul was sitting in a booth by himself.

"Remembered me after all," he said.

"Come on."

"No. You come on. That's the Boulevard, I guess. Gotta expect people to disappear."

"It's not that you know."

"What then?"

"Just, things happened. Good things. Really good things. I'll tell you."

"Can't wait," Paul said coldly.

"Hey, it's not like you had a number I could've called." She slid next to him in the booth and kissed his cheek. She noticed a battered brown leather bomber jacket on the seat next to him.

"Nice jacket."

"Got it at the Frenchy's thrift store."

"Way cool. Looks warm."

"Is. Have some fries," he said. "How'd it go?"

"I decided something."

"Yeah?"

"I'm not doing any more dates," Casey said.

"Good. Do it."

"And I think you should stop too."

"And sit on the sidewalk begging nickels? No thanks. I liked the room we had."

"That's the other thing I wanted to tell you. I got us a place we can live. A squat. Wanna go see it?"

"Can't. I got a date."

"Now?"

"Yeah. It looks like real money."

"Later?" Casey said.

"There he is."

He headed for the door where a shiny blue Mercedes had pulled up outside.

"You forgot your jacket," she called after him.

"No I didn't."

"Sure you did."

"Nah—I got it for you."

She couldn't believe it. No one had ever given her something as great as this. She ran after him to give him a huge hug. He smiled to end all smiles, and went out towards the Mercedes. Casey thought, nice car, real money—things were improving.

29
Jimmy

The clock behind the security guard in the black marble Century City tower entrance read 5:55. Perfect. The cherry wood paneled elevator flew up in a whoosh that made Jimmy's ears pop as he and Erin rode up to the forty-first floor. When the doors slid open Jimmy saw an enormous reception desk with Miller & Lodge, LLP across its front in brass letters. Behind the desk was a floor-to-ceiling window with a view all the way to Santa Monica. As they approached the desk, the receptionist, a tall, athletically-built kid with movie-star looks was stuffing a script into his bag. Jimmy told them who they were.

"Mr. Lodge's secretary is about to go home for the day," the receptionist answered.

"Sorry, but can you let her know we're here?"

He noisily exhaled . . . but at 5:58, his first job was making it to the gym, yoga, acting lessons—anything but arguing with two cops.

Lodge's secretary was a nice-looking, well-dressed, Filipino

lady. Her coat was already on and she was clicking off a game
of FreeCell when they reached her desk. It made sense to
Jimmy that she wasn't swamped with work—how many calls
a day do you make for a boss who's dead?

Erin gave her a kind smile and said, "We know how late it
is, but we've been completely overwhelmed and just haven't
been able to make it here earlier. We were hoping to go
through Mr. Lodge's things. See if there's something that
could help."

"Tomorrow would be much better. If you come in the
morning I can stay with you all day."

"Yeah . . . Tomorrow doesn't really work," Jimmy said.

She looked torn.

Erin added, "We're really sorry. Can we buy you coffee at
Starbucks downstairs? We'll try to finish as fast as we can."

"It's okay."

She took off her coat and went back to her FreeCell. Jimmy
and Erin entered the office. Displayed on the walls were
undergraduate and law school diplomas from UCLA and a
large framed certificate honoring Lodge's appearance before
the California Supreme Court. There were also framed pictures which Lodge must have taken on vacations: giraffes in
Africa, mosques in Turkey, gondolas in the rain in Venice.
Lodge wasn't a half-bad photographer. They started plowing
through his files. It was slow going. A real-estate deal here,
another one there. A contract the size of a small city's white
pages. Endless notes for on-going negotiations.

The secretary stayed outside at her desk, moving from Free-
Cell to solitaire, back to FreeCell again. Every now and then
she would stick her head in. At 6:30 she was pleasant and
offered them sodas or water. By 7:00 her smile had faded. At
7:15 she was pacing with her coat on behind her desk. Around

7:45 she was cranky as hell, and by 7:55 she asked them if they could lock the door behind them on the way out. Which is what Jimmy wanted in the first place.

Now they had the run of the office. Miller was in Vegas for the day with the mayor, the others in the firm had long since left, and Jimmy could hear the distant hum of the cleaning people's vacuum cleaners. But for all the freedom, two hours later Jimmy was sitting in one of Lodges red leather chairs surrounded by a pile of useless files—half a dozen for a huge new office tower under construction on Wilshire, and a knee-high pile of contracts for building casinos.

"How are you doing" Erin asked from behind Lodge's desk where she methodically searched his computer.

"He's got more gambling business than an Indian chief, but bullshit when it comes to something for us. You?"

"He either clean or clever," Erin said.

"So far."

As he plowed through yet another stack of files Jimmy thought about an assignment he did in New York with another undercover named Ron Chang. Ron was obsessed with the city's massage parlors, almost all controlled by the Hong Kong tongs. He had a right to be. The gangsters would go into tiny Chinese villages and basically buy teenage girls from their parents. The tongs would smuggle the girls into the US, where they were made to turn tricks in massage parlors to repay the money their parents took, plus what it cost to smuggle them into the country. It could be twenty or thirty thousand dollars. The girls were young, scared, and incredibly naive. Jimmy did the math and figured they'd have to work seven or eight years, fucking one asshole after another just to pay back the gangsters that brought them into this misery in the first place. The girls weren't officially slaves, but they were

Goddamn close, and seeing it broke his heart. There were eighty-two massage parlors in the precinct and systematically Ron or Jimmy would go in undercover looking for a massage, and get them to offer 'something extra'. They got offered the 'something extra' in eighty-one of them. But the way a cop's mind works is—not thinking the eighty-second place was clean—no way. It's just their technique wasn't working on eighty-two. Jimmy kept going back in—he and Ron were on a mission to nail number eighty-two. But after nine or ten trips back to the place, they realized it really *was* just a massage parlor. That's all. As Jimmy sifted through Lodge's notes, he was haunted by the possibility that the same thing could be happening here. Sure Lodge gets iced somewhere he shouldn't have been. But what if at the end of the day, he was clean, and this was massage parlor eight-two all over again?

Erin pulled up Lodge's appointments from the day he was killed. It was virtually empty. When she went to three days before—she leaned back in her chair and smiled.

"He sees Cat Cassandra? Now *that's* bizarre."

"Who's Cat Cassandra?" Jimmy said.

"He cuts hair. I saw him a couple of times."

"Something strange about it?"

"You might say that. But when I saw him—it was the only time in my entire life I was stopped on the street—twice—by someone asking me who cut my hair."

"But you didn't stick with him?"

"It was a little much."

"How?"

"Cat was the last appointment our vic had—or at least the last official appointment, right?"

"Sure. But what's the deal on Cat?"

"Know something, Jimmy—you could use a haircut."

30

Jimmy had been to the Roosevelt Hotel dozens of times, but he had never been in a room like 401. The door swung open to give him a view of Cat, a tall Filipino man wearing a fluffy Helmsley Palace bathrobe, and whose face was fully made-up, compete with ultra-long fake eyelashes. Cat led them inside the tiny room, no bigger than a standard–issue Manhattan studio apartment, with a folded-up futon couch and a beauty shop chair that faced a large mirror which had a chest in front of it holding clippers, brushes and the usual hairdresser's supplies. Below the chest legs was a collection of high pumps, all of them black or red. On one side of the mirror was the largest TV Jimmy had ever seen. An old black and white movie played—a young Shirley MacLaine was running down a Manhattan street with a blissful smile. Leaning against the TV was a six-foot stack of straight and gay porno tapes. On the other side of the mirror was a display case packed with figurines of angels, the Virgin, and saints and crosses.

"Honey, you have been gone much too long." Cat said to Erin. He had a faint accent.

"I know, but my new partner, Jimmy, he needs it a lot it more. Right?"

Cat cocked his head like a beagle. "You have a smart partner." He extended his hand, indicating the chair and Jimmy slipped in.

Erin checked out the angel case. "This is new."

"I still do all these Filipinos. They come here for their hair, but always wanna buy the saints too. What am I gonna do?"

He threw a plastic beauty-shop sheet over Jimmy.

"You want the same, honey—but better, right?"

"Right."

"Cat was the hottest thing in Manila," Erin said.

"*Years ago*, darling" he said with a laugh. "*Years* ago. I had three shops there. But *thank God* somebody still remembers me."

As Jimmy looked around the room he knew how a Jew must feel at a Catholic mass. It was a world familiar to lots of people, but it sure wasn't him. Reflected in the mirror behind him was a gold trophy nearly as tall as Cat.

"What's the trophy for?" Jimmy asked.

"Miss Castro. I came in second place."

"That's impressive." *Good God*, if his dad could hear him now, complementing this drag-queen on his beauty contest success.

"But you know who I lost to . . . ?"

He couldn't wait.

"Miss Gay America. We went out for two months after that. But he was *such* a user—just laying around and looking beautiful, like some pussy cat. Use me, use me, use me, that's all he ever did. Finally, I had to throw the lazy bitch out."

Stuck in the mirror, was a picture from the LA Times of the

West Hollywood Halloween parade where a stunning Imelda Marcos was striding down the middle of Santa Monica Boulevard. Jimmy realized she was none other than the guy cutting his hair.

"You always go out as Imelda?"

"No!!" he said it as if he was shot with a bullet. "I used to. Every night—for years. But American men they don't appreciate *class* any more. They want *trash*. So now I go out as Sharon Stone. Ugh. But it works."

"Yeah . . . I guess." What else could he say?—We American men really do appreciate class, and you were so wrong to abandon Imelda?

Erin flipped through a Harper's Bazaar on the couch. "We heard you did Mark Lodge," she said.

"Honey, I didn't *do* him. I just cut his hair." Turning to Jimmy, he said, "She tell you how many cops I do?"

"You're kidding." As soon as he said it, Jimmy realized his answer should have been, *I didn't know that,* and kill the conversation. It was too late.

"Oh yeah. In uniform—and on duty. You cops love it. It's a nice little dirty thing. Makes the night go by faster."

"You tell them what you are?" Erin said.

"God yes!—I always says to them this hot chick got a hot dick. I don't want no surprises later."

"And they don't mind?" Jimmy said.

"Nah, that's what they there for."

"What about Lodge?" Jimmy said.

"He was nothing. His secretary sent him to me the first time. I couldn't believe he came back."

"What did he talk about with you?"

"Pfff. Borrrrring. Too, too Valley. But he liked the book, so he wasn't a complete nothing."

"What book?"

"What book?—*The book*. You never saw it? Right there on the table."

Erin picked up a large red photo album—and pulled back.

"See what I mean?" Cat grinned.

"Show it to your partner."

She held it open for Jimmy. On the first page there were half-a dozen Polaroids of men of all different ages and races, but all in the same basic pose—on their backs, stretched out the same couch that Erin now sat, and naked. The book was packed. It looked like he had half the city in there.

"Okay. I get it."

Erin shut the book.

"Sure you don't wanna see the whole thing," Cat said. "Might find someone you know."

"That's what I'm afraid of," Jimmy said. "Those are all cops?"

"Not all—but plenty."

"Lodge was interested in it?" Erin said.

"Honey, *everybody* but you two is interested. That book is worth a million dollars . . ."

Not to me, pal, Jimmy thought

". . . If I wanted to sell it, it would be bye-bye shopping Betsey Johnson and hello *owning* Betsey Johnson. All these closet queers with wives in the Valley? Name your price."

"Lodge ever talk about what he was doing?" Erin asked. "About work or anything else?"

"Nothing, honey"

"You're sure?"

Jimmy was about to pump him for more info. Then he stopped. Whatever Lodge was, he wasn't an idiot, and Cat had to be the most indiscreet man in Hollywood—hardly the person you confess anything to.

Jimmy had about all he could take and started to get up. He looked into the mirror and realized that for all the craziness—this drag queen was giving him the best haircut he ever had. Maybe he'd come back sometime.

31

Jimmy drove towards the stationhouse, cutting through a light rain misting over West Hollywood. Erin was staring out the window, trying to catch sight of any kids she knew who could tell them something . . . When the streets were this quiet, every house seemed to have a memory for Jimmy. As they drove down Seward he passed a big place with a nice white picket fence. Six or seven years ago he was the first one on the scene where a young Japanese woman with an eight-month-old baby, had been pistol-whipped during a break-in, and her husband shot in front of her. Every time he drove past the house, Jimmy thought about the woman as he arrived—the baby crying in her arms, the husband on the floor still bleeding from a shot to his cheek, her screams tearing into the night. That image, a snapshot of unimaginable pain, he figured would be with him till the day he died.

The light changed. Jimmy shut his eyes a moment and tried to push the woman's screams away. It worked. For now. But they would be back. There wasn't a street in Hollywood that didn't have a memory that Jimmy wished he could shake. An apartment building where a waitress was stabbed in the vagina by her jealous boyfriend and left to bleed to death in the bathtub; a nice tiny house where a raging drunk kicked his nine-months pregnant girlfriend so hard in the stomach that the baby died. Over the years Jimmy tried to change his route home—so he wouldn't keep seeing the same ghosts, but there was always some house, some park, some spot where the ghosts found him.

"Striking out—the rain, " Erin said, pulling him out of the horrors.

They drove in silence for a block. He could see the side of her face from the corner of his eye and wondered what she was thinking. She turned to him. "How come you moved out here?" she asked.

"I had an incident in New York." Lousy way of putting it, Jimmy thought, but it was the best he could do.

"Bad?"

"I guess."

"If you don't want to talk about it, that's okay."

"No. It's alright. I was coming back from a break-in with my partner Angelo in the East Village—or the Lower East Side—that's what it was called when my father and uncles used to be cops there. And I see this little twelve-year-old girl who comes running up to me screaming there's a guy at the bodega at the corner chasing after a kid with a nine. Angelo hits the gas, and the girl was right—at the end of the block, there's this fat black guy waving the gun and running after a fourteen year old kid yelling, 'Gimme that the fuck back.' But the kid kept running. Angelo pulls the car onto the curb across the street from the bodega. I jump out and squat behind the open car door for cover. Angelo pops out the other side, and leans over the cruiser with his arms stretched out on the hood pointing his gun at the perp. Angelo yells across the street to the perp, 'Drop the gun, buddy.' The perp is a nasty-looking guy, his pants are unbuckled and hanging half-open, and his face is covered with scrubby white stubble. 'Drop it!' Angelo calls over again. But the perp just stares at us with the strangest Goddamn look. But then, he does like he's told and drops the gun onto the lid of a dumpster. So we relax a little. Another scumbag with a gun, but at least he was giving it up without a hassle. Angelo yells, 'Just walk way from it, man. With the hands up.' The perp takes a step away from the dumpster. I feel for my cuffs on my belt—and then the perp scoops up the gun and aims it right at my head. What was it?—a tenth of a second. Less? And that tenth of a second was *filled*. Filled with thoughts of my wife being a widow, my kid, the person in the world I cared the most about, growing up without a dad. I pulled the trigger—but before the shot was even out, Angelo's shot had already hit. Then mine hit. Then two more of Angelo's. And the perp was dead. No question."

"Hell to pay?" Erin said.

"God, yeah. Complete shitstorm. It took over seventy cops to calm the neighborhood—they had to bring in guys from three other precincts. Two white cops shoot a fifty-three year-old black guy. If that won't rip the city apart, nothing will. Before the shooting, he was just another drunk from the neigh-borhood, but the second he hit the ground, he became a com-munity leader. That's all the papers wrote about—cops shoot community leader. The autopsy showed he was off-the-chart drunk, but that only made things worse—what kind of cops shoot a drunk? That night I dreamed about it. I dreamed about it for weeks—more. I'd taken a human life. He may have been a perp chasing after a kid with a gun when it happened, but the truth was, he still was somebody's father, grandfather. I'd lay in bed at night thinking, what right did I have? I wondered what my wife thought—what did she think of me now that I had killed someone?

"We got a thirty-day suspension and Angelo and I couldn't be partners any more. The captain called it a bone they had to throw to the neighborhood. But the city just got too hot. I was on the front page of Daily News for a week—the guy who killed the community leader. I could've stuck it out. But I kept asking myself, is this was really where I wanted to raise my kid? LA was looking for cops—they had all these flyers on the station-house bulletin board, and suddenly it didn't seem so bad."

"That's hard. Really hard."

"Sorta . . . Yeah. I don't know." Jimmy felt it in his stomach. He hated going back to the shooting again—but telling her was like letting go a huge breath of air. And no one had asked him about it for a long time—until Erin.

32

It was pushing three in the morning when Jimmy finally made it home to Santa Monica. He had a small house on Yale, where they moved into when they first came to LA nine years ago. When they bought the place, most of the houses on the block were like his, with low fences around the yards, kid's toys on the lawns. Over the years, one at a time, the houses were being torn down and replaced with lousy-looking, overpriced apartments.

For a while, things here were pretty good. But that was before Rancher fell into the abyss. Rancher was fourteen and went to a party at the beach where one of his buddies passed him a crack pipe. He had smoked some pot and drank a little, but nothing serious. Crack was a whole other animal. After the first hit, he did another, and then one more. When he woke up the next morning, all he could think about was how to get the next hit.

First he emptied his bank account, then he stole all the cash in the house. And after that he stole Jimmy's ATM card from the dresser while they slept—anything for the rock. It was hell for Jimmy and Shannon. Rancher was a solid "A" student before this, and two weeks later he wasn't showing up at school. When Jimmy confronted him, he was still together enough to realize what he was doing with his life, and Jimmy got him to agree to go into a treatment program. After two nights, Jimmy was woken up by a call from the treatment center at one in the morning telling him that Rancher and a girl had busted out. It didn't take a genius to know where they would go.

Jimmy hit Hollywood. He drove down countless dark streets passing pack after pack of strung-out street kids, slowing the car to a crawl, to see if Rancher was with them. He went by dozens of crack whores and their scumbag pimps. He drove past every crackhouse he knew—fifteen or twenty of them—but from the outside there was nothing. Not the tiniest hint of whether Rancher was inside. An enormous knot of pain was in his stomach. He cruised the streets endlessly, eyeing every kid he saw, praying that one of them would be his. These were the same streets he worked everyday as a cop, only then he was dealing with someone else's problems, not his own.

He rolled up on the baby transvestite Gina as she was getting out of a car. He could make life miserable for her and she knew it. For fifty bucks Gina told Jimmy about a kid who fit Rancher's description she saw earlier at a crackhouse on Wilton. Jimmy knew the place: the SWAT guys in his precinct had raided it half a dozen times. It had a door like a battleship's, and there were God knows how many guns in there from crackheads trading them for rocks. There was no way Jimmy was going to be able get inside on his own. He parked the car half-way down the block hoping that Rancher would eventually come out. No luck. The sun came up and when it was eight, Jimmy called Charles. It was a call he hated to make, but what choice did he have? Charles told him the SWAT team was serving warrants starting at nine, but the place on Wilton wasn't on the list. Without a second hesitation, Charles added it on. Fuck a search warrant, Jimmy's kid was inside.

An hour and a half later, twenty cops in black fatigues, Kevlar helmets, bullet-proof vests, and M-16 machine guns charged the door. The lead guys screamed *Police—we have a warrant!* A second later, two guys behind him smashed the door down with a steel battering ram. The cops raced in yelling *Get on the ground!*, and *On the ground, asshole—now!* His gun drawn like the rest, Jimmy followed the SWAT team in. He had been in plenty of crackhouses, but this was a bad as they got. The place was strewn with garbage, empty cans were all over the place, along with rotting remnants of fast-food burritos and burgers. It smelled of shit and piss. In the first room he went through, a guy with a scraggy beard lay on the floor already cuffed, and beside him was a girl still in her teens, sitting on the floor with her knees pulled to her chest. She must have been seven or eight months pregnant. A cop was kneeling next to her holding up a crack pipe he found in her boot. She was crying and saying, *I try to stop . . . I'm trying to stop.* Jimmy walked past her into the living room where two Latino guys faced the wall as the lieutenant was speaking Spanish and holding up a gun which he took off one of them. Jimmy made it to the back room. There, sitting on the rattiest mattress he had ever seen, in a room with stench so bad he could barely stand it, was Rancher. He was completely strung out. Beside him was a pretty Hispanic girl with waist-length black hair who must've been a nice kid too before she got into this. She was wearing only a tank top and panties—so it was obvious how she paid for the shit. Rancher's eyes met Jimmy's, not with surprise or even hate—but like he barely recognized him. Jimmy felt like screaming at him, he felt like hugging him. How could this be the same kid he taught to ride a bike, whom he read to every night, whose little league team he coached, whose laughter and kisses were the happiest parts of his whole life? . . . He helped him to his feet, then reached across the mattress for up a pair of corduroy pants and passed them to the girl. As she slipped them on, Rancher looked up at him. His eyes were distant and drained of life. Somehow, it all began to register. He said, "I'm sorry," and leaned his head on Jimmy's shoulder.

The girl, Mary, was returned to her parents in San Diego, and when Rancher got home, he slept for almost a day. When he came to, he asked Jimmy for one more chance. Jimmy begged the treatment center to take him back. If Jimmy wasn't a cop, they probably wouldn't have gone for it. Rancher went back in, saying he was completely committed to making it work. But six days later, Rancher bolted and was back out on the street. This time for good.

Jimmy paced his house. He couldn't sleep. He opened the refrigerator. Lots of condiments—pickles, mustard, relish— but little else. This is what happens when you live alone. He threw out some tangerine beef from Wok Fast that should have been tossed last week. He walked some more. He thought of Erin—tried to stop. He picked up a picture on the mantelpiece—the family on the beach in Florida. Shannon, looking as good as she ever did, her arm around his waist as Jimmy held a seven-year-old Rancher. They were happy then. Jimmy flopped down on the couch and pushed the clicker.

Bond and some babe racing through a building exploding all around them. Next channel, Australian rules football. Who cares? Next, a cute blonde in some cheeseball Showtime movie running her hands all over her breasts in a sauna. Jimmy used to like bumping into shots like this, but now it made him think of Dani, and all the shit she had to do. Back to Bond. The building was still blowing up. He thought about Erin. Wondered what she was doing now. Was she with the husband? Probably. Was she sleeping? The phone rang.

"It's Erin. I hope it's not too late to call."

Jimmy felt a jolt in his chest. Should he tell her he was thinking about her, or play it cool. Better not say anything. But he did it anyway. "I was just thinking about you."

"Yeah?"

"Yeah."

"I guess we're on the same wavelength," she said. "I couldn't sleep. I was thinking about the Chateau girl who the busboys told us about. What I would do if I was in her shoes."

"And?"

"She'd have to be unbelievably hardcore not to tell anyone about it. It would have to be burning a hole in her."

"You think she spilled it?" Jimmy said.

"It's worth checking out, right?"

Jimmy imagined Erin—sitting at her kitchen table in Chatsworth; the kitchen probably had blue and white wallpaper; glass cabinets with perfectly lined up coffee cups; dark but for one light above the table where she sat in a T-shirt— and he wondered if he would ever get her out of that kitchen, and himself off the fucking couch in Santa Monica.

33
Casey

Casey and Dragon found Tulip sitting on the low wall by the Chinese Theater. She looked bad—her arms rested on her knees as she bent over to light a smoke. It was ten or eleven and Hollywood was just starting to come alive. Tulip was by herself at one end of the wall. At the other, were a bunch more kids. A couple of skinheads were coming out of Mickey D.'s. Gina, Barbara and two other baby trannys were heading for Joey's. As Casey came closer to the wall, she could see Tulip was more than tired, she was hurt. Her right eye was purple and swollen, the sort of major black eye that cartoonists draw when they're exaggerating what a black eye really looks like.

"What happened?"

"Date. I thought it was straight. Nothing bad. But this jerkoff wanted to piss on me. I told him no way. He gets like, 'Look you fucking whore, that's what I'm paying you for.' And he wouldn't let it go. Like an idiot, I yell, 'Go fuck yourself, pervert.' And this is what I got back. Fucking asshole."

"You gotta get some ice," Dragon said.

"Nah. I'll be okay."

"You gotta. We can get it at Joey's. It'll make the swelling go down. You'll feel better."

Tulip pushed out a smoke. She wasn't going anywhere.

"She's right," Casey said.

"You'll feel a lot better—really," Dragon said. "I'll get it."

Tulip looked up, and with the faintest smile said, "I'm supposed to be the one who takes care of everyone around here."

She got up and they started towards Highland, when Tulip stopped.

"Hey—where's Paul? I could definitely use a mega-dose of the Saint right now."

Casey felt it in her stomach. "He get married and leave us all behind? " Tulip continued.

"Nah, " Casey said. "He's got some old rich dude hot for him and he's riding it for all it's worth."

"When you see him—tell him we need his cute ass back here—"

Tulip then saw whipping around a corner, and flying to a stop at the end of the block, three cruisers. A pack of cops jumped out and before anyone knew what was happening, they grabbed a couple of the skinheads and two or three others. *Fuck!* Casey could see more cop cars father down the Boulevard, all doing the same thing. *This was it!*

"Shit!" Tulip yelled. Dragon froze. Casey turned around towards La Brea—and coming down the Boulevard from the other direction were two more cruisers. Tulip scrambled over the wall and sprinted into the parking behind the Chinese. Casey and Dragon followed, and the three girls raced through a line of parked cars. Casey looked back and saw a cruiser had jerked to a stop by the wall, and two cops were coming over it after them.

As she ran, Casey felt a panic like she never had before. The other kids might get popped for being runaways or doing dates—big deal—what they wanted her for was a million times worse. She kept running, but then she realized it was crazy—how could they ever outrun the cops?—the parking lot was only so big, and in seconds they'd be back in the open on a street. Then she saw it. A cool old Impala convertible that someone was stupid enough to park with the top down.

"Here!" Casey called to Dragon and Tulip. She dived over the Impala's door, into the back seat, and the other girls followed. Casey and Dragon were huddled together, tight and low on the right side of the bump, and Tulip was on the left. Casey's heart was pounding and she was so close to Dragon that her arm could feel Dragon's chest going up and down as she tried to catch her breath. They heard a girl cop yelling to her partner.

"It was this row, Manny?"

"Yeah, " her partner replied. A guy with a Mexican accent. "I saw them. Definitely."

Casey's heart was racing so loudly you could hear it for a mile. She wanted to lift her head up to see. But didn't. She could hear the soft crunching of boots on gravel as the girl cop walked down the row of cars. Her boots were moving slowly . . . very slowly, and every footstep sent a jolt through Casey. She thought, one minute you're sitting on the wall chilling with your friends, and five minutes later, they got you. Forever. The steps were getting closer. She could now see the cop—she was in her twenties, intense, with black hair in a tight braid tucked under her hat. She slowly moved through the row of cars, towards them. Casey held her breath and kept saying to herself, *keep going . . . keep going . . .* And she did. But then, she stopped. Right at the hood of the Impala. The cop stood only a few feet away, her walkie-talkie was squawking away. Casey looked over at Dragon and Tulip. They were all holding their breath. Dead quiet . . . All the cop had to do was turn her head and they were busted. Her hand resting on top of her gun, she started to turn around . . . *Shit. Run for it? Now?* A second later, Casey heard the sound of someone running in the distance—and the cop took off. Casey lifted her head to see it was a skinhead. The cop's partner caught him and was cuffing him. The girl cop was helping out. Casey leaned her forehead into the back seat of the Impala, her heart pounding, body trembling.

34
Jimmy

I n the large central room of the police station, a dozen cops at gunmetal desks all had kids sitting in the chairs beside the desk. In the interview rooms down the hall, half-a-dozen more cops had kids with them. Jimmy, in charge of it all, was in the big room, across from June Bug who was sitting on her hands, squirming on the chair. On the desk in front of her was a picture of Lodge.

"Where were you Monday night?" Jimmy asked.

"You expect me to remember that far back?"

"It was three days ago."

"That's what I mean," June Bug said.

"Just try."

"The street. I was on the street. How's that?"

"It's a start. Now what were you doing on the street?"

She gave Jimmy a look of total boredom and looked across the room at Dog-Face, who was seething as he sat on a bench waiting his turn. At the other end of the room was the mayor's guy Miller, watching over everything. Jimmy turned back to June Bug.

"Okay," Jimmy said, "let's try this again. It's the day Mark Lodge was killed. Where are you?"

"Know something? I'll save you a lot of time—I killed him."

"You did, huh?"

"The jerk deserved it," June Bug said.

"Why are you saying he's a jerk? You knew him?"

"All these guys are jerks. I know them all."

"You giving it to me straight up? About knowing him?"

"I told you. I know all these guys."

"That's not what I asked. How about answering my question?"

"Or what?—You're gonna tell my parents?"

"Where are your parents?" Jimmy said.

"Can't remember."

"You don't think I can find out?"

"In Tucson."

"They know you're here?"

"They know I ain't home."

"What do they do in Tucson?"

"My dad's an artist. My mom . . . my mom . . . she's just fucked up."

"But if they were ever hurt, you'd want to find out who did it, right?"

"Suppose."

"Well this guy wasn't a john, or a jerk. He had a wife. A baby. Help me out here . . ."

"I seen him around," June Bug said.

"Around?"

"He was one more guy I seen talking to kids on the Boulevard."

"Who—which kids?"

"Can't remember."

"When did you see him?"

"Dunno. A month ago?"

"Ever see him pick up kids?"

"For dates?"

"For anything," Jimmy said.

"Nah."

"Sure?"

"Sure I'm sure. Why would I cover for a jerk like that?"

Across the room, Erin had Dream and was asking the same questions. Erin looked nervous. Dream was probably giving her the same garbage, and he knew she felt responsible for the slow going. It was Erin's idea to pull everyone together and do the raid. Jimmy told her if it got them something, anything—great— but if it didn't, it was all part of the investigation. Still, she desperately wanted some leads to come out of this. But after a couple of hours, none of the cops had walked up to Jimmy, put an arm on his shoulder and said, 'come over here, I got someone you should talk to.' And Jimmy had his private disappointment. When Charles approved the raid, Jimmy had secretly hoped Rancher would get caught in the net. No such luck.

Jimmy caught Erin's eye and gave her a subtle shrug that said, 'don't worry about it'. He selected Dog-Face as his victim. He knew the kid by sight, but had never spoken to him. Then he knew why.

"You think you got the right to pop anyone you fucking want, and then fuck with them any way you want!," Dog-Face snapped.

"You finished?" Jimmy said.

"Fuck you."

"Hey. Enough about me. Let's talk about you. What were you doing when the mayor's buddy was killed?"

"What are you saying, man?"

"I'm not saying anything. I'm asking. What were you doing Monday night?"

"I was fucking your old lady."

He nearly screamed it. Everyone, cops and kids alike, turned to them. The room went strangely silent for a second.

Jimmy sucked in his breath then leaned into the kid and in a harsh whisper said, "You know something. You're a piece of shit. I know it. Everyone in this room knows it, and deep inside, you probably know it, too. And pieces of shit like you don't deserve to breathe the same air as I do. Your ass belongs in jail. And unless I start seeing a little change here, I'm gonna put you there. And I'm not going to break a sweat doing it. So consider this your get-out-of-jail card, asshole . . ." Jimmy then lost his whisper and spoke to him in his usual voice— "Now, what were you doing Monday night?"

"Actually, I kinda do remember . . . I wasn't fucking your old lady after all . . . I was watching her suck off a crackhead!" The kid sprang up, kicked over his chair and snapped, "I'm outta here!"

That's what he thought. Dog-Face's right wrist was now handcuffed to the leg of a bench in the far corner of the room where he sat on the floor rhythmically banging the cuff back and forth. But having sufficiently annoyed everyone, he finally stopped. He sprawled out on the floor and shut his eyes. Across the room, Jimmy took Casper, the little skinhead, to his desk. Where was Charles' Chinese stress ball when he needed it?

35

Nothing was coming his way. Jimmy had been at it all day. He had talked to nine or ten street kids himself, not to mention how many Erin, and the rest of the guys had interviewed. The room was now cleared of the kids except for the one asshole still cuffed to the bench and passed out asleep on the floor. And for all the back and forth, cajoling, threatening and sweet-talking that went down, they had little to show for it. Jimmy leaned back in his chair, his legs up on the desk and looked across at Erin who was entering her report. She was the last cop left. He knew she felt bad, but it wasn't her fault. It was still a good idea—the hardest core thugs, not to mention the nervous first-timers— they *all* need to talk. If it wasn't for that, police work would be a thousand times harder than it was already.

Jimmy started to walk over to Erin, when coming towards him was Charles, along with the mayor's guy, Miller.

"How you doing?" Charles said.

"We're doing."

"What do you have?" Miller asked.

"We got him I.D.'d on the Boulevard by three kids before he was murdered. Any ideas what he might be doing up there?"

"Ideas?"

"Yeah. Hollywood Boulevard isn't exactly the Bel Air Country Club."

"You're not serious?"

"I am."

"Mark Lodge was on the West Hollywood Redevelopment Commission. Don't you read the newspapers?"

"I've been busy." *Fuck*, Jimmy thought.

"This is pathetic," Miller said, "The one piece of information you have—the million people who read the *LA Times* already know. What are you doing?"

"I got the same question for you. What exactly are you doing here?" Jimmy said.

"I'm trying like hell to get this case solved."

"You're doing a great job."

"Jimmy, take it easy," Charles said, bringing some calm back. "Just let us know what you're coming up with."

"We're pretty sure the perp's a female. A lefty. We're getting a piece here. Bit there. Little things. But little things add up. You know that . . ." It was bullshit. All the little things they had added up to next to squat. "But we keep going like this, all the pieces will come together and we'll get the killer."

Across the room Erin quietly got up to leave. She offered Jimmy a sympathetic glance and rounded the corner out of sight.

"I hate to say this," Charles said, "but we're just—"

"I know, not moving fast enough for the mayor," Jimmy said.

"Jimmy, maybe, you know, we should get someone else to

straighten this thing out. We gotta get this one taken care of. Know what I mean?"

"Cap' we're moving. We got a perp in lock-up whose prints match the knife? No. Are we getting closer—absolutely."

"The mayor is anything but happy with the speed this is running," Miller said. "Every morning and every night, without fail, I get a call from him wanting to know what's going on, and why the hell it's taking so long."

"Jimmy, we gotta break this one. You know how it is. So—"

Jimmy slowly exhaled. The time had come. He looked right at Charles. "Look, I got something else. Yeah, we've been doing all the regular stuff. Street interviews, forensics, inform-ants . . . but on top of that, I still got my top ace to play."

"Which is?" Charles said.

"I can't say."

"What do you mean, you can't say?"

"I can. But only to you."

"What is this?" Miller said.

"Sorry," Jimmy said.

"Jimmy," Charles said, "this man represents the mayor. The guy who signs all our checks. Let's hear it, man."

Speaking very softly, Jimmy said, "We got someone inside. An undercover cop working it too."

"How inside?" Charles asked.

"Completely inside. If the street kids give up anything up at all, we've got the perp nailed."

"He coming up with anything?"

"It's deep cover. I'm waiting for the heat on the street to come down before I risk making contact."

"You feel good about this cop?"

"This is as inside as it gets."

Charles nodded. He got it.

36
Casey

The girls sailed through the long aisles of a Rite-Aid on Fairfax, with none of the security guards saying anything. Either they somehow looked respectable, or the guards were too lazy to follow them around.

"I can't believe how close that cop was," Dragon said exuberantly, "if she had looked an inch more—*an* inch—that would've been it."

"It was great," Tulip said. But she said it weakly. Casey knew she was down.

They stopped at the makeup counter. Tulip took one of the testers, leaned into a mirror, and smeared some Revlon stuff over her bruise.

"You can still see it, right?" she asked.

"A little," Dragon answered.

Tulip applied another layer and finally got it covered. As she put on the makeup, she looked carefully at her face in the mirror. When she finished, she kept staring at her reflection.

"You alright?" Dragon said.

Tulip looked away . . . but a moment later she turned back and leaned in closer.

"I look in here and know what I see? . . . My mom."

"Your mom?"

"Yeah . . . she was a receptionist for some big surgeon in Fort Lauderdale and then married this gym manager fucker who became my stepfather, who messed with me. My mom caught him, and for one time in the whole history of the whole fucking world, the guy went to jail for it. But two weeks after he went in, the other guys in there stabbed him, 'cause that's what they do to child abusers in prison, and he bled to death. My mom couldn't keep it together after that. A couple of months later, I go into her bedroom and she's holding a gun in her mouth. I begged her not to do it. I cry, I scream, I beg—but she says, 'I'm sorry darling,' and pulls the trigger . . . Now, every time I look in a mirror, I wonder if I'm cracking up like she did?"

Casey kissed her on the cheek. "You're not. You know you're not. You're the greatest."

Back on the Boulevard. Back at the wall. Tulip and Dragon were sharing a Big Gulp cup of Mountain Dew. The kids who the cops had picked up were coming back. No one seemed too bothered. "Hey!" The scream came from the parking lot behind them. The girls turned and saw Rancher and Mary.

Casey had never ever seen Mary so whacked out.

"Can I have a sip?" Mary asked softly.

Tulip passed her the Mountain Dew.

"What happened with the modeling thing?" Casey said.

"Wasn't a fashion shoot at all, but just some sleaze who wanted to take pictures of me with nothing on."

"You do it?"

"I shouldn't have. But, you know . . ."

"Fucked up," Rancher said. "All fucked up. Rock's all gone. And now we got nothing."

"Wouldn't say that," Tulip said, "Least you're out here. Half the kids on the Boulevard ain't, thanks to—"

"My dad? Give me fucked-up dads for two hundred, Alex."

"Your dad?" Dragon said.

"Oh yeah. Big fucking detective. His number one gig—making life suck for us."

Mary looked like she was going to cry. Tulip put her arm around her and said, "Let's get some pancakes or something."

While they went to Joey's, Casey headed for the Koreans. At the cash register was the boy, and like always, his head was buried in a math book. He was majorly shy, but nice looking. The boy's mother called over to Casey, "Apple, you want apple?"

"I have money, "Casey said.

"You take apple. Free," she said. The lady then spoke in Korean to her son, starting with 'Chan June'—that had to be his name. He got her a Fuji and went to wash it off. He didn't look at Casey, but she sensed something. Casey looked at him and thought, *what if? What if* a miracle happened and somehow they could go down to the beach together? They could body surf in the big waves, and then they'd come out and he could read his books. She could curl up next to him. She would read something, too—back home she used to read all the time. The sun would be beating down on them. It would get too hot and they'd take another swim. Ride the waves some more. And once they got cold, they'd come out, get warmed up under one big towel, and watch the sun go down over the water.

He handed Casey the apple.

"Thanks." She smiled at him.

He shyly looked down. "You're welcome," he said, barely loud enough for her to hear . . . but then he lifted his head and smiled back. Progress.

But as fast as it happened, he turned back to the cash register to ring up a security guard. Casey went out into the street. It was getting colder. She glanced back at the market. The boy, brightly bathed under the store lights, was weighing the salad of a kid with dark blond dreads and an electric guitar case strapped on his back. After he bagged the salad he went back to his book. Casey thought, she'd give anything to be in his place. He'd go to college. After that, maybe he'd go to law school, or maybe become a doctor. Definitely a doctor. And what was she?—a fucked-up whore on the Boulevard.

It was really getting cold now. Casey pulled her jacket zipper all the way to the top, making a high collar of soft leather where she could hide her face up to her nose. The green chairs— that's what she needed. She found Dragon, who was sitting by herself on the wall, freezing too. Casey took her along. She should know about Starbucks on Santa Monica and its great green chairs. Paul introduced her to it. Her breath danced in front of her face, and all she could think about was Paul.

37

A month earlier—which she'd give anything to return to—Paul left Casey in Joey's and went out to the guy in the blue Mercedes. She sat by herself in the booth finishing his fries. He was *so sweet* to give her the jacket—actually, he was so sweet, period. Then something strange happened—she started getting mad at Paul. Every night, he was doing the same stupid thing, going out there and risking his life. Doing dates off Santa Monica without protection?—because that's the way most of the johns made you do it—that was a one-way ticket. She also did the dating game, and she was stupid too, but at least she recognized it. Now, she was trying to make things better. She came up with a place for them to stay—the Fountain squat. It wasn't paradise, but it they wouldn't have to freeze their asses off on Wonderland either, and they could stop doing the dates. Maybe even get some sort of real jobs.

She stayed at Joey's for as long as she could get away with it, then went to hang out at the wall. The more time passed, the madder she got. Paul was acting like a jerk. If he was so smart, how come he couldn't see that what he was doing was crazy. When he came back, she was going to tell him just how stupid he was.

Two hours later, maybe more, Casey looked up to see Paul coming towards the wall. She was still mad. When he got close, he broke into jog, sailed over, and kissed her forehead.

"Let's go!"

"Go? Where?" she said.

"Only the best Starbucks on the planet."

"Come on." He took her hand and started pulling her up from the wall. She stayed put. But he just pulled harder. He smiled at her. He had the sweetest, greatest smile on earth. And she couldn't be mad anymore. She let herself go, and landed hard, but nice against his chest. He wrapped his arms tightly around her and she wished she could put that feeling in a bottle. Later, when she thought about it, she was never sure what love meant—whatever it was, she wasn't given a ton of it—but at that instant, when she was so happy to be held close in Paul's arms, Casey realized this must be what love means—there's one person whose presence makes your whole life worth living. He was the air in her lungs, and all she wanted to do was be with him.

He took her down to the Starbucks. They had biscotti with chocolate on one side of them, hot chocolates and croissants. It was heaven—they called it Maui. Paul had lots of money in his pocket. The date was no hassle. All from Mr. Mercedes.

"He's a pimp?" Casey asked.

"Sorta. He's plugged in. Not some jizbag who has you do truckers by the freeway. Last night I was in Beverly Hills. Two hundred and fifty."

"No way?"

"Oh yeah. Two-five-zero. And there's more coming. He gave me a pager so I don't miss any. Got one tonight. You wanna come?"

"And do what?"

"Just hang while I do the guy. Then we can go someplace nice."

The car was a Beemer, given to him for the night by the guy sending him out. Casey couldn't believe it. Here was Paul, a street hustler used to sitting on a newspaper box with his shirt open on Santa Monica, and now *he's* driving a Beemer? The radio played a new, cool, version of *Chapel of Love*. The car *was* kind of a chapel of love: speeding up the Strip, radio blasting, and heat cranking from the vents—a beautiful unending stream of flowing hot air. Sunset was a lot better when you were seeing it from inside a Beemer. Casey was loving it all. But suddenly, she felt bad—Paul was doing exactly what she said she wouldn't do again. How could it be good enough for him, but not for her?

"You sure you wanna do this?" she said.

"Sure I wanna be cruising LA in this ride, about to make another two-fifty? You bet."

"But—"

"Casey. I'm not gonna be some kinda creepy old hustler—losing my hair, and giving blowjobs behind Krispy Kreme. I keep doing this, we can get a place. Get the fuck off the streets. Do something real. This thing dropped out of the sky, and I'm not gonna let it go."

Casey was in the car by herself. The street was lined with large trees with brown leaves. Casey thought it was one of those strange LA things—this was the middle of winter, but the trees still hadn't lost their leaves. Everything—even nature—was twisted here. She found a lever under her seat and gave it a pull, which sent the seat almost flat. Paul had told her not to run the engine, so she wasn't bathed in the great heat, but slipping into the soft leather, the tinted windows sealing out the city, still felt good. The street was quiet, no cars were moving. She knew they were in Beverly Hills, but beyond that she didn't know where exactly they were. Paul was in a huge, super modern house just up the driveway ahead of her. Casey shut her eyes—then, she thought she heard a noise. She looked around. Nothing. Just a deserted street lined with parked cars. Casey looked up at the house. Inside, through a tall, very narrow glass window, she could see Paul sitting on a couch. Some old jerk, who was maybe sixty, walked over to him. Paul was laughing at something the guy was saying. Paul was good—the john was happy, but she knew all Paul was thinking was, how fast he could get it over with and break with the bucks. She heard the same noise again. Then she saw it. Up the street, on the far side of the driveway, was a parked Jag. There was a guy inside, hanging out with the engine off, like she was. The noise was the sound of its window sliding partially down. Casey looked closer at the Jag, but couldn't make out the guy inside. She saw a glimmer of something and looked closer. Suddenly she got worried. Glimmer—silent guy in a car. He had a gun! What was going on? Casey lunged for the door handle—but stopped. It wasn't a gun. It was a camera lens. The camera pushed a tiny bit outside the window and clicked away at Paul and the john inside the house. Strange. Casey curled up on the seat and tried to sleep. Everything was just too fucking strange.

The car door swung open. Casey was asleep, a deep good sleep. She looked up to see Paul leaning over her. The cold came in with him, and she shivered a little.

"So pretty when you sleep."

She curled up tight against the cold, not wanting to wake up.

"Some of us get to work, some of us get to sleep," Paul said as he slipped inside.

"And some of us get to be in photo shoots as we work."

"So?"

"You knew there was a guy taking pictures of you?"

"For what they're paying me, they can shoot 24-7."

He tossed Casey slim pile of folded bills. She unfolded them—three crisp hundreds.

"One date?"

"Oh yeah! We're moving into a whole other zone here."

Casey rolled the bills around her finger. This was one date? It was more money than she had ever held.

"What do you wanna do?" he said. "We're rich—anything you want."

"Anything?"

38

The Beemer limped around in a big crooked circle on the roof level of an empty parking lot next to the Third Street Promenade in Santa Monica. Suddenly, the car lurched forward, then, a second later, screeched to a halt. Casey was at the wheel, smiling as she drove.

"Shit," she said.

"Don't worry about it," Paul said, "just gently give it the gas—nice and even."

She did, and the car took another clumsy leap forward.

"Shit! But I'm gonna get it. I'm gonna get it!"

"You're getting it." But an instant later, he yelled—"Watch out!!"

Seconds from them—was a cinderblock wall. Casey snapped her head towards it in a blind panic—and an inch before impact—she swerved hard to the left, just clearing it.

"Sorry. Sorry. Sorry. I know I'm gonna get it."

The sky was beginning to lighten. Tall aluminum lights on the roof cast wide orange beams, revealing the air heavy with morning mist. The Beemer cruised all over the lot, turning left, then deftly going right, coming to stop, and then going in a smooth circle which took Casey and Paul by the railing at the edge of the roof, where they could the glistening lights of the Santa Monica Pier and the placid ocean. Casey began to laugh—"I'm getting it."

"You got it!"

"I got it!"

The car made another graceful circle and Casey kept on laughing.

She and Paul sipped sweet coffees as they sat in white plastic chairs at Perry's, next to the bike path along the beach. The day's first rollerbladers and bikers were gliding past them. A tall surfer kid with a German accent was wiping the morning moisture off the chairs, as the smell of baking muffins floated over the tables. The coffee cup felt warm in Casey's hands. The beach was empty and pretty, and for the first time in a long time, everything was peaceful and nice.

Paul lifted his cup to toast. "To the judge."

They clicked coffee cups.

"He was a judge?"

"Think so. Had all these plaques with the thing they bang down with . . ."

"A gavel?"

"Right, Gavels. Mounted on them."

"Messed up," Casey said.

"Why?"

"I don't know. A judge? It's sorta respectable."

"Yeah, right. Everyone's respectable till they want to get sucked off. But, yo, he gets the same thing as I give everyone else, only he pays ten times more. Gimme a judge—any day."

39
Jimmy

Charles told Jimmy to go home. Only Jimmy didn't want to go home. Too much was swirling around his head and he knew he'd never sleep. He pushed open the door to the stationhouse lot and saw Erin leaning against her white Jeep, having a smoke.

"You weren't waiting for me?" he said.

"Yeah. I was . . . sorry about today."

"Don't be. It's the game. And we got some stuff that'll help."

"It work out with the brass?" she said.

"Shit rolls downhill."

"It's not like we're not trying."

"It's okay. You going home?" As soon as he said it, Jimmy thought he sounded like an idiot. Where else was she going. A strip club? Run an ironman?

"I guess. You?"'

He looked at her and thought, why not ask her? . . . Why not—because he'd feel like an asshole if she said no.

Erin took out her keys and said, "Good night."

The key slipped into the Jeep door.

"Hey, you want to . . . to go eat or something?" Jimmy said.

"Sure. That'd be great."

The hostess at the Peking was supposed to be taking them to the table, but for now she couldn't be bothered. She'd get to them right after the girl on the TV game show blew the question that could give her fifty G's. The question keeping them from Jimmy's favorite booth was "what is a sphygmomanometer used for?" Jimmy thought, not in a million years would he get that one—questions like this is how they kept the money out of the contestants poor hands, and in the hands of the rich producers. While the girl on TV was shaking her head, Erin turned to Jimmy and said. "It's the cuff and gauge that measures blood pressure."

A second later, the buzzer sounded. The contestant couldn't even make a guess and the smarmy host, who acted like he knew the answer all along, but Jimmy figured without his cheat sheet, was as clueless as the contestant, said, "I'm sorry, Heidi, a sphygmomanometer is the device that measures blood pressure."

Jimmy looked at Erin.

"Let's get a drink," she said. "I'll tell you."

The hostess put them in Jimmy's booth. Same tear in the leather, the gaffer's tape covering it, a bit more frayed. But this booth at the Peking was where Jimmy most wanted to be. Away from the stationhouse, away from all the pressure and the mayor's prick buddy. Away from the street kids and the horrors they see and the evil they do. Away from the assholes who specialize in fucking over the kids. Away from the heartache of Rancher. Just away. And being alone with Erin.

She took a sip of red wine. It left a dark maroon film on her lips and when the tiniest part of her tongue slipped through to trap a wayward drop and bring it home, Jimmy felt himself pull in a short, deep breath.

"My dad was a cop." Erin said. "Old school. He had the mustache all the guys—well not you—but most cops have. He was big—six-three—and since he was a boy, always wanted to be a cop. He was LAPD for thirty years. In the first twenty-five, he pulled his gun out of his holster, like he was ready to use it, maybe three times. He fired it once. Missed the guy. I think he was secretly happy he did. But things had started to change. In his last five years on the force, all of a sudden, he's got his gun out all the time."

"And compared to what the crowd on the streets got, his gun's nothing."

"Sure. My dad would always say, they got us out-gunned and out-manned, and nobody gives a damn. But it still looked pretty exciting to me, and when I was a senior in high school, and told him I wanted to go onto the force, he was incredibly unhappy about it. He couldn't bad-mouth it entirely—after all, it was his life—how he paid for my sisters, my mom, and me to live. But at the same time, the idea of his little girl becoming a cop was more than he could bear."

"What he want you do?"

"Be a nurse. What else?"

"Ahh. Starting to make sense. Were you interested?"

"Actually, I was. And since I'm still the dutiful daughter, I go to Northridge and major in nursing. It's not so bad. But without telling my dad, I do a double major. And the other one's in criminology."

"Bad girl."

"Very," she said with a smile.

"What he say when he found out?"

"I didn't tell him till I was about to graduate. By then I had already applied to the academy. I mean, I hadn't really lied to him. I did the whole nursing thing—graduated with honors in it. I just did criminology too. He was torn. There was a side of him that was proud his girl wanted to be like him, but he was also scared for me, that every night I would be facing down the kind of stuff that in his time, he hardly ever had to deal with."

"He was right in a way."

"He was more than right. When I was doing my nursing training in the Cedars emergency room, I saw lots of terrible things. But at least there was some time between the shooting and when we saw the vic. The blood wasn't still coming out of a hole in his head and you see pieces of his skull on the ground. And by the time they got to us, it was all about the treatment. Guy comes into the ER, the job of the team is to try to save him. That's it. It wasn't, who's the shooter? Oh God, there's a little girl who watched her mother get shot? But I didn't listen, and went straight to the academy."

"Sorry you did?"

"Not now."

Jimmy drove down them down Boulevard, back towards the stationhouse. When they hit La Brea, Jimmy passed a weird sculpture he always liked—four life-sized silver girls in a circle. Who knew what the hell it meant? Probably something to do with actresses and the movies, but the girls were hot enough, and it definitely beat looking at generals on horses. He jerked the car to a stop. Inside the circle of silver girls, sitting on the feet of one of the statues, was Mary. She was eating chips from a bag. As soon as she saw Jimmy, she got up and started drifting away.

"Mary," Jimmy called.

She looked back at Jimmy and walked faster down the Boulevard. Jimmy followed, piloting the car slowly after her.

"Mary." She didn't answer and kept on going.

He turned to Erin, "This'll only take a minute. Sorry."

Jimmy pulled the car over and jogged down the sidewalk after Mary.

"Haven't seen you around," Jimmy said.

"Haven't seen you."

"How you doing?"

She shrugged.

"Rancher around?" Jimmy said.

"Yeah."

"Where?"

"Around," Mary said. "You know."

"I don't know. Where around?"

"Around."

"He okay?"

"Yeah."

"What's he doing? Where are you staying?"

"He's okay. I told you."

Jimmy looked at her. A young, pretty girl—and completely cooked on crack. His one thin connection to Rancher.

"Tell him to find me, alright?"

"That's up to him."

"I know it's up to him. But tell him. Please—"

"How 'bout some money?"

"For food?"

"Yeah. Sure. And a room. It was freezing last night, you know."

"No drugs."

Mary shook her head.

What were the chances? But he reached into his wallet and emptied it. Sixty or seventy bucks.

"Now, what are you going to tell him?"

"I'm gonna tell him to call his daddy."

"Look," Jimmy said, "just tell him I wanna talk. That's all."

Mary started to walk away. Jimmy called after her, "And tell him he can come home, both of you, if you want. The door's always open."

"Sure."

Then she stopped and turned around.

"Wanna know something?" she said. "You're gonna be a grandpa."

"What?"

"Yeah. That's right. Me and Rancher, we're having a baby."

"What?"

She smiled and headed for the corner.

"Wait—"

Jimmy ran after her. "Mary—stop."

He put his arm on her shoulder. She screamed, "Get away! Get way from me!!"

Jimmy let go. She raced across the street.

Jimmy slowly walked back, wondering where and how it all went wrong—he tried so hard to do everything right. He slipped inside the car, and for a moment, silently stared ahead, down the lights of the Boulevard. He turned to Erin. "I've been doing this job for eighteen years and I'm still naïve enough, stupid enough, or crazy enough to think cops help people. But the truth is—I can't even help my own family."

40
Casey

C asey was back on the Boulevard with Dragon, Jumper and the others. The walking back and forth drove her crazy. Stores where they couldn't afford to buy anything, restaurants where they couldn't eat, hotels where they'd never stay. What was the point? But what else were they supposed to do? So they walked. Coming towards them, taking fast bites from a glazed donut, was Dog-Face.

"Doggie," Jumper yelled, "they keep you in there all night?"

"Assholes," Dog-Face said.

"That's big news."

"Fucking assholes."

"Cops gave you some fine food though—" As he said it, Jumper snatched away what was left of Dog-Face's doughnut.

"Fuck you, Jump, this is serious, man. They're fucking obsessed with getting the dude who greased the mayor's buddy. And they got someone on the street."

Dream laughed. "They got lots of guys on the street, you dumb fuck."

"No, bitch. Undercover."

"Come on," Tulip said.

"No, come on. I was there," Dog-Face said.

"What—they told you?" Dragon said.

"I was lying on the floor all handcuffed and they forgot me—thought I was asleep. Yo, this is super-fucked. Someone's out here spying on us."

"Hiding in our closet?" June Bug said, "They'd be pretty bored."

"No. On the street."

"Actually," Jumper said, "I know that already."

"You do?" Dog-Face said.

"Sure."

They all looked at him.

"Sure. 'Cause that person's me."

Jumper got the smiles he wanted.

"No, man," Dog-Face said. "This is serious"

"So am I."

"Asshole, this is real."

"Doggie, that's bullshit. Cop shit," Jumper said. "Let's go to Joey's."

Casey looked around. Everyone was enjoying the show. Not her.

She suddenly felt sick, like when she was a little girl and had a bad fever, and every muscle, every bone, her head, her skin, and her stomach—all felt sore.

They kept walking. But Dog-Face held still.

"Hey, man," Dog-Face said, "How *do* I know it's not you, Jump?"

"It is."

"No, really."

"Dog, if it was me—I would've turned your sorry ass in a long time ago. Let's eat."

41
Jimmy

Jimmy stood in line at Kinko's Copies. He couldn't believe there even was a line. One-thirty in the morning, and the rest of America was sleeping, but in Kinko's on Sunset it might as well have been noon. Two guys in their late-twenties were buzzing with energy as they went back and forth over what color their screenplay cover should be. A rock band complete with the big hair, circa mid-80's, dressed entirely in leather, and with spiked wristbands was picking up a two-foot high pile of posters announcing a gig. And of course, there were the knock-your-socks-off beautiful girls in the self-service area, Xeroxing resumes and stapling them to the back of their headshots. The pictures all had the same basic look. Glossy eight-by-ten black and whites of fresh-faced girls from places like Wisconsin or Texas with pearly white teeth, a lot of them wearing tank tops, and nearly all with long hair, laying over their shoulders. Everywhere Jimmy went in LA he saw them—from the breakfast joints at the Farmers' Market to the corner dry cleaners. There were so goddamn many girls, most of whom could stop traffic in their home towns, and every day the Hollywood pond was restocked. How do you break out of the pack. With talent? Good luck. It was a crap shoot all the way, and the woods were full of assholes who were ready and eager to prey on girls who didn't know shit, but had the killer looks. Girls like Dani, chasing the dream, but at this second, was swinging naked around a pole at the SR Club. Sometimes the girls gave up and went home—they were lucky. Others got lucky by checking out of this bullshit, like he wished Dani would, and instead they managed restaurants, became teachers, went back to college. The unlucky girls just descended lower and lower, and in Hollywood that was the porno world. They would be barely out of high-school and banging for the camera one guy after another. Ask them about AIDS, and they'd say, everyone has to be tested. Great. One test, six months ago, and after that they were free to get it and spread it. Was it really worth it? Fucking whoever they told you, and every time you did, playing Russian Roulette?

A girl to the side of the cash registers was attaching her headshots to a pile of resumes. Jimmy could see her top credit was playing Marion in *The Music Man* in Redding—wherever that was—California. The girl was in her early-twenties, model-tall, with long strawberry-blonde hair. Their eyes met for a moment and she smiled at him. She was beautiful. Jimmy smiled back, and hoped he would never have to deal with her as a victim, the way he had with so many cuties, so many times before.

When he got to the counter, a friendly girl with a pink and blue Mohawk and an English accent ran his order. He walked out of Kinko's with fifty green sheets.

The first place he went was the corner of Hollywood and Vine. A few months ago, Jimmy took one of his nephews from Brooklyn around, and this was one of the places he wanted to see. Allegedly it was famous, but when they got here the kid said, 'this is it?' There was a star for the astronauts who first walked on the moon, but the rest was nothing, just some seedy, forgettable stores.

Near the corner was a tattoo parlor. Its lights were still glowing, and Jimmy could see a buff woman in a tank top with plenty of tatts herself, inking Chinese characters onto a guy's shoulder. On a light pole in front of the place, Jimmy taped the first poster. On it, was a picture of a big, friendly Akita. Below the photo was printed, "Lost Dog. Carrie. Reward if found" and a phone number. For the next hour, Jimmy went down the Boulevard, every couple of blocks, putting up another green poster.

42

His car was parked on the fourth level of the Beverly Center lot. The oldies station was playing as usual, and some girl whose name he forgot or never knew, was singing *Save the Last Dance for Me*. Jimmy opened a Fatburger bag he picked up on the way over and looked across the parking lot to see families laden with shopping bags coming down the escalators that ran up the outside of the enormous mall. They'd get off, the parents talking, the kids fooling around, and go to their minivans. Lots of happy families. Shopping together, hanging out together. Fuck. It didn't seem so hard for them—what was the matter with him? He thought about Shannon and when they met. Pretty, with long curly red hair. She was a first year law student at Fordham and was observing in a courtroom where Jimmy was testifying. The first night they went out, he knew—they both knew—this was the real thing.

Her father was crazy, a con man who had done time, and when he wasn't screwing up other people's lives, he was wreaking havoc on his own family. Shannon got as far away from him as she could, becoming a lawyer, marrying a cop. He was moving up fast in the NYPD, and she was an assistant DA in the Bronx. They had a son, Liam, and for a while they were happy too. Liam was a great kid in every way. His favorite book was *Pecos Bill*. Jimmy must have read it to him a hundred times. One night, as Shannon sat on the edge of the bed folding laundry, and Jimmy read to him, Liam turned to Jimmy in the middle of the story and in his high voice said, "I don't want to live in New York anymore, I want to go and be a rancher." The name stuck, and from then on he was probably the only Rancher in the Five Boroughs.

They took trips together: New Hampshire to see the leaves change, Disney World for Rancher's seventh birthday, and Ireland for ten days. But after Jimmy's shooting and the shitstorm that followed, things began to fall apart. He kept playing the shooting over and over in his head, seeing it every night in his dreams. He and Shannon were hardly talking. He was going to choir practice. Far more than he should. Shannon told him to see a shrink. He had zero interest; choir practice was working just fine. He was pissed that she couldn't understand what he was going through, the way the guys at the bar could. Then one time he took a skater from Disney on Ice, who somehow ended up in their bar, back to her hotel room. He didn't fuck her, but he came close. He told himself that other guys would be proud they didn't go through with it. But Jimmy felt like shit that he went as far as he did.

When they moved to LA, things were better for a bit, but then it was the same. Shannon was once the love of his life, and now they fought all the time. More and more, on the nights they were all home together, he would read to Rancher in his room and once Rancher fell asleep, Jimmy would fall asleep beside him. Half the time it was because he was wiped out from work, but the other half it was because it was a lot easier sleeping next to sweet Rancher than arguing with Shannon. She was miserable, he was miserable. What was the point? After the divorce they shared custody of Rancher. A year later, she married a lawyer, which is what she should have done in the first place. Jimmy would stop by her new house in Encino whenever he knew something about Rancher. Usually he didn't have much to say, and it was tough having the conversation with a picture of a beautiful nine-year-old Rancher snuggling with Shannon in a Dublin café, looking down on them from the wall. It was a big house, nice furniture, nice yard, nice husband. They had a beautiful, whip smart two-year-old boy, who Shannon worshiped. She loved Rancher, of course, and would do anything for him, but it was clear to Jimmy, her goal in life was not to fuck it up with her new son like they had done with Rancher. Sometimes it pissed him off, but most of the time, he understood.

The passenger door opened. Jimmy jerked his head to the side. Slipping in the car, was Dragon.

"You the guy with the lost dog?"

"You got him?"

"I wish. He's cute. Is he yours?"

"My next door neighbor's. Good to see you, Robin."

"That's Dragon, now." She had the street kid look down. Jimmy would defy anyone to make her as a cop.

"Must be doing something right to get a street name like that. You doing okay?"

"Yeah. Basically."

"You're looking kinda thin. You eating enough?"

"Sure."

"Yeah?"

He passed her a bag from Fatburger holding two burgers, two bags of fries, and a huge shake. "This is for you."

"Thanks." She tore right in.

"When I was doing this, it was with wise guys in Brooklyn. They may have been murdering scum, but you never went hungry."

"I wish."

He looked at her. She was too thin. Dirty. Tired.

"Now, how you really doing?" he said.

"Good."

"Hey, just you and me here," Jimmy said.

"Sometimes it's hard to keep up the act."

"Sure. It's a rough goddamn assignment. You gotta give a performance worth an Oscar and I send you out there with what?—an hour's advance warning?"

"But I wanted it. I still want it."

"You all the way in?"

"Definitely."

"Good girl."

"But one thing's bad—they know there's an undercover on the street."

"You're kidding. How?"

"A kid overheard something—Dog-Face."

Fuck! Jimmy thought. The asshole on the floor.

"We gotta take you out."

"I can't. Not yet."

"It's too risky not to."

"Jimmy, please. I can't."

"You're on the force what, three months?"

"Four."

"Okay, four. Listen to me, you'll get other whacks at this stuff—."

"But not like this."

"Robin, sweetie, hear me out. When you were still playing with Barbie, I was doing the same thing you're doing. And one thing I learned from my boss, and hopefully you'll learn from me, is there comes a time when *every* deep-cover *has* to come out."

"The kids know there's a cop. Sure. But they don't know it's me. This isn't the subtle crowd. If they had made me, I'd know by now."

"And when they do know its you, you know what's going to happen, right? You'll be lucky to get out of there alive."

"But they haven't made me. And they're not going to."

"No guarantees on that."

"I got too much going to quit now."

Their eyes met. If something happened to her, Jimmy would never forgive himself. On the other hand, she was good, she was crucial to the investigation, and she was also right—if they had made her, she would've known it in two seconds.

"Okay," Jimmy said. "But, the *barest, tiniest* hint of them making you—someone even looks at you the wrong way—and you gotta get outta there as fast as your legs will go. Deal?"

"Deal. Thanks."

"What do you got?" he said.

"I got a kid who's been telling me about someone on the Boulevard who I'm pretty sure is Lodge."

"That's good."

"With chicken meat."

"Boys or girls?"

"Boys."

"Naturally. What else?"

"Not much. But kids are starting to open up. I got that kid, Dog-Face bragging about a murder."

"No shit. Who'd he kill?"

"A bouncer at the X Club, who was also dealing."

"Nice. I remember that one, we had nothing. Good work. We break this case, we'll move onto that."

"Look, I know things are coming way too slowly. But they really are coming."

Jimmy knew it was true. But he also knew, unless he got somewhere soon, they would pull him off. This was a career-making case—you don't get too many of them—and if he was replaced, it would be a huge blow to any chances he had for moving up.

"It's okay," he said. "We got a waiter at the Chateau who has a girl in the room with Lodge, the night he got whacked. She was wearing two earrings in each ear. Long brown hair, cute."

Robin smiled.

"I know it's not exactly look for the six-foot-five Samoan with Bugs Bunny tattooed above his wrist. And one other thing, our stud coroner's got the perp as a southpaw."

"That's something," she said.

"Who gave you Lodge with chicken meat?"

"A girl named Casey. I was with her the night you popped the teacher."

"Oh yeah. Nice acting. Very convincing."

"What happened to the perp?"

"Out the next morning. Scum's probably back teaching. This girl, she have a street name?"

"No. Just Casey."

"What's the deal with her?" Jimmy said.

"She's okay. Sweet."

"They all are. Till they stick a knife in your heart."

"I guess. She was tight with a kid named Saint Paul. Know him?"

"Don't think so."

"He doesn't seem to be around anymore. I'm sitting on her. She's opening up."

"Better get me something soon. The mayor's crawling all over his pal. The pal is crawling all over the chief. The chief's is crawling all over the captain, who's crawling all over guess who?"

"And you're crawling all over me."

"Of course. Gotta get me something, sweetie."

"I will. Soon. I promise. Can you give me a couple of bucks?"

"I like the way you say that. You're good."

"I'm supposed to be hitting up the tourists. Can't go back to the squat with nothing."

Jimmy took out all the coins he had, then opened his wallet and gave her a twenty and a small wad of singles. She passed back the twenty.

"It's too much."

"Take it. Tell them it's from some French tourist who didn't know any better."

"Thanks."

"Be careful, huh . . . Really careful."

She nodded and swung the car door open.

"Wait," Jimmy said. "I got something else . . . you ever met up with a kid named Rancher?"

"Yeah."

Her eyes lowered. She knew, Jimmy thought. It was the worst kept secret in Hollywood.

"I'm sorry," Robin said. "It must be hard."

"It ain't easy. Next time you see him, let me know right away. Okay?"

43

When Jimmy came home his bathroom looked like the health club steam room. Dani was in the bath and running a natural sponge hard over her body.

"Scrub my back, baby?"

He took the sponge and ran it across her skin. The soap foamed up in small bubbles, leaving a milky film.

"Little harder."

He went back across. He knew what was going on. She was purging the creeps from the club: their grubby hands, the money they rammed into her G-string, the awful things they said to her. No matter how late it was, and how tired she was, every night when she came home Dani scrubbed and scrubbed, till the coating of dirt flowed down the drain.

"I called Santa Monica College for you," Jimmy said, gliding the sponge in an arc across her back.

"You did?"

"They got a teacher education program that starts next week. You missed the regular registration, but I spoke to the assistant director of the thing, and she said they still got a couple of places open. If you go down and speak to her, she'll probably let you in."

"That's so sweet of you."

She turned around, and he ran the sponge over her stomach, her breasts.

Jimmy looked at her, and in the quiet of his mind, took a picture. What they had was good in its own way, but it wasn't the real deal—for either of them. And he always wanted to have this snapshot of Dani—so beautiful—in his head.

Jimmy stood at the kitchen table making tea. Dani came in wearing blue checkered pajama bottoms and a long Angels t-shirt, and from behind, kissed him on the cheek.

"Jimmy, sweetie, I've been thinking . . ."

It's coming, Jimmy thought, it's coming.

"That program sounds great. And I really want to do it. But next week I got these two auditions."

"I didn't know."

"Yeah. One's for a horror film. I would play a sorority girl. It's probably terrible, but some of those films are really cool. The other's an open call for this Fox pilot where the star's girl-friend from sixth grade comes to LA to visit him after all this time apart. And she's from North Carolina—pretty near. So that's good for me, right? . . ."

Right, Jimmy thought. In the horror flick she'd be topless in the locker room, hot tub, bedroom, sauna, someplace—and then get killed by thirty knives flying at her, or from a bucket of acid, a machete. And the chances of Dani getting the part? Slim to nil. The sitcom was an open call. A thousand girls would be going for it. Lots with real experience. All stunners. Dani's chances: less than nil.

"What do you think I should do?" she said.

"It's tough. But if you're gonna get out, this is opportunity knocking."

"I want to. You know that. But . . . I dunno, maybe I could do it next semester. Give myself another couple of months to try and make it. I figure for the sitcom they're looking for someone to play like they're from North Carolina, but I practically am. I think I've got a real shot at this one."

"Sure—you never know."

"Thanks, baby."

Jimmy passed Dani her tea. He was beat. He thought about adding brandy into his. It was something he enjoyed. But after seeing Mary on the Boulevard, he didn't feel much like enjoying himself right now.

"How was your night?" Jimmy said.

"Like always. Except Sean was even more on a jerk than usual."

"Now that's hard."

"He's was saying when the gambling comes in, he's really gonna be kicking ass."

"He's probably right about that."

"He's gonna put in a special club room," Dani said.

"What's that?"

"It's like a private club within the club."

"Private? What do you have to do to get into this exclusive club—pay an extra fifty at the door?"

"Basically."

"And what do you get there?" Jimmy said.

"He's calling it lap dance plus."

"Plus what?"

"Hand jobs, blow jobs. Probably more. But I'll be long gone before it happens."

"We'll keep an eye on the asshole. Sounds like he's about to go way over the line."

"He's already is, with all the under-agers. He just hired two more."

"Yeah?"

"Sure. That's what guys want. Nineteen, twenty—that's too old, now. They want fifteen, sixteen. It's sick."

"How many girls like that does he have?"

"Five, maybe. You met one of them before—Tara. Remember her?"

"Sorta."

"She's a cutie. But she's doing so many dates she's ready to quit dancing."

"How old's she?"

"Sixteen. But looks younger. She's really in demand."

"You know who she's dating?"

"Guys with serious money."

"You think she'd talk to me?" Jimmy said.

"You're a cop. She has to."

"No. Really talk."

"About the dead fellah?"

"Yeah."

"I thought about that already. I asked her if she knew him."

"You did?" Jimmy was surprised and touched. "Really?"

"Sure."

"Thanks, baby—you've been hanging around me too long." Jimmy said.

"Way too long," she said with a smile.

"Wha'd she say?" Jimmy said.

"That she didn't know him."

"Think she was lying?"

"I couldn't really tell."

44

Casey

E veryone was back on the wall except Tulip, who had a date. Casey knew she *had* to get out. Otherwise she'd look back and think she was the idiot that stayed around when any sane person would've bolted. She thought about Montana. She'd work at a preschool in some pretty, little town. She'd take long walks with the kids and bring them through a beautiful field to a small stream at the edge of the woods. In the stream there'd be little frogs. She'd crouch down and put her hands into the water and catch a frog, then hold it in her cupped hands for the children to see. They would surround her, a little scared, but also curious. An adventurous little girl with light-blonde hair in a long braid would bravely reach over and gently stroke the frog. She'd giggle, loving it. A couple of boys would follow her lead, and then the whole group would take turns. The kids would feel brave and be happy and when she'd release the frog back into the water, her kids would call out "Bye frog," "Bye-bye froggie." The frog would disappear up the stream, and Casey and her kids would head back across the field, stopping to pick the prettiest purple wildflowers—

"Yo! Where'd you go?" It was Dog-Face, breaking the spell, as he yelled across the street to Dragon as she crossed from the other side of the Boulevard.

As Dragon weaved through cars stuck in traffic, she was bouncing a tennis ball.

"At the Bev' Center," she said. She fired the ball at Dog-Face. "Catch."

Dog-Face's right arm shot up to grab it and he threw it right back.

"I never heard of anyone going down that far," Dog-Face said.

"You never heard of lots of things."

"That's a hike," June Bug said. "What's down there?"

"Dunno. I figured it was someplace no one else would be . . ." She tossed the ball to June Bug who caught it and lobbed it to Dream. "So, like, why not?"

Casey thought the Bev' Center sounded like a pretty good idea. At least it wasn't the same stupid wall. Coming right at her was the tennis ball. She reached up with her left hand and tossed it back. Dragon had a funny look on her face . . . but Casey figured, sure she would, having to deal with idiots like Dog-Face, who thought walking a couple of miles to the Bev' Center was like going to Japan.

"I think it's weird going down there," Dog-Face said.

"Let it go, Dog," Dream said.

"Yeah?" Dragon said, "then check this out—"

Dragon dug into her pocket and came up with a killer haul.

"Not fucking bad!" Jumper said. "Someone gave you a twenty?"

"They didn't even speak English."

"Shit, nice going."

"Mickey D.'s?" Dragon said.

"Abso-fucking-lutely!" Jumper yelled.

Everyone was off the wall ready to go. Casey too, even though she hated the place. But it was better than sitting alone. Then Dragon turned to her. "You wanna get a salad or something while they go to Mickey's?"

It was the best offer she had in days.

As he headed away, Jumper said, "Where's Paul been?"

"With this rich dude—like one giant date," Casey said.

"The dude have any friends?" Jumper opened his hands wide, but then turned, hearing someone running—and saw Rancher, looking even crazier than usual.

"Looking ratty, dude. Gotta go slow on that shit," Jumper said.

"Got a problem, man," Rancher said, out of breath.

"What?"

"Mary. She's in the hospital. Something inside her's all fucked up."

"What, Ranch?" June Bug said.

"It's fucked, man."

"What is?" June Bug said.

"Mary, she was gonna have a baby—"

"Mary?" Dream said.

"Yeah. She was way into it at first. She loves kids. But then she started freaking about it. She says, 'I can't do it. No way.' So, there's the bitch that works at that tattoo place by Vine, and she tells Mary she can take care of it for twenty-five bucks. We go to the shop. She puts Mary up on the table, uses these nasty looking doctor things and . . . She don't know shit! Oh man, there was blood everywhere. Mary looked like . . . like, I never seen her looking before. Like blue almost. I go to call

911. The tattoo bitch says don't call them, we're all gonna get in trouble. I say, fuck you, and call them anyway. She grabs her shit and takes the fuck off. They come, and take Mary to the hospital."

"How's she doing?" Casey said.

"I dunno."

"You've been there already, right?" Jumper said.

"No, man."

"You know which hospital?"

"Cedars or something?"

"Cedars-Sinai—down by La Cienega," Casey said, "Ranch, you gotta go."

"I want to . . . . But you know, I figure, I go there, they're gonna give me some kinda dope test or something, and I end up in jail, and what the fuck good does that—"

"Ranch!" Jumper said, "Listen to me. Casey's right. You gotta be with Mary. Forget that other stupid shit. They ain't gonna put you in jail."

"She needs you—go! You gotta help her through this," Dragon said.

Rancher stood immobile, biting his nails.

"Go, Ranch," Casey said.

"Yeah . . ." And then he took off running.

45

The Denny's waitress came over with two salads. Dragon's was piled high with chicken pieces and Casey's veggie-only was overflowing with extra dressing. Casey started putting it down fast, but then, forced herself to slow down. What good was it to go so fast? Where was she in such a rush to go? Everything sucked. There had to be a way out—but the *hows* of it all were nowhere to be found. She missed Paul. You can be surrounded by people—even people you really like, and still be lonely as shit.

"Where are you?" Dragon said.

"What do you mean?"

"I dunno, it just seems like you're someplace else in your head."

She got that right. She was far away, and wanted to be farther. "I was just thinking about a friend."

"Yeah?" Dragon said.

"Paul. The best. I can't stop thinking about him. Couple of weeks ago he taught me to drive."

"Cool."

"The greatest. And for a while, it was the greatest day."

"What happened?"

Casey didn't want to say. But also, she did. A lot. She told Dragon about waiting in the Beemer while the jerk took pictures of Paul with his date, and how afterwards they went down to Santa Monica . . .

Coming back that day, they picked up Sunset where it began at the beach. When they hit Beverly Hills, Paul turned to Casey and with a wicked smile said, "Close your eyes."

"Why?"

"Why do you need to know why?" Paul said.

"Because—"

"Because you don't trust me?"

"C'mon."

"Then do it . . ." He reached over, gently lay his fingers on Casey's eyelids, and lowered them. "You won't regret it."

The Beemer suddenly whipped ahead. They sped around curves, over hills, and weaved in and out of traffic. Paul hadn't made any sharp turns, so they had to be still on Sunset, heading towards the Strip. With her eyes closed it felt like a fantastic dream—the speed, being with Paul, the light smell of the beach still in his hair. She felt safe with him, and every time the car slowed down, she hoped the trip wasn't over. He could drive to San Francisco, Chicago, Boston—just keep moving. She heard the turn flasher go on, and a moment later the car took a left, moving slowly up a steep hill.

When the Beemer came to a stop, they were still on the hill. Paul told her he'd be five minutes, max, and to still keep her eyes shut. Casey was dying to open them, but did what he said. It seemed like he was gone an hour. She felt for a switch and lowered her window a bit. She could hear people talking the distance, in English and Spanish, and also something else—German maybe. She could smell trees and flowers—strong, sweet scents, like they were beside a huge garden.

Paul came right back, and with her eyes still shut, he led Casey into a building. She gripped his arm, wondering what was ahead. She could feel big stone tiles under her feet. They climbed a flight of stairs, also with tiles on them, and she could hear their steps echo around the hallway.

"What is this?" she whispered.

"Shhh . . . you'll see."

Casey held his arm tighter. She could smell more flowers and in the distance, bacon and eggs. Paul stopped. She could hear a key going into a door, and the door opening.

"Okay," Paul said. "Open them, now."

Casey did, and saw a room at the Chateau Marmont. A big beautiful room, with a huge bed with a thick, white comforter; a boomerang-shaped desk with a silver vase holding a purple and white orchid; and a high-tech desk chair with only three legs. Tall French doors led to a small balcony which overlooked the Strip. And just below the hotel, holding his lasso and overlooking the city was the huge Marlboro man—her god and protector.

"What do you think?" Paul said.

She started smiling and couldn't stop.

46

Casey stood tall in the shower, steam rising all around her. The water was so hot it almost hurt—God, did it feel good. The heat seeped into every pore. She lifted her head, letting the water cascade over her face, then turned around to let it coat her back. Through the thick glass shower door, she could see a polished brass sink and above it an enormous, fogged mirror with two ultra-thin vases mounted on it, each holding a yellow orchid stem. It was all so beautiful. Casey raised her arms and spun around and around as the steam and water flowed. The Boulevard was gone, and she was clean and warm.

She stepped out of the bathroom wearing a thick white bathrobe she found on the back of the bathroom door. Her skin glowed from the shower and the bathrobe was so soft and comfortable she never wanted to wear anything else. Paul was lying on the bed, and he offered her an apple slice from a bowl of fruit on a room service tray.

The slice was crisp and juicy. They even had the apples right here. The tray had more plates, all covered with metal lids. Paul lifted one, showing her a fat steak.

Casey groaned.

"C'mon," he said, "I'm from Minnesota, remember? *This* is real food."

She sat beside him on the bed, and as he cut into the steak, she piled whipped cream onto apples, strawberries, raspberries and huge blackberries. Paul may have thought his steak was great, but every piece of fruit—coated with the world's sweetest whipped cream—no way could anything be better than this.

Casey kissed Paul's cheek and said. "You're the greatest."

"Shitty way to pay for it. But what the fuck."

He lifted another tray cover. A plate of cookies.

"Oatmeal-raisin. I love these," Casey said.

"Me too."

"When I get my preschool, me and the kids are going to make these cookies all the time."

"All the time? That doesn't sound so healthy."

"Alright. Once a week, then." She stuck her tongue out at him. "As a special treat. And we'll also make healthy stuff. Banana bread, or whole wheat pizza. And you know what else, I want to have a little vegetable garden, too. The kids and me will plant tomatoes, corn, cucumbers—everything, and then, take care of them. Watch them grow. And later on we'll all get to eat what we grow. Like a farm. What do you think?"

"I think they'll love it. I think I'd love it."

"Come with me. We could get jobs together someplace."

He shrugged.

"Life here is so great? C'mon—" Casey said.

"Life sucks. But I'm not going to be dating forever. I'm going to go to college. Don't ask me how, but somehow. I saw a sign on a bus saying LA City College is like fourteen dollars a unit. That doesn't sound so expensive, right?"

"You could probably pay for a year on what you've made the last couple of nights."

"Fuck yeah. And when I get there, I'm gonna kick ass. I was good in school before all this shit. And when I finish, I'm going to go to law school."

"Really?"

"Definitely. Way I see it, everyone always gets fucked here 'cause they don't have any power. But the more power you got, the less people are going to take advantage of you. I'm going to be a lawyer for, you know, people who really need help."

Sunlight streamed through the window. Casey slept most of the day under the great comforter cuddled tight against Paul. A few times she woke up for a minute, and hearing the traffic below on the Sunset Strip, she felt her stomach tighten. This was all going to end. Now she was warm in a fluffy white bathrobe, tomorrow morning it was back to the Boulevard . . .

When she woke again, steam was slipping out from the crack at the bottom of the bathroom door. Casey pushed the door open and saw Paul at the mirror shaving, surrounded by a warm mist. He had a towel around his waist, his hair was wet, and droplets of clear water glistened all over his body. She slipped behind him, put her arms around him, stood on her toes, and rested her chin on his shoulder. Casey liked the feeling—the bathrobe surrounding her like a heavy white cocoon, her breasts tight against Paul's back. She looked at the two of them barely visible in the steamed-up mirror. She smiled at the picture. She pulled away to take another shower—and stopped. As good as she felt a second ago—now she felt ten thousand times worse. "Oh my God."

"What?" Paul said.

"Oh my God."

Paul saw Casey staring at his back. He spun around, twisting his shoulders towards the mirror, and saw it—a small purple bruise between his shoulder blades. He rubbed it, trying to make it go away. It didn't. He rubbed some more. Still it wouldn't disappear.

He backed away from the mirror, and as though his knees could barely hold him, dropped to the edge of the bathtub.

"This is it," he said weakly.

"We don't know. It could be other stuff."

"Other stuff?"

"Yeah. You and me—we're not doctors."

"You don't have to be a doctor to know what AIDS is. Hanging out for fifteen minutes on Santa Monica is all you need."

"It could be anything," Casey said.

"What?"

"I don't know. Maybe you banged up your back or something."

"I didn't."

"Or you don't remember. Or it could be like a cut that got infected and didn't heal right."

"It's not."

"It could be!"

For a second, he calmed down—the tiniest bit hopeful.

"I dunno . . . maybe . . ." Paul said, turning his back towards to the mirror again, "maybe it could be—"

He stopped cold. A couple of inches below the bruise there was another one. A little smaller. Casey felt it like an electric shock.

"Fuck!" Paul screamed. He swirled around and smashed his fist into the mirror. The glass shattered. Casey screamed. The mirror went red—and blood ran down his arm. Casey lunged for a washcloth.

"What are you doing?" she yelled. She wrapped his hand.

"What's it matter what I'm doing? I'm going to fucking die."

"You won't! You can't! We'll go for a test. There's that place on Cahuenga. Please, we don't really know."

"No. We do. We both know."

"Don't say that."

"It's the truth. I'm dead. It's just a matter of time."

"You die, I die."

"Hey, this isn't some poem. Your heart's breaking, and it feels like you're dying too—this is the real fucking deal for me."

Casey looked right into Paul's eyes. They were wet. She took his cut hand, pulled it to her lips to it and swallowed a mouthful of his blood. It was salty. But also sweet—it was Paul. She couldn't make it without him. If he was going to die, she would too. His blood was in her.

"Casey," he said, ". . . I'm so sorry."

47

At the free clinic, there was a young Asian doctor—Dr. Lee. He was in his late twenties good-looking and kind of cool. Casey and Paul sat together on the padded table in his tiny and clean examination room, waiting for him to come back with the test. She gripped Paul's hand. Casey couldn't remember praying for something since elementary school. But this was different. If Paul's test came back negative, she promised God she would change completely. She'd make up with her parents, move back to Seattle. Paul could come too. She'd go back to school. She would never sleep with a boy, or drink, or do drugs. Or anything else bad. *Just let the test be good, just give Paul this one break . . .*

The door pushed open—and Casey knew. Dr. Lee sat across from them and talked just like every other doctor. He said things like, "It's important that we look at the entire HIV picture," and "Paul, naturally, at this instant your emotions are running very high. It's completely normal. But we should take a moment to look at your situation in the context of treatment, safe sex, and what's the best way to take care of your health in the future." Paul was silent. He rocked back and forth on the table. Casey held his hand still tighter. His breaths were fast and deep, like he was trying to pull in as much air as he could.

Dr. Lee kept talking. Softly and nice. But it's easy to be nice when you're on that side of room, Casey thought. Try being like Paul over here, and you're seventeen and it's time to start thinking about dying. Try looking out the clinic window and see a street full of people who are going to make it to fifty, sixty, seventy, eighty. They're going to have millions of laughs, millions of kisses, millions of good times. They'll get to do something with their lives. Casey ached like she never ached before. She felt like she was in some kind of movie and she was playing somebody else's part—only this was real. And you couldn't walk outside into the sun and forget it all.

Dr. Lee continued talking in his caring doctor's voice, but she and Paul only heard only one word, which pounded over and over like a hammer—AIDS.

They didn't check out of the Chateau after all. This was one night they weren't going to spend on the street. Paul sat on the bed, flicking through the channels. He stopped at *Mr. Rogers' Neighborhood.*

"I used to love this show."

"Me too," Casey said.

"He's such a dork, but there's something about him that's . . . I dunno . . ."

"Real?"

"Yeah. Real. And he's not ever gonna lie to you. You can always trust him."

Paul's pager started beeping. Casey picked it up from the table beside the bed and read the number to Paul.

"It's Lodge," Paul said. "Fuck him."

Her thoughts exactly.

Casey turned towards Paul. He was staring at Mr. Rogers. A toy train was going around a track. Mr. Rogers was talking about *always, always, be kind to the people around you. It will make their day brighter, and yours.*

A few minutes later the pager went off again—this time with 911 at the end. Casey didn't care how many times the thing went off, she was never going to answer it. But then she said, "Hand me the phone."

"You're not gonna call him?" Paul said.

"Yeah, but not for what he thinks."

When Lodge answered, he was pissed he got her and not Paul. He wanted to know where Paul was. Casey felt like screaming at him. Instead she said, "He's too sick to talk right now."

"What do you mean, sick?"

She hated his voice. He sounded rich and smooth. But so what? In reality, he was just another pimp.

"Really sick. He's been throwing up all day."

Paul leaned in close to hear.

"Let me speak to him," Lodge said.

"He can't."

"Can't? Oh please."

"He's in bad shape. Listen, he needs some money for a room."

"I'm starting to get it."

"Get what?"

"The shakedown. How long are we talking?"

"I don't know. A week? He's in bad shape."

"When he's better, tell him to call me."

Paul lifted his hands and pushed them closer, to say, 'make it smaller.'

"Look, Casey said, "even a few days would help."

"Really?" Lodge said.

"Yeah."

"I'll tell you what . . . I think he's full of shit. I think you—whoever you are—is full of shit, too."

Paul heard the answer, got off the bed and paced the room. Asshole, Casey thought.

"There's one other thing," she said. "Paul wanted to let you know, if we can't get any money for a room, we might have to see if anyone's interested in hearing his story."

Silence . . . scary silence. She held her breath, too nervous to breathe. She looked at Paul. Their eyes met as they waited . . .

Finally, he exhaled and followed it with, "You give Paul a message from me, okay? You can tell him he's a fucking street hustler and there's nobody out there who'll care about his story. You tell him to get well soon, or he can forget the car, forget the biggest paydays I guarantee he's ever seen. He's going to be back selling his ass on Santa Monica with all the other hustlers, and when he comes begging to come back, I'm not going to take him—"

Casey slammed down the phone. She was shaking.

"Fuck!" She felt like crying. She hated herself. "I'm sorry."

"Don't be," Paul said. "You tried. He's just a complete asshole."

Mr. Rogers walked to the coat rack at the door and took off his red sweater. He was singing. *It's a beautiful day in this neighborhood, a beautiful day for a neighbor. Would you be mine? Could you be mine?*

Paul walked to the widow and looked out over the Strip.

"You know, I hate every john I ever did. They're all freaks. But what am I going to do, infect them?"

"You can't," Casey said.

"They deserve it."

"You can't. Right?"

"My hustling days are over. And what do I got?"

"Let's get out of here."

"Sure," he said in a whisper.

"Yeah. Come on. Let's do it."

"What?"

"Get out of here. Go to Montana."

"And do what there?"

"I'll get a job babysitting or working in a preschool. We'll be outta here."

Paul leaned his head against the balcony door.

"Come on . . ." Casey said, "let's not just sit around letting shit happen to us. We'll go and—"

"Right. Go to Montana to die. Just what I need."

"No, jerk. People live a long time with this. Ten, twenty years. Or more. That's what the girl doctor who saw me said."

"But you didn't test positive."

"It doesn't mean she wasn't right. It's a long time. Ten years ago, where were you?"

Paul looked at her. A smile came to his face—the first one she had seen in a while.

"I was seven. It was my first year of Little League T-ball. I loved it. I was pretty good. Whenever I got a home run my teammates would jump up and down like crazy and run over to high-five me at the plate . . ."

His smile faded. "A lot happens in ten years."

"It's a really long time," Casey said, "We'll make it a great ten years. They'll have a cure for AIDS by then. They gotta. And we'll be so far from Hollywood, it'll seem like some kinda dream. What do you say?"

"We're both through with dates, right?"

Casey nodded.

"So we're going to be poor as shit?"

"I'm used to it," Casey said.

"Then let's go in style."

48
Jimmy

Jimmy and Erin snaked through the mob at the SR club. Girls were swinging around poles on three stages, mind-numbing techno was cranking. At first, Jimmy didn't want to tell Erin where he got the tip—he figured he would seem like some crummy cliché, cop pushing forty dating a starlet-stripper half his age. On the other hand, it was the truth, and thanks to Dani, they had a lead which might actually go someplace. But the main reason he told Erin, was maybe, if somehow, the planets miraculously lined up, he might have a tiny prayer of a chance with her, and this time he wasn't going to screw it up by telling half-truths and leaving things out. Those days were behind him.

When he told Erin, she gave him a mischievous smile which he thought might be saying, he was yet another guy-going-gray taking advantage of the local beauties—pretty sad. But the look also could have meant that she understood what he had with Dani was only a substitute until the real thing came along.

Dani was off tonight, thank God. Jimmy scanned the crowd, trying to spot Tara. It was also time to rattle the boss' cage. Every hell had its Cerberus, and Jimmy saw Sean, who waved for them to come to his usual booth in the back room. Jimmy leaned over and whispered in Erin's ear, "After he shakes your hand, count your fingers."

Sean had a Guinness in front of him and was wearing a Manchester United jersey.

"My partner, Erin," Jimmy said.

"Moving up," Sean said.

"I feel like that every time I come in here," Jimmy said.

"Load of bullshit, mate."

"Hey. Would I pull your chain? I was thinking about you the other night."

"More shit," Sean said.

"Nah. I was watching a special on the 80's on VH1. Your old band was there."

"Jesus, that was on at three in the morning. I thought I was the only fucker in the city watching."

"Least two of us. Feel like helping one of your fans out?

"Always."

"Let's not get carried away."

Jimmy showed him a picture of Lodge. He was standing next to the mayor at some trendoid party on the beach in Malibu. Jimmy could have used a shot with just Lodge, but he figured having the mayor in the picture, would crank the pressure.

"Know this guy?"

"From the paper," Sean said.

"Nothing else?"

"Nothing."

"If you had seen him, you'd tell me, right?"

"Sure, I would. You're dating one of my girls. You're family."

Not my family, Jimmy thought.

"We've got someone putting him in here the night before he was killed," Erin said.

Good move, Jimmy thought. Completely untrue, but it would be nice to know how Sean would take it.

"Lots of people come in here, missy."

Your basic non-denial denial.

"When he came by, he ever taste?" Jimmy said.

Sean leaned back into the booth and lit a Dunhill. He shook out the match and said, "Guys, whoever told you he was in here—he's got it wrong."

"He's reliable," Erin said.

"Your guy may have seen him, missy. I sure as shit didn't."

A six-foot tall girl in a zebra print bikini came over, took Sean's bottle and replaced it with a fresh Guinness. Jimmy looked around and thought, what would happen if they did an old-fashioned raid to nail this prick for the underage girls? They'd probably bag a couple, but the prick would say, they had I.D. when he hired them, he had no idea. Jimmy could probably shut the place down. The underage girls would be given court dates which they'd never make, and the legal ones would scatter to the other clubs. The celebs would find a new hang. Two weeks later, the place would reopen with a new name. Same set-up, brand new girls. A raid would be a dumb fuck thing to do, but still, it frothed him that this asshole got away with whatever he wanted.

"How's business? Jimmy asked.

"See for yourself."

"I can. And I gotta tell you, we keep getting calls from the neighborhood, complaining about the noise, traffic, and drunks getting out at 2 A.M. and pissing on their lawns. And now they got this idea that you've got underage girls working.

For the old folks around here, that's too much." In truth, a month ago they had two calls, and both were about people pissing on lawns.

"They got their facts wrong, mate."

"That apply to the underage?"

"Absolutely."

"Seems like everyone we talk to has it wrong about you."

"Mates, I'm in the pretty girl business, not the going to jail business. I don't need that kind of headache."

"Then you don't mind if we ask around?"

"Ask away."

They got up and started for the main room, where on the center stage a redhead was on her stomach, naked and slithering like a snake.

Sean called after them.

"Jimmy, why you doing this shit?"

"Why? Because call me fucking old fashioned—but I think you should be able to go to the Chateau without someone sticking a knife in you twenty-nine times."

As he walked away, Jimmy exhaled. He thought about the autopsy x-ray that Christian showed him his first day on the case. All those stab wounds, and how the guy must've died. LA is a fucked place, and who knew what Lodge was up to, but murder is murder. Take a life, you pay the price. Jimmy wanted to know what happened, but more than that, he wanted to catch whoever did it. One way or another the perp deserved to be in jail—and he'd use everything he had to make it happen.

They found Tara as she was about to enter the dressing room. She was small and cute, with long black hair and beautiful blue eyes. Most of the young girls slather on the heavy makeup, affect the attitude, and do everything they can to seem older. Not her. She *was* young, looked young, and was playing it for what it was worth. She had just finished her turn on the pole and was holding two fistfuls of bills. Mostly twenties. She didn't look happy to see Jimmy and Erin.

Across the street, in a booth at Moon Coffee, Tara wore a leather jacket over a silver bikini. A couple of kids with large cobalt blue cappuccino cups were at by the front window, surfing the net. The place was nearly empty, and the girl who made the coffees sat at the counter typing on her laptop, her face lit by a faint blue-white light from the screen. Tara sipped a hot chocolate loaded with whipped cream.

"You know I'm a friend of Dani," Jimmy said.

"She told me."

"Then you don't mind talking to us?" Erin said.

"Nah."

"How do you like working at the club?" Erin said.

"It's great."

"Good money?"

"Most nights," Tara said.

"Looks hard, though."

"Not, really."

"How long you been doing it?"

"I just started. Less than a year."

"That's still a long time," Erin said.

"Not compared to some of the other girls."

"If you don't mind me asking, how old are you?"

"Eighteen—almost nineteen."

"Eighteen," Erin said. "Really eighteen?"

"Really eighteen. Got I.D. to prove it."

Right, Jimmy thought.

"Dani told me you might be able to help us," Jimmy said.

"Yeah, but I don't really know anything."

He slid the picture of Lodge over. "You ever remember seeing this guy."

"Nah."

Bingo. She answered too fast. She sees more guys a day than a New York subway token seller, and she shoots right back, that she never saw Lodge? No way.

"You're sure?"

"Sure."

"You know who he is?"

"Nah."

"Tara," Jimmy said, "I'm gonna ask you another question, and with this one, you gotta answer us honestly, okay? And I'll tell you why. Why is—a less than honest answer could make me and Erin do a *real* check on your age, find out exactly where and when you were born. And if by some crazy mistake we find out you're not eighteen, there could be some trouble. Now, honestly, and only between us here at this table—you do dates, right?"

She looked directly at him, then over to Erin. Erin and Tara's eyes met.

"You do, right, sweetie?" Erin said.

"I've done some."

"These dates," Erin said, "they ever involve the guy in the picture?"

Jimmy thought about jumping in, but Erin had the ball. He wasn't going to take it over the goal line—she was. He stayed quiet. So did Erin, letting the question sink in.

Tara held her cup to her lips. She looked like she wanted to speak, but couldn't do it . . .

Finally, she put down her cup and said, "I gotta go. I got my turn coming up."

She pulled her jacket zipper all the way up. But Erin slid the picture a little closer to her.

"Take another look, okay? Please."

She did. Her lip quivered the tiniest bit.

"Look," Erin said, "the world of the clubs and dating, you probably know a thousand times more about it than I do . . ." Tara smiled for an instant. "But one thing I do know is, lots of kids who come to Hollywood think they can take anything, and most of the time, they're probably right. But there's also some other stuff that they get involved with, that makes even the toughest kids say, woah, this is too much. There's stuff that goes on here that *I* feel that way about. I can't even imagine how a sixteen or seventeen year old feels. And maybe you know a girl who's tough, tough in all sorts of ways—dances with the older girls, maybe does some coke or meth' from time to time, does dates. But maybe she had a date with some guy she thought was rich and safe, but later on, the guy ends up dead. And maybe she thinks that if she says anything about the guy, the same thing could happen her. She's afraid—who wouldn't be? Now say that's the case. Well, I'd want her to know the person who killed the guy isn't some big time hit man, but probably someone who just lost it. Maybe even a kid. Who, as far as we know, could be a thousand miles away from here by now. We may never get this guy, but it's our job to find out what happened. There are a lot of jerks out there— way too many of them—who take advantage of kids. I'm guessing you've met a bunch yourself. And me and Jimmy are trying to do something about it . . . And, if it's okay with you, I want to try something. You mind?"

Tara nodded.

"Here goes . . . I'm going to count to five, and at the end of that five, if you knew the guy in the picture keep on stirring your hot chocolate, like you're doing now, but if you didn't know him, stop stirring."

Tara looked right at Erin. Not saying a word. Jimmy watched the stirrer in her hot chocolate. It was moving. Erin began to count.

"One . . . two . . ."

The stirring continued. White cream circling in a tiny whirlpool of chocolate.

". . . Three . . . four. . . ."

Jimmy glanced up at Erin and then back down to the stirrer.

". . . and five." The swirling went on.

Erin's gaze was locked on Tara. The girl's eyes were the tiniest bit moist, and it looked like she was on the edge of losing it. Erin crossed to the other side of the table and put her hand on Tara's arm. Tara truly looked her age now. Then softly, so softly that Jimmy could barely hear, she said, "He sent me out on dates."

"Sent you out?" Jimmy said.

"He got them. I went wherever he told me."

"Where'd you go?"

"All over. Nice neighborhoods . . ."

Erin and Jimmy both stayed quiet. The best interview technique Jimmy knew was after someone gives you an answer, don't rush in with the next question. Leave a gap, and half the time, the person you're asking will feel obligated to fill in that space.

A moment later, in a voice even softer, Tara said, "There's something else."

"What?" Erin said, her voice matching Tara's.

"There was something sicko about him. He sent me out on all these dates, but it wasn't only that. After I went in, he hung around and took pictures."

"Pictures?" Erin said.

"I would go inside the houses, and they were always all fancy, I was supposed to somehow get the john by a window, so he could get a picture of me and him."

"What for?" Erin said.

"He was sick. Lot's of them out there."

"Where'd you meet him?"

"Sean. Thanks a lot."

"Anything more about Lodge?" Erin said.

"Yeah. Usually after a date, when I left the john's house, he'd fuck me too. Asshole."

Jimmy looked at Tara. She was still just a kid. Jesus Christ.

"Why don't you quit early tonight?" Jimmy said. "We'll take you home."

"I can't. Sean promised to get me a part in a movie. If I don't come back, you think that's gonna happen?"

49

Jimmy and Erin sat on the same side of the coffee house table looking over his small notebook. They were the last customers; the counter girl had closed her laptop and was loading the dishwasher. Jimmy had written down all they knew. The pictures, the Sean connection, the autopsy report—everything. Erin leaned over, and with her pen, drew an arc between Tara's story and the girl with the two earrings. As she leaned in to write, Jimmy felt her breasts brush against his arm. He sucked in his breath. It was strange—tonight he had probably seen dozens of girls with their tops off. Fabulous breasts, out there for all to admire. But the tiniest brush of Erin's, wrapped in a bra, and covered by a thick sweater, had his head spinning.

50
Casey

asey looked across the Denny's booth at Dragon. The
future sucked, the past was worse. She thought time
would help her forget. It didn't. That night, the night
that changed everything, was burning inside her. And Dragon
would understand . . .

The Chateau room service guy, a Mexican kid, a few years
older than her, brought them a packed tray. Casey tipped him
and brought the food over to the bed. There was a fat steak
for Paul, some great-looking apples, a huge bowl of strawberries, a silver bowl of cream, two pieces of strawberry short-
cake, a bottle of champagne, and some sodas. The feast of a
lifetime.

On their little balcony, Paul popped the cork. It was Casey's
first time. The bubbles on her tongue felt good, and the cold,
sweet champagne sliding down her throat made her smile.
The strawberries, bright red, and full of juice, tasted even
better. Back inside, the sleek radio played an old Neville

Brothers song. The cold wind whipped her long hair behind her, then across her face and then straight back again. Paul put his arms around her waist. They swayed to the music, and then they were dancing. The guy from the Neville Brothers had the sweetest voice on the planet.

If you want me to love you, baby I will. You know that I will. Tell it like it is . . .

Casey buried her head in Paul's shoulder. They moved in a tight circle. God, it felt good. Yeah, he had AIDS, but so do lots of people. And Dr. Lee was right, people live a really, really long time with it.

Tell it like it is. Don't be ashamed. Let your conscience be your guide. Deep down inside me, I believe you love me . . .

They were going to pull through. With each other. They'd start a whole new life. As they danced, Casey caught a glimpse of the street below. People were small. The Marlboro Man was big. He was on duty as usual, having a smoke. Watching over the Strip, watching over them.

You know life is too short to have sorrow. You may be here, and gone tomorrow. You might as well get what you want. Baby, baby don't leave. Baby, Baby don't leave . . .

She felt tears rolling down her face. She and Paul would make it. They'd—

Their room at the Chateau did a fast fade. Something big was going on outside of the Denny's. Casey and Dragon looked outside. Jumper, Dog-Face, Dream and the rest were sprinting down the street.

Dragon was first out the door and Casey followed just behind. She was nervous and confused, but she knew if the other guys were running, she should be with them. She ran down off the Boulevard, turned into the Carl's Jr. parking lot—and stopped short. In front of her was a long ribbon of bright yellow police tape, pulled taut and bouncing in the wind. Cops wearing black LAPD jackets were hanging out. Pressed against the tape was a line of kids. Casey hurried towards them. Afraid. She slid between June Bug and Jumper and saw a sheet on the ground over a body. The sheet didn't cover the body entirely, and barely visible, was a tiny bit of a girl's leg, wearing fishnet stockings—Tulip. Tulip! What the fuck?! Why? Why Tulip?

Casey felt an arm slide around her waist, June Bug's. And from the other side, Jumper's. A cop in a purple polo shirt and jeans came over to them. He glanced down at a notebook. "Girl's street name was Tulip. Know her?"

"Yeah," Jumper said.

"Know anybody that would want to do this to her?"

Jumper was silent. June Bug was silent. Casey was silent too. What could she say—that there's ten thousand assholes on the Boulevard that treat them like shit? Any one of them could have done it. One more dead street kid and they could care less . . .

There was nothing to say.

A couple of hours later. The cops were gone, the police photographer had left, and the guys who worked inside the Carl's Jr. The cameramen from KABC and Fox were also gone—they both stayed about ten seconds, long enough to get a shot of the body before jumping back into their vans and heading for the next body. The yellow tape was gone. And Tulip's body was long gone.

But the street kids were still there. Dozens of kids. And where Tulip's body once lay, there were hundreds of candles—burning into the night. Spread throughout the sea of candles were just as many tulips—red, yellow, purple, and white. Casey sat on the parking lot curb next to Dragon, gripping her arm. Beside Dragon were the others from the squat. Kids from all over the Boulevard kept coming and slowly walked back and forth, weaving through the flowers and candles.

Casey was transfixed on the candles.

She turned to Dragon and said, "I just saw her. A couple of hours ago."

"She was such a good person," Dragon said.

"The best," Casey said.

"I can't believe it."

"Some john greasing you, OD'ing, getting raped, killing yourself—everyone ends up the same."

Casey looked back at the candles and kept staring at them until they slipped out of focus, making the city disappear . . . A dozen flickering, yellow ovals filled her darkness . . .

"I got so much shit I can't get out of my head . . . Never goes away, no matter what."

51
Jimmy

Tara was sleeping across back seat sleeping as Jimmy and Erin drove Sunset towards Beverly Hills. As soon as she finished her last lap dance, she found them in the parking lot. Jimmy grabbed a glimpse of Tara in the rearview mirror and thought, if you didn't know any better, you could almost believe they were a family returning late from a long trip—only the daughter asleep in the back was a baby hooker and the parents were anything but married.

Erin sat low in the seat with her black cowboy boots up on the dashboard. She looked silently out the windshield, watching the Strip slide past. Jimmy wondered what was she was thinking. In his mind one thought above all—Erin. He was looking at forty and had been through too many relationships. Some were real, like Shannon, until it wasn't. Others were about hammering down half a dozen tequilas at a party, falling instantly in lust with the cute blonde in the kitchen, and then doing everything he could to get her naked in his bed by the end of the night. He had lived with two women besides Shannon. One walked out when he wasn't ready to get married again—at least not to her, and the other, a pastry chef from Sydney, went back home after a year, breaking his heart. All those girls had faded far away—and the one of his dreams was right next to him. But she was married, and he was always going to wonder what could've been?

"Think it's time to wake sleeping beauty?" Erin said.

"Sure."

She leaned over the seat and gently touched Tara on the shoulder. "Sorry, baby. But this won't take long."

Tara rubbed her eyes and figured out her bearings.

"Go down there," she said.

Jimmy turned just past Rodeo. Two blocks later she told him to take another left. And then another.

"I think it's right around here."

"You remember which side?" Erin said.

"I'm not sure."

Jimmy slowed the car to a crawl. Tara leaned forward to look at the houses draping her arms over the front seat. At the end of the block was a 'No Outlet' sign and Jimmy circled the car back around.

"I know it's around here someplace. It had a cool door knocker."

Any other time, a line like that would've bugged Jimmy. A cool door knocker—that's a great description. Now, it didn't phase him at all. It was three in the morning, the streets were quiet, and with Erin beside him, he felt a strange calm. He was in no rush.

They drove all around the tony neighborhood, passing one huge place after another, Jimmy slowing at each one to check out the doors.

"That's it!" Tara said.

"That *is* a cool knocker," he said. A green iron dragon with its tongue shooting out decorated the front door. The dragon's spiky tail curled into a loop, forming the knocker. They were in front of an enormous Tudor-style house.

"You're sure this is right?" Erin said.

"Oh, yeah. I was here a couple of times. I wish I could remember the guy's name."

"That's okay," Erin said, "We'll get it."

"He probably gave you a phony one anyway," Jimmy added.

"See the big window, upstairs on the left?" Tara said, "that's where he got his picture taken."

"You're absolutely sure?"

"Definitely. Mark said he wished all my johns had such big windows."

Jimmy wondered where those pictures were now, and how many other johns' pictures were in the same filing cabinet.

"Thanks, sweetie," Erin said.

Jimmy didn't know if Tara even heard her. She had dropped back down and was instantly asleep again.

They dropped Tara off at a crummy apartment building on Cherokee, just above the Boulevard. On the way back to the stationhouse, Jimmy realized in all his tiredness, he fucked up.

"I screwed up," he said. "I should've gone behind the house to see if there were any cars to run the plates."

"I should've thought of it too."

"Nah. It's my bad. I'll drop you off."

"I'll come," Erin said.

Jimmy was about to go into how it was his mistake, and he should do it—but then he told himself, *shut the fuck up. She's coming.*

"Really?" he said.

"I don't mind."

At this time of night, it took fifteen minutes to shoot back to Beverly Hills. They went down the alley behind the house and by the garage there were two Mercedes. Of course. Erin wrote down the plates and as they drove away, Erin turned to Jimmy.

"You tired?"

"Yeah. Sure."

"That's okay, then . . ." she said.

He turned to her. She was barely visible in the dark. A floodlight mounted on a garage cast a soft white light though Erin's blonde hair and fell onto the side of her face. She was looking into the distance, as though not only her gaze, but her thoughts were someplace else. She was as beautiful a woman as Jimmy had ever seen.

"What is?" Jimmy said.

"Nothing. Just wanted to know if you wanted to get a cup of coffee or something?"

52

Instead of staying at the 24-hour Peet's, they took their coffees and drove to a little park on Sunset. Dawn was still a couple of hours away and they had the place to themselves. They sat on an old-fashioned iron bench and looked across a small field of closely cropped grass, and beyond it, framed by gently swaying palms was the Beverly Hills Hotel. The hotel was from Hollywood's glory days in the twenties, Spanish-style and lit by a wash of green and amber lights. Every window was dark. This was as calm as LA got, as peaceful as it would ever be.

"It's pretty," Erin said, sipping her coffee.

"You been in there?"

"Once. I went with a doctor."

"Not bad." Of course she would be dating doctors.

"It's not what you think," she smiled. "For work. Back when I was going to be a nurse."

"You could still be doing that. Most cops, they don't have any other choices."

"Or they think they don't."

"Right."

"You ever wish you were doing something else?" Erin said.

"Sometimes . . . There's days when I can't stand it. It's like we're emptying the ocean with a teaspoon. But even worse than that . . ." He stopped.

"What?" she asked.

"Just . . . my son. And if that doesn't make you feel like a failure, what will?" The instant he said it, Jimmy wondered what was wrong with him—yeah, it was true he felt that way—every day—but he had never told anyone before how he really felt.

"You're not a failure," Erin said.

"I dunno."

"You're not. You can't think that way. I know. Because I had the same kind of thoughts myself. All the time. After my baby, I kept thinking everybody else out there can produce a normal, healthy baby. What's the matter with me?"

"But that's not right. You know that."

"Sure, in your mind you know it. But deep down inside, you know you're a complete failure. When the baby was alive, I had a focus, a mission. Everyday I was at the hospital. All I thought about was, how do I make his short life better? What can do I for him today? And I think I was pretty good at it. But when he died, you're left all alone. Your failure. And then feeling that way back on the street . . ."

"Seeing the shit."

"Seeing the shit. And at the same time, thinking about my beautiful baby. Take in the shooter, the guy bloodying his wife. Drag yourself home. Rick's a good guy. But he's in his own world. He's do anything but talk about our baby. If I brought him up, Rick would change the subject. So I learned not to. I just tried to sleep and forget. But it's so hard to sleep. When you finally do, and the alarm goes, getting out of bed is the last thing you want to do. But two things happened to change all that."

"What were they?"

"The first was, as crazy as it sounds, I was found a kind of strange comfort on the streets."

"Helping?" Jimmy said.

"Yeah. A thirteen-year-old girl is raped by some horrendous animal down her block. The perp is in jail, but nobody cares about the girl now. Not her own family, and definitely not Child Protective Services. I stop by, we have a Coke, just talk. She's incredibly grateful and I feel like I'm doing something. Or the little Guatemalan kid whose dad was shot in the liquor store on Gardner, I would go by and see him too. It's not changing the world, but it is something. To them and to me."

"What's the second thing?" Jimmy said.

"The second is, this case . . . and working with you. I wish we'd been made partners a long time ago."

So did Jimmy. Like nothing else.

They sat in silence for a moment. Jimmy felt like a teenager, a knot in his stomach. After all this time, had he finally drawn the royal flush? He looked over at the hotel and then back towards Erin. She was looking at him. He brushed a strand of hair off her face. Her eyes held his. He didn't know what they were saying. . . . He leaned over and put his lips on hers. She pulled as close as she could—and then closer, like she had found what she wanted and was never going to let go. Jimmy always wanted to feel this way—it was the first kiss of the rest of his life.

53
Casey

The sky rolled out of black into electric blue and Casey and Dragon were the first customers into Starbucks when the UCLA kid unlocked the door. Casey needed her big green chair, to fall into its felt, be sheltered by the soft cushions. The kid gave them the coffees for free, and in huge mugs. She slipped into her chair and Dragon sat on the couch next to her. The chair's soft prickles on her back felt good— about the only thing in her life that did. Tulip filled her head and would always fill her head. Dragon looked into Casey's moist eyes. Casey took a sip of the coffee. It warmed her. But did nothing for the pain.

"It's more than Tulip," Casey said. "It's Paul . . . and the jerk . . . It's everything."

And then Casey told her . . .

Back at the Chateau. Casey was dancing with Paul. The Neville brothers were singing their sweet song.

You know life is too short to have sorrow. You may be here and gone tomorrow. You might as well get what you want. Baby, baby don't leave. Baby, baby don't leave . . .

It was their last night in the great, soft bed. Casey jumped in first, still wearing the bathrobe. Paul was still on the balcony, looking down over the Strip. He took a big swig from the champagne bottle. Casey had drunk only a little, but Paul had almost finished it off. Tomorrow they would be on their way.

"Coming?" she said.

"In a second."

They would travel together. It would be like being married. Not really married, but sort of. Live together, cook together, and if Paul wasn't seeing anyone, sleep every night in the same bed.

She fell asleep. At some point, she woke up as Paul kissed her on the forehead and said, "I love you, Casey." The words surged through her veins like wave of heat, and she slipped back to sleep.

Bright rectangles of light shot through the French doors, stretching across the carpet. Casey was alone in bed, but heard dripping water in the bathtub. She slid off the sheets, pulling the bathrobe belt tight, and opened the bathroom door. And saw Paul in the bathtub, the water crimson with blood. She screamed and raced to him. His head was just above the water. She yelled his name. But nothing. She dropped her arms into the water and shook his head. Nothing. She shook him again. Still nothing. She lifted Paul's arm and saw a jagged cut on his wrist, and on the other, the same thing. She called his name over and over and over again.

She sat on the floor, her knees pulled to her chest and her arms wrapped tight around them.

She stayed that way. She had no idea how long. She felt as though someone was sawing into her heart, her guts. A pain that would never get any better. Then she saw it. Beside the bathtub was the razorblade Paul had used. It was tiny, like it had come from a disposable razor. It was stained with Paul's blood. Casey slowly rolled the razor in her hand. It had to be sharp enough to take care of more than one person. Home was worthless. Asshole father. A mother who cares more about her jerk boyfriend than her own daughter. Come to Hollywood, get raped by Dennis, get raped by his disgusting friends. Sleeping in a freezing construction site. Have to suck dicks. All shit. What good was there anywhere? . . . Paul. All she had was Paul. And now what? Nothing. Take the razor. Be brave. It was on her wrist. It doesn't feel so bad. It doesn't feel like anything at all. Just push down hard and slice across. Go. Use it like he did, and that's the end of the shit and the end of the pain. It has to be better than this. It couldn't be worse. Go . . .

The telephone rang. Casey looked up, the spell broken. The razor was pressing down on the vein on her wrist, about to break through. The phone rang again. She let it ring until it stopped. She looked at Paul in the bathtub. Still so cute. She put the blade in her bathrobe pocket.

Night came. Casey was in the exact same place. Hours ago, the maid had knocked and Casey said they didn't need anything. A lady from the desk downstairs knocked and asked when they were checking out. She said 'tomorrow,' and that was fine with them. The telephone rang a bunch more times, but why should she answer it? Who did she want to talk to? Who on the whole planet was really going to care that when they opened the door in the morning, there would be two dead kids and not one?

She went over to the tray on the bed for what was left of the strawberries—strawberries that they shared last night. She wiped the meat residue off Paul's steak knife and cut a piece of apple. And then she went back to where she felt best, sitting on the cold tiles, beside the bathtub. She reached in her pocket for the razor. It felt good, having it there. She pulled her knees tight against her chest again.

There was a knock. She ignored it. But the knock came again.

"I told the lady before, we have everything we need."

She heard noises. A key went into the lock. The door opened and shut, and before she could get up, standing in the bathroom doorway was the guy with the blue Mercedes—Mark Lodge.

He looked at Paul. "Oh, shit."

Casey scrambled to her feet.

"What did you do?" he yelled.

"What did *I* do? What do *you* do? Pimp kids, then fuck them over."

She hated him. She pushed past him, heading for the bedroom. As she flew by, Lodge grabbed her arm.

"Where you going?"

Casey couldn't even look at the asshole. She pulled away from him. She was out of here.

"Where you going?" he said again.

Then she got it. She wasn't going. Not yet. She grabbed the phone.

"What are you doing?"

"Calling 911. Gonna tell the cops what you did. What you did to Paul."

There was fire in his eyes. But a second later, he seemed calmer.

"Look," Lodge said, "let's talk this through."

"What for?"

"So we don't do anything dumb."

"Dumb?" Casey said.

"Let's look at the facts. You're here with a dead boy in the bathtub. How do you think that looks?"

"Know something?—I don't care! I'll tell them the truth."

She leaned over to dial.

"And you think they're going to believe you had nothing to do with it?" Lodge said, getting angry again.

"I don't care. I don't fucking care!"

Lodge went over to her. "Give me the phone. Come on—"

Fuck him.

"Give it to me!"

Fuck him. She punched the numbers. It was ringing.

"I said to give it to me!"

He lunged for the phone and jerked it out of her hand. He slammed it back down. As Casey reached for it again, he thrust her down hard onto the bed with a strong open palm. Her head fell onto the room service tray, sending apples rolling to the floor. Casey jumped back to her feet.

"Take the phone!" she yelled. "You gonna take every phone in the whole city? The cops are gonna know what you did to him. How you killed him, you pervert!"

"Fuck you, you little whore."

"Little whore?—now we're talking about something you know all about. How many other kids you pimping? How many other kids you kill?"

She took a wild swing at him. He grabbed her fist before it hit, and took Casey by both arms and threw her back down, slamming her head against the bed backboard. The pain was sharp. She could feel her blood. "Help!" She yelled it as loud as she could. When she yelled it with Dennis, it didn't do shit. But now she was in a fancy hotel. This time it would work. She started to shout again—but Lodge grabbed a pillow and threw it on top of her face. She screamed, or tried to scream. Barely anything came out. Lodge lay on top of her forcing the pillow down. The louder she tried to yell, the harder he pushed.

"Going to shut up now?! Going to shut up?!"

She was never going to shut up. She fought to break free—trying with everything she had to somehow get out from under him. But he was too strong. The pillow was coming down harder. She needed air. She couldn't scream any more. She couldn't breathe any more. He kept pushing harder. Air. She had to have air. And once she got it, she would scream and scream and scream until someone came.

Air wasn't coming. She struggled, but he had her pinned. Her fingers spread out fighting the pain. Then they felt something. The steak knife in the sheets. She hated this asshole. He killed Paul and now was going to kill her. She lifted the knife—and drove it into Lodge's back. His mouth popped open with an awful groan, and he let go of the pillow and reached back to take the knife out. Casey gasped for air. Lodge was still stretching for the knife—but before he could get to it, Casey did. She pulled it out and then rammed it in again. And again. And again. And again.

She slid from under him and scrambled off the bed. Blood still oozed out of Lodge's back onto the bed. Her hands were covered in blood. She hated herself. She was fifteen and a murderer. But she had to get out. For her—for Paul.

Casey stood at the bathroom sink. The bar of burnt-orange Neutrogena getting slimmer as she scrubbed the blood off.

She threw water on the back of her head, cleaning off the blood from when Lodge slammed her into the backboard. It would be dawn soon, and it seemed like she'd been washing up forever. The one thing that asshole was right about—no one would believe her—no one. And there was still blood on her—Lodge's, Paul's, and her own.

She cleaned everything off she could, then washed down the area around the sink. She looked at herself in the mirror. There was water all over her face, but no blood. She pushed her hair back looking for more. Only water.

She headed for the door. But then stopped. Casey looked over at Paul. Her last look at him. She kneeled down beside the bathtub. More than anything, she wanted him back. For an hour—ten minutes—*one minute*—just to tell him what a jerk he was. They could've gone off together. He didn't have to do this. Why did he abandon her like this? But also, she wanted that minute to tell him how he was everything in the world to her. She leaned over the red water, put her lips to his cheek, and said, "I love you."

Casey opened the door a crack and looked down the hall. No one. She found a door that led to the driveway. She glanced up at the Marlboro Man, cool, calm, and together—completely unlike her—and started running. Down the hill and into Hollywood.

As she finished telling her, Casey lifted her head and saw Dragon looking at her with a look she had never seen on Dragon before. Of confusion or shock—both, maybe . . . But of course Dragon would look that way—how often does the girl next to you tell you she killed someone?

"He deserved it, right?" Casey said.

"Definitely," Dragon said softly.

Casey then felt an emptiness, a loneliness in every pore of her body. But telling everything somehow made her feel the tiniest bit better. She was very tired and the chair was nice. So soft, so comfortable.

54

Casey woke up when someone dropped down on the green chair's arm. She opened her eyes to see Dog-Face. Where was Dragon?

It was pouring outside, and Dog-Face was soaked. Water from his coat ran down the chair to Casey's jeans.

"What's that?" Dog-Face said.

Casey didn't answer. She was too tired.

"Over there," he said.

Casey looked at the counter and the UCLA cutie was letting Dragon make a phone call. Dragon saw them, hung up and came over.

"Calling in late for school?" Dog-Face said.

"Yeah, right."

"Who you calling?"

"What is this?" Dragon said, sounding angry.

"I just asked who you calling?"

"I called the hospital where Mary is."

"But you didn't talk to anyone?"

"You paranoid or what?"

"What they say?"

"I got a machine. The message said it's too early to call patients."

"And you really thought they were gonna let you speak to her?"

"Yeah. Why not?"

Dragon got pissed. "I tried something. It didn't work, so what? Hey, I don't need this." She looked over at Casey and headed for the door.

Casey rubbed her hands over her face, pushing the heels of her palms into her eyes. It was starting all over—the same people, the same shit.

When Dragon reached the glass doors, she looked back at Casey.

"Doggie, you can be such an asshole," Casey said, leaving the chair.

She'd rather be out in the rain with Dragon than inside and dry with Dog-Face. Any day.

55
Jimmy

Jimmy could hear the shower running. He stretched under the blankets and looked around the hotel room. It was almost as if no one had been here last night. Two unopened Pellegrino water bottles were on the dresser. The TV armoire door was sealed tight, and so was the mini-bar. But he *was* here—and he couldn't believe that the woman you hope—pray—dream—will be in your arms—actually was. That your imagination doesn't match reality. She wanted to be with you as much as you with her. That her skin was softer than you could have imagined, her kisses had more heat than you could've imagined.

When they were making love, for a second, he felt a sharp pain between his shoulder blades—her nails. Digging in. Not letting go. She apologized, but she didn't have to—if he had nails that weren't so short, he would have done the same thing. And for the first time that he could remember—when he woke up he didn't hear the same chorus he heard every morning for years—I hate my life. It was gone.

Jimmy didn't want to check his beeper. He did it anyway. He rolled onto his stomach, and stretched his arm down to the carpet to retrieve the pager. To see what misery awaited him, what was going to be the boot to kick him out of heaven.

A message. Shit. He pushed the button to retrieve it, then he felt a weight on his back. Erin. With her hair still wet, and wrapped in a towel, she lay on top of him. Her legs matching his, her head on his back, her lightly freckled arms draped over his.

"Forget the beeper," she said.

"My dream." He let it drop back to the rug.

"I'll make a deal with you," Erin said.

"Accepted."

"You haven't heard it yet."

"I still accept. What is it?" Jimmy said.

"We turn off the pager. Turn off the phone, bolt the door and just stay here."

"Till when?"

"Till the hotel runs out of food."

She kissed the back of his neck, then his shoulders, and then the top of his head. He turned and found her lips.

She slipped off.

"Better check the beeper, detective," she said.

He pushed the button.

"What's it say?"

"My deep cover."

"You have one? On this case?"

"I should have told you, but . . ."

"But never tell *anyone* about a deep cover," Erin said.

"You're not anyone. I'm sorry. Her name's Robin English and she's hanging out with the street kids. She's new, couple of months out of the academy, so nobody knows her face."

"How's she doing?"

"Don't know. But she wants to meet tonight."

They pulled onto Sunset. Rain was crashing down, slowing the traffic to a crawl. Jimmy glanced to the side and saw Erin staring out the window.

"You okay?" he said softly.

"Just thinking. You know, about Rick."

"What are you gonna tell him?"

"For now, that I worked all night, and had court in the morning. It wouldn't be the first time. Only usually, I sleep in the benches outside the third floor courts."

"It's tough."

"The writing's been on the wall for a while. It wasn't going to last. But sure, it's still tough."

She lit a smoke. And Jimmy knew he had to deal with it too. But strangely, he sort of knew the way it would all go down—there are people you know forever but don't ever truly know—his dad for example, and then there were others you just know everything about. Dani was like that. She wasn't going to do cartwheels when they broke up, but in her heart she would get it. And in Jimmy's heart, he prayed that she would get out of all this shit which was making her so unhappy. Become that teacher, maybe even in LA. Then she could still chase the dream, and if the stars miraculously lined up, he might see her in a sitcom or even a movie. Someone as great as Dani deserved some like her, someone her age, and ready to go the distance. And maybe he'd get a birth announcement from her some day. Was it going to be easy—no way—he could already feel all the pain and heartache, but they both knew what they had was never going to really last.

Erin ran her palm down the side of his face, maybe reading

his mind. He nodded, and then dialed his cell to check in with Charles. He gave Jimmy the latest: Tulip's murder.

Jimmy felt it like a punch. She was a good kid. Yeah, she was a tough street kid, but in her own way she was a sweet, nice girl. He told Erin and it hit her, too. Anyone who spent more than two minutes with Tulip would have the same reaction. She was a ruby in the muck, so of course, some asshole greases her.

"Who you with?" Charles said.

"Erin."

"You guys getting anyplace?"

"For once, yeah."

"Well hurry up. This shit's bad," Charles said. "First the mayor's pal, then, a day later, that hustler kid Saint Paul, and now Tulip. Fucking Wild West time."

"Wait a second. Paul too?"

"New case. The kid committed suicide."

"I just heard that name."

"Well it's too late to interview him," Charles said.

"Where'd he off himself?"

"Your favorite spot—the Chateau."

"And he's smoked the day after the mayor's buddy?" Jimmy said.

"I told you—it was a suicide."

"Fuck me . . ."

56

It was leaking all over in the morgue. Jimmy thought it was bizarre that a basement could have so many leaks, but walking down the dimly lit corridor, you needed an umbrella. But almost everyone here was dead, so it wasn't going to bother them. He and Erin squeezed past a long line of parked gurneys, dodged some major puddles, and finally reached Christian's office. The radio was on and playing opera of all things. Some diva was belting it out; whatever was happening in her life, she sure felt the passion. But Christian was gone and his secretary's desk was empty too.

"Tough life," Jimmy said. He looked up at the clock. It was ten-fifteen. "Coffee time. Can't miss that."

He dropped into the secretary's chair and reached for the computer mouse.

"Think it's okay?" Erin said.

"He won't mind. We're buddies."

You didn't have to be Bill Gates to figure out the morgue

computer. Jimmy was sure it was this simple for a reason—if the best secretary job in LA was sitting outside the office of the president of some movie studio, this one, corpse-adjacent, had to be the worst. They didn't get the cream of the crop down here. Erin leaned over his shoulder as he scrolled through the records of each day's new arrivals.

"There," Erin said. She pointed to the top of the screen, where Paul was listed. Jimmy clicked on his name, and the details came up.

"Woah. Jackpot."

"Hey! What the hell are you doing?" he heard behind him.

Jimmy turned around and saw Christian, Starbucks cup in hand, rushing towards them.

"I rang the bell for service, but nobody came."

"You can't do that, Jimmy."

Then Christian glanced at Erin. He held the look, a second more than he should, and Jimmy saw his chance. Jimmy introduced them, and Christian gave Erin his best 'I'm interested' smile. But he put his interest on hold long enough to stretch past Jimmy and click the screen back to the desktop.

"Can't go in there, kids."

"Why not?" Erin said.

"Because they're our records."

"I didn't know they were restricted from the LAPD."

"They're not," Christian said.

"So we can see them?" Erin said.

"You can. But you have to go through channels." He was getting a lot less interested.

"Christian," Jimmy said, "those files—they honest?"

"What kind of question is that?"

"Straight one. Are they?"

"Yeah, they're honest."

"Then let me ask you something. A kid named Paul McCloskey—you remember him?"

"Vaguely."

"Vaguely?"

"We do a volume business here."

"Well, he supposedly dies the day after the mayor's pal, "Jimmy said. "And you know what the particulars were?"

"Tell me."

"According to the sheet, not only did Paul die the very next night, but it was at the very same hotel. Different room, but same floor. That's one hell of a coincidence."

"What are you saying?"

"You tell me—what do you make of all this?" Jimmy said.

"A kid kills himself? Happens as often as you go to Starbucks. We don't exactly send out press releases for cases like that."

"So everything's copasetic on his case?"

"Sure."

"You know what Paul did for a living?" Erin said.

"No idea."

"He was a hustler," she said.

"So?"

"So, Jimmy said, "I think it's too much of a fucking coincidence. You'd have to be some sort of idiot to believe that kind of coincidence."

"Tough shit, Jimmy—that's the way it went down."

"That's what the computer says, that's what you say. I'll tell you what I think—I think our boy may have died in the *same* room as the mayor's buddy. And then someone moved him."

"Come on."

"Come on? Hey, once the body is taken in for an autopsy, it doesn't require a Watergate-sized cover-up. It just requires the coroner to say the kid died twenty-four hours later. Who's gonna care about a tiny, little, truth-stretch like that? Now everyone who watches the eleven o'clock news doesn't have to hear how the mayor's best buddy was whacked by an underage gay hustler who then goes into the bathroom and kills himself."

"Finished?" Christian said.

"Yeah, I'm finished."

"Well I got news for you—the kid hustler, maybe he *was* there. I don't pick up the bodies, they just come in and I do them. As for the time and date of death—that's a guessing game.

"Bullshit it is."

"It can be."

"You're the hotshot," Jimmy said, "You can Goddamn well figure out the time. It's only a guess when someone wants it to be."

"Kids, listen to me—Lodge was killed by a B-pos' southpaw. Paul's a righty. And his blood is O. Yeah, he might have been in the same room—not that I told you that—but take my word for it, Paul didn't do the kill.

57

The wipers slapped back and forth. The windshield became obscured in a wave of rain, and with the passing of the wipers Olympic Boulevard, gray and covered in a river of water, appeared again.

"Moving bodies, that's pretty wild," Erin said.

"How many more times can we strike out?" Jimmy said.

"Lodge's body stays, but Paul's moved?" She rested her head on her palm and looked out into the heavy rain.

"And what was Lodge doing with him?" Jimmy said. "He liked girls—at least that's what Tara said—that's what we thought."

"Except for Cat's book. That was full of boys, and he was plenty interested."

Erin lifted her head. "Jimmy—what if it wasn't the boys in the book he was interested in. But just having his *own* book?"

Another wave of water hit, and the city disappeared.

58
Casey

H alf-jogging, half-walking, Casey and Dragon hurried down Santa Monica Boulevard. Water rushed down the sidewalk; drains were backed up, creating small lakes at every corner. They were soaked through, and half the cars that passed shot back waves of water drenching them further. At the same time, they saw it—Circus-Circus Books at the end of the block.

There were more magazines in here than anyplace. By the door was a high cashier counter where a young gayboy, wearing a leather vest and a white t-shirt, watched over the store. He was incredibly interested in the boys who went into the gay porn section, but could care less about what happened in the rest of the store. As far as he was concerned, you could hang out and read all day.

Casey slowly walked past the racks. Elle, Vogue, Marie-Claire—the girls with the perfect faces—perfect bodies section. She was never going to look like that, never going to have that life. She found the travel mags. On the cover of

Travel and Leisure was a kayaker on a lake in British Columbia. It wasn't Montana, but it looked pretty close to what she thought Montana would look like. As Casey flipped though the pages, she felt herself salivate. She couldn't believe it. How stupid can you get? Salivate over a guy or something. But over a field of wildflowers? Casey looked behind her and saw Dragon leafing through *People*. On the cover was *The 50 Most Beautiful People*. But she wasn't looking at the pages. She was staring at Casey.

"Find Dog-Face's picture in there?" Casey said.

"Oh, yeah. There's a shot of him relaxing with a Corona at the Fountain."

"He can be an asshole sometimes," Casey said. "Don't worry about it."

Dragon gave her a 'I know' shrug.

Casey liked her. She wasn't like the rest. Smarter, more together. And not stupid enough to do what she did. Dragon would've run right past Lodge—straight out the door. Not her. She had to go at it with him . . . She heard Lodge's groan as the knife went in. The feel of the blade sinking deep into his flesh. It was haunting her . . . She tried to shake it—but her hand still held the knife, wet with blood.

The rain was gone, or at least they thought it was gone. After hours in Circus-Circus, Casey and Dragon had just reached the Fountain's rusted fence when it started pouring again. They squeezed under the fence and made a run for it, splashing across the yard which the rain had turned into a shallow pond.

Casey pulled back the boards on the crumbling porch, dropped down into the basement—and landed in a sea of mud. It covered her shoes, past her ankles. Before she could call back a warning, Dragon had dropped down beside her. Dragon instantly lost her balance, rocked backward, and just managed to grab one of the wood pillars and catch herself from falling into the muck. Water, cold and miserable, was streaming in all around, and Casey couldn't wait to get inside.

She pulled herself up through the living room floor and Dragon followed. Everyone was there—Jumper, June Bug, Dream, and Dog-Face. They were sitting on the sleeping bags and talking rat-a-tat-tat, like she and Dragon showed up in the middle of a fight. But as soon as they came through the hole, the talking stopped. All at once. Casey looked around. Everyone had strange looks. Something bad happened.

"Hey," she said.

"We were worried about you," Jumper said.

"I was with Dragon. Doggie didn't tell you?"

"You know, everything's crazy now," Jumper said. "Paul's gone. Tulip gets it, and there's like a thousand cops still trying to figure out who taxed the mayor's buddy."

"That's the truth," Dream said. "The Boulevard's gonna be all fucked up till they get that guy."

"Something was wrong, Casey thought. Definitely.

"They didn't bust the squat?" Casey said.

"They didn't have to," Dog-Face said.

Casey looked around. Everyone was staring at them. Did they know?

"What are you talking about?" she said.

"We got a cop right here. Remember. I told you that before," Dog-Face said.

"On the street?"

"No. Here. Right here"

"Right."

"He *is* right," Jumper said, "For once in his fucking life, Doggie is right."

"What?" Casey said.

"Know how you and Dragon were hanging at Starbucks before I came in?" Dog-Face said. "And remember how you guys looked at me like I had fucking AIDS when you saw me?"

"What are you taking about?" Casey said.

"I'm talking about two bitches all happy together, and then I come, and they take the fuck off. But when I showed up, what was Dragon doing? . . ."

Casey didn't answer.

"Come on, tell me—"

"What's it matter?" she said.

"I'll tell you what she was doing—she was on the phone. I ask who she's calling. She says the hospital where Mary's at. So after Dragon gets all pissed and blows, and you follow her, I go up and ask if I can make a call, too. Guy's okay. He says, yeah. I hit the re-dial button, and guess what? No hospital. I get a tone for a pager. She didn't call the hospital. She was checking in. She's a fucking cop!"

"You saying I'm a cop?" Dragon said.

Casey looked at Dragon. She was a kid. Just like them.

"Come on, Dog," Casey said, "you're unbelievable."

"I'm unbelievable? Hey, we've been fucked by her!" he yelled. "*I've* been fucked by her."

"Dog, man, I'm *not* a cop!" Dragon shot back.

Casey didn't know what to think. Dog-Face was an asshole. Most of what he said was complete bullshit. But then, Casey became scared. She knew it wasn't true—but what if it was?

"We're all fucked," Dog-Face said. "I didn't trust her from the first day she came here."

He stood up and started towards Dragon.

"I'm not a cop—you're crazy!" Dragon yelled. She was shaking.

"She is," Jumper said, "in here spying on us."

"Guys—she's not!" Casey screamed, and turned to Dragon. She couldn't be. No way . . .

But then it hit her—Dragon *did* make that call when she was sleeping. Calling the hospital? No street kid would ever call a hospital—they'd just go. And when did Dragon show up on the Boulevard—right after she killed the jerk . . .

At that moment, Casey knew that Dragon *was* a cop.

She was fucked. She had told her everything. *Everything.*

"Jumper, I'm not." Dragon said, her voice lower, trying to calm things down. "Fuck you're not!" Dog-Face yelled.

He pulled his knife from his boot.

"You're crazy, Dog!" Dragon yelled back, staring at the knife.

"Cops don't have real enough shit to do?" Jumper said. "You gotta come here and fuck up our lives?"

"I'm not, man! I'm not!"

"I think you are."

"Dog—I'm not!"

"Gotta spy on a bunch of kids? Admit it—you're a cop." Dog-Face yelled.

Casey looked at his face—the knife—Dragon. The knife shot up from Dog-Face's side and, yelling, "Don't fuck with me!" he lunged at Dragon.

Dragon jumped out of the way, but Dog-Face still sliced her right arm with it, slashing a gash from her shoulder straight down to her elbow.

Dragon screamed in pain. Her shirt instantly ran red.

Dragon staggered backwards, holding her bleeding arm— when running up behind her was Jumper. He grabbed Dragon around her waist, so the next time Doggie stabbed, he wouldn't just get her arm.

Dragon screamed, "Don't do this! Don't do this. Please!"

Casey knew they were going to be her last words.

Doggie was going for her—all rage. This time he'd ram that knife in Dragon's throat, her stomach, her heart.

Paul. Tulip. And now Dragon?

"Doggie!" Casey yelled with everything she had, "Stop it, man!" She ran at him—and threw her whole body into his chest, dropping him to the ground. And in that instant, Dragon sank her teeth into Jumper's arm.

"Fuck!" he screamed, and let Dragon go.

Dragon spun around and kneed Jumper hard into his balls. He popped over in pain. Dragon scrambled across the room and jumped through the hole in the floor. As she dropped down, she threw a look back at Casey—and then Casey ran as fast as she could, past Dog-Face, past Jumper, past them all, and dropped through the floor after Dragon.

Dragon was a few feet ahead of her, pushing through the mud. She could see Dragon struggling to get traction, ducking under low beams, and grabbing the wood pillars to pull herself forward. Casey could hear somebody—it had to be Dog-Face—jumping down through the floor just behind her. Out of breath, Casey struggled through the mud. Dragon glanced back over her shoulder, and looked surprised to see Casey. But she waved her hand for Casey to catch up. Casey knew they were after her too.

Casey tried to run faster—but her feet were slipping. Dog-Face was just behind her. Fuck the mud. Fuck it all. She quickly looked back. Dog-Face was getting closer. She had never seen him this crazy. Her lungs were throbbing. Her legs were running out of juice. She was freaking-out scared. Dog-Face was gaining on her—and her feet slipped out from under her, and she fell down into to the mud.

This was it. Her knees, hands, everything, was covered in mud. Stopped cold. She turned back to see Dog-Face charging her, faster than ever. *But no way was it over! Not Lodge! Not Doggie! Not anyone!* She scrambled back onto her feet, and as much as she hurt, she was back running.

Dragon was ahead, by the hole leading out. Casey now ran like she had spiked track shoes on. Dog-face was almost close enough to grab for her. But fuck it all! She reached the hole out. Dragon's good arm dropped down for her to grab. She took it and was out of the hole.

Rain was crashing down all around. Casey was just out, when she saw Dog-Face—just behind her. He jerked his body through the opening, and stood up looking for them—when from behind Dragon swung a long two-by-four board straight into his side. Dog-Face screamed and fell to the ground. Dragon raced through the rain, across the yard, and out under the fence to the street. Casey followed her to the street—running, stumbling, heaving for breath.

59
Jimmy

The car was stopped dead in traffic. The wipers shoved off another wave of rain. Erin slid the back of her palm across the windshield to clear a swath of fog, and leaned forward to try and figure out what was holding them up.

Jimmy scooped up the Chinese stress ball. He gave it a shake, and as the vibrations went up his arm, he went over all they knew for certain, and what was unproven but undeniable—like Erin's take on the book, which almost twenty years of being a cop told him had to tie in. Even by LA standards, this case—with its baby hookers, a covering up coroner, and camera-happy vic—was crazy-fucked-up. Jimmy hated wacky conspiracies, not to mention the jerks that make their living promoting them. If with Kennedy, there was another shooter along with Oswald, how come in the all the years since it happened, miraculously, not one person ever came forward? No way. People's mouths are too big. Same for O.J.—they want you to believe that with amazing speed and efficiency, half the

275

LAPD was supposed to have gotten together and worked out a completely flawless plan to frame him, and then not a single cop spills the beans. Bullshit. Big conspiracies don't work. But little ones, with a tiny enough group, they worked just fine. He wondered if that was what was going on here.

The traffic crawled another two feet.

"Oh, that's great," Erin said.

Jimmy leaned forward to the windshield's clear spot and saw what she did. Ahead was the nastiest intersection in West Hollywood: La Cienega and Third, with San Vicente slicing through at a diagonal. A very thin truck, little more than a rolling billboard, was trying to make an illegal left turn. It was jammed in the middle of the intersection, surrounded by honking cars in an untieable knot. Of course, Jimmy thought, the one thing in traffic that didn't have to actually go some-place, was messing it up for everyone who did. The rolling billboard read, *More Police Officers. More Firefighters. More For Our Schools. YES ON 120—WE NEED IT.*

"I'm ready to vote no just on the basis of this truck," Erin said.

"Why doesn't he go into Beverly Hills and screw up traffic up there" Jimmy said.

"Casinos? That's a headache they're smart enough to skip."

Suddenly, Jimmy was transfixed on the truck. The wipers slammed back and forth and all he could see were those big letters screaming at him—*YES ON 120—WE NEED IT.* The skinny truck finally started to make the turn and Jimmy watched it go. Only now he was back at the SR club, having a Sam Adams with the kid who wrote the awful horror film scripts and spent every night down at the poker tables . . .

A rib-shattering honk blasted behind him. He wasn't moving, and a cement truck on his bumper was giving him a

500-decibel reminder. Jimmy hit the gas and shot through the intersection.

He looked at Erin, "What you just said—"

"What?"

"That's a headache they'll skip. You're absolutely right. But what about here?"

"Here the city needs the money,"

"Right," Jimmy said, "I got a buddy who drives down to Gardena every night to gamble. There's tons of people just like him. If 120 goes through it's great for them. Great if you own a casino. But would you want one of them on your block?"

"No. Who would?"

"No one would, if they could help it . . . so if you want it, you better pull out every stop. And where did we see a giant stack of casino contracts?"

Jimmy looked ahead. Traffic had cleared.

60

Jimmy ran into Circus-Circus. He figured he'd skip the gay porno and just pick up the *LA Times*. He got back to the car and it took them all of five seconds to find a full-page ad for LA's favorite proposition. At the bottom of the page, in microscopic print was a telephone number.

Erin dialed her cell, and Jimmy could hear a lady answer, "Yes on 120, how may I help you?"

"Yes, my name is Maria Abraham from the Los Angeles Times. We have a question regarding tomorrow's advertisement. Can you tell me who's your legal counsel?"

"One moment, please."

Jimmy wrapped his hands around the back of his neck, meshed his fingers together and squeezed them tight. He slowly exhaled, praying he wasn't about to bloody his nose again, smashing into one more brick wall.

The lady clicked back on.

"That would be Miller and Lodge. Do you need their number?"

61

Miller was standing arms-crossed and leaning against the front edge of a battleship-sized desk. He was wearing a pink shirt, and dark suspenders decorated with grapes, wine bottles, and naked, dancing nymphs. His Century City office was so high that the storm was nearly below them. Jimmy and Erin were standing up too, and Jimmy made sure they were close enough to make Miller uncomfortable.

"You can spend shovelfuls of money on 'Yes on 120'," Jimmy said. "Run the TV ads for months, put billboards at every bus stop, make it so you can't turn on the radio or drive down the street without hearing why it's so Goddamn good for you. Get everyone to think having casinos in West Holly-wood is the secret to funding the schools, firemen, and God knows what else. And get people to vote for it. But there's going to be lots of other people pissed as hell about it. Maybe they don't think modeling LA on a shit-hole like Gardena is such a great idea. And the day after it gets voted in, there's guaranteed to be court challenges. And as sure as the sun's gonna shine, a lot of people at the top of the LA food chain are gonna do whatever they can to prevent LA from turning into some kinda Vegas wannabe. And if you wanted to make sure the proposition still flew, despite the shitstorm guaranteed to follow, what would you do?"

"Tell me," Miller said.

He looked directly at Jimmy, his eyes flat and cold. He wasn't giving anything up.

"You know what I'd do? I'd make sure that I had a situation where when LA's powerful started talking morality, going on the news and saying gambling isn't the magic potion to solving the city's problems—I could call that person, and say, 'Guess what? You're so moral? How about if we let the world in on the pictures we have of what you do in you spare time? Or if its not you personally, maybe it's your law partner, your best friend, or maybe one of the guys you play golf with. And what's that hobby—sex with kids. Somewhere, there's a hell of a book of those pictures."

"You're joking," Miller said.

"I'm not."

"Then you're delusional. You and your partner were asked—no, make that *told*—to solve a brutal murder and when you can't do it, you come up with some horse shit theory with nothing to back it up."

"Nothing?" Erin said.

"Nothing I've heard."

"We have a sixteen-year-old hooker who told us Lodge set her up so he could take pictures of her with the johns?"

"You expect me to believe that? Please."

"I wouldn't believe it myself," Erin said, "Except for one thing . . . Lodge had a taste for kids himself. He *liked* doing the dirty work. And he did the exact same thing to a girl he was setting up. Only no one was there taking pictures."

Miller shook his head. "So you've got teenage hustler with a crazy story. Great source."

"Yeah? Well, we got another source," Jimmy said. "Someone who's not a teenage hustler. Someone who went to Dartmouth, followed by UCLA Medical School—that respectable enough for you?"

Nothing from Miller. Not even a hint. Man, he was tough.

"Who?" Miller said.

"How about the deputy medical examiner."

A flash in the eyes. Jimmy was getting somewhere.

"What did he say?"

"He didn't say anything—he's too much of a political animal to give up something like that. But the records on his computer said plenty."

"What?"

"That there was another body down the hall from where they found your partner. You're following me, right?"

"If you say so."

"I say so. Way I see it—this hustler, a seventeen-year-old boy named Paul McCloskey actually dies in the *same* room as your buddy. He commits suicide. But someone moves his body to another room, and big surprise, the boy's not discovered till the next day. You don't have to be Sherlock Holmes to know something happened in there—something that led to the murder. You still following me?"

"I'm trying. But I haven't the slightest idea what you're talking about."

"Jesus. You're denying knowing anything about this?"

Miller stood silently.

"You gonna deny it under oath? I mean, we still got a job to do. And as dumb as it sounds, I still want to know who killed your buddy. I still think murderers should go to jail. And you're not giving me shit!"

Miller turned towards the window, wrapped by gray storm clouds. Not a word came from him.

"Know something—" Jimmy said. "This is your basic high-profile case. Maybe someone like KCBS or KTLA would be interested in what we've already got."

Jimmy saw Miller's hands tighten around the rim of the desk.

"Or Fox," he continued, "or KNBC. One thing we got in this city are lots of news stations, who all have three hours of news to fill every night. They'd kill for this story."

"We got the sixteen-year-old to turn," Erin said. "She may be a prostitute, but she's believable, cute, and looks her age. And she'll tell anyone we ask what Lodge had her do."

Miller's fingers let go of their grip. He pushed himself away from the desk.

"This conversation," Miller said, "it's off the record?"

"Your buddy's dead, the boy is dead, and the killer's still out there—and you're worried about the record? Is it off the record? Fuck the record! Yeah, it's off the record. Just tell me what you know about the boy and the night Lodge was killed."

"I'm telling you this strictly off the record . . ." Jesus, Jimmy thought, the Goddamn record again. ". . . Because this is a tragedy that involves a prominent member of the community, and I'd like to save his family any embarrassment."

"I get it. Now, the boy was working for Lodge, right?"

"The kid's job had certain risks."

Miller was dodging.

"*Was* he working for Lodge?"

"He worked for whoever had fifty bucks. That's Hollywood."

Miller walked over to the widows. Pellets of rain drummed across the glass.

"Look," Miller said, "Mark was having some sort of trouble with the boy. Someone drove Mark to the hotel and waited in the car. When Mark didn't come back, that someone may have had to go upstairs to find out what happened."

"And who might that someone be?"

"I can't say, of course."

"Who are you covering for now?" This guy was unbelievable. Then Erin jumped in.

"Could that someone be professionally involved with underage girls?" she said. Good call, Jimmy thought.

Miller gave a barely perceptible nod.

"And does that someone supply these girls out of a strip club he owns?" she said.

Another nod. Thank you. Sleazy Sean thought he was in business with the one guy in LA who would never yak. Think again, buddy.

"Then what happens up there?" Jimmy said.

"There may have been a situation."

"A situation? What the hell does that mean?"

"It means that some money may have changed hands to facilitate a result that was the best that could be expected under the circumstances."

"Speak English," Jimmy said.

"I have no firsthand knowledge of this, of course . . ."

"Of course."

"But five thousand dollars may have went to the desk clerk . . ."

Mr. Nehru jacket, Jimmy thought, the man who remembered nothing about Lodge.

". . . As it could have been embarrassing for Mark's family if the other body was found in the room. You can understand that, can't you?"

"How about the boy's family?" Jimmy said. "Anyone care about them? Anyone care that your partner was running teenage hustlers?"

"No one's completely clean."

"Completely clean? This is about underage kids!"

"And this is reality. Once people found out he had this connection, his phone was ringing all the time."

"So it wasn't his fault at all," Jimmy said. "He was just a prince among men. Helping LA neediest."

"You know something," Miller said, "I'm not going to take morality lectures from a cop with a crackhead kid."

Jimmy could feel his whole body tighten up.

Miller bashed on. "The story I heard is this detective's kid and his crackwhore girlfriend are up to all sorts of illegal activity—dealing the crack, using it, pulling armed robberies to pay for it. But somehow they never get arrested. The kid clearly has protection."

"That's complete bullshit."

"Maybe. Maybe not."

Miller plucked his cell phone from his desk and scrolled through the stored numbers.

"Know who's on here?"

"Tell me."

"The mayor, the police chief, the president of the city council, the publisher of the LA Times, the owners of the Lakers and Kings, and the presidents of two television networks and three movie studios. You find out who killed Mark, and you won't just be a detective any more. You'll be on your way up the ladder. You and your partner. I can *guarantee* it. You'll deserve it."

This guy had his balls in a vise and was cranking the handle. Jimmy felt like throwing his arms up in the air and screaming, 'Hey, I'm just a lowland-fucking-gorilla compared to you guys. You win!'

Instead, he said, "We gotta go."

As they headed for the door, Miller called after them, "You're still on the case. The mayor wants justice. And he wants it soon."

62

They waited in the car in the Beverly Center parking lot. The sun had just gone down and Dragon could show up in five minutes or in five hours. Erin was sleeping, her head resting on Jimmy's chest. Jimmy hoped like hell Robin had the killer made. They'd pop the perp, and that asshole, Miller, was right—he, Erin, and probably Robin too, would get their promotions. And this would all be behind him.

He was exhausted. And his head was spinning with the case. All the lies, all the sleaze, and the fuck-over-everyone bulldozer of LA money and power were never clearer. He felt like a protester standing in front of a line of tanks—you can hold them, but sooner or later, they're gonna to roll. But at this minute and in this place, he loved the feel of Erin sleeping against him, a wisp of her hair brushing his face. Dragon could take the five hours. She could take twenty-five hours.

Casey sat alone on a bus shelter bench on the Boulevard, her hands tucked between her legs, trying to keep them warm.

It was getting dark. Dragon was long gone, running off once she escaped from the Fountain. She wondered how she could have been so stupid, not figuring it out about Dragon. She hated Dog-Face and Jumper and the other guys. Well, not really, she loved them—but trying to kill Dragon—that was crazy.

She was shivering and wet, and didn't know what she was going to do. She had twenty-six dollars. Where she was going to sleep? Maybe on the loading dock at Thrifty's. It would be freezing, but at least it would be dry. In the morning she'd go down to Santa Monica. Sleep on the beach for a while. Warm up. And even though she hated the idea more than anything, she'd go back to Sunset and do some dates. Just the thought of it made her want to puke. But no money, no Paul, can't go back to the squat, cops still looking for her. Gotta make enough to get out of Hollywood. She felt like there was a hundred-pound barbell laying on her chest, and every breath was packed with pain.

A shadow fell over her.

Dragon. She knew it was coming.

Dragon didn't say anything. She sat on the bench beside her.

A tremble rolled through her—it was all over.

"Thanks for back there . . . ," Dragon said.

For the stupidest thing I ever did, Casey thought.

"I don't know where I'd be if you hadn't," Dragon said.

"How's your arm?" Casey said. It was wrapped with a gauze—but stained completely red.

"Hurts."

"Bad?"

"Kinda. Not always."

Dragon pushed her wet hair back. As she did, Casey could

see her hands were red with streaks of blood. Dragon was as soaked as Casey, and water was dripping off her hair onto her jeans.

"Casey. . . ." She stopped.

A second later, she tried again, ". . . I'm sorry."

"You're a kid! At least I thought you were."

"I'm twenty-one."

"I trusted you—I told you everything. Now what are you going to do?"

"I'm really sorry. It was my job."

"What are you gonna do?"

"What can I do? I'm a police officer."

"I can't believe it . . . What you told me, about your father. And about your stepfather, and what he did to your sister—it all sounded so real."

"It *was* real," Dragon said, "All of it. That's why I wanted to become a cop in the first place. I wanted to see jerks like him go to jail for what they did."

Dragon put her hand on the back of Casey's hair. "You and me—we're different . . ."

"That's the truth," Casey said.

"The difference is, you had the courage to get on a bus and leave. I didn't."

A tear slid down Casey's face and disappeared into all the drops from the rain. She should've killed herself when she had the chance. Every person she ever trusted—except Paul—fucked her. This can't be the way it's supposed to be.

Erin stirred and woke up. "Hey," she said. "Anything?"

"Not yet," Jimmy said.

"You want me to go to Peet's? Get us something—"

She stopped. Standing at the car window was Dragon—

Robin. Her face was dirty, with a faint streaks of blood. There was also blood all over her shirt.

"Jesus!," Jimmy said. "What happened?"

"I got stabbed." She held up her arm. The gauze was wet with blood.

"Holy shit—you okay?"

"Sorta."

She pulled open the door and slipped into the back. Jimmy was pissed at himself. He should've known better. He knew the risk, and what did he do?—let her go back in. Some boss.

"Lets go get that taken care of. Cedars is right around the corner."

"Two minutes. It can wait a little."

"It's unbelievable, what you did," Erin said. Jimmy introduced them.

"Unbelievably dumb. Managed to get cut up by a kid. Sorry."

"Come on," Jimmy said, "you went into the lion's den with no gun, no backup, no nothing. Something most cops would never do. You got nothing to apologize for."

"Jimmy, I know where Rancher is."

"You do?"

"His girlfriend had a botched abortion—she's at Cedars."

"Christ." He couldn't even imagine the horrors a Boulevard abortionist could do. "She okay?"

"Don't know."

Robin was trembling.

"Let's go get you fixed up," he said.

"Later. Please. First tell me what you know?"

Jimmy gave her everything. As he told her, he looked at her bloody gauze-wrapped arm, and then up at her face, which had aged ten years in a week, and thought—what price does a cop have to pay?

"How about you?" Jimmy said, "that girl help out? Her name was Casey, right?"

"Yeah."

"She give you anything?"

"Some stuff."

"She give you who smoked the mayor's buddy?"

At that instant, in the rearview mirror, Jimmy caught a glimpse of someone. Partially appearing from behind a thick concrete pillar, for a quick glance around, was a girl. She looked fifteen or sixteen. Long brown hair. And Jimmy would bet everything he had, that if he got closer, he would see two earrings in each ear—her blood type was B-pos', and when they'd run her prints, they'd be the ones all over the Chateau room and Lodge. The girl saw Jimmy, and ducked back around the pillar, hidden from view.

Casey leaned her head against the back of the pillar. Shaking. He saw her. They would pop her, put her in jail forever, and go home and kiss their kids, and not think twice about it afterwards.

Jimmy looked where the girl jumped back.

"I hung out with her a bunch," Robin said. "I thought she knew, and sooner or later would give it up."

"But? . . ." Jimmy said.

"But the kids made me. That's how I got stabbed. They would've killed me—but it was Casey that saved me."

"Knowing you were a cop?" Jimmy said.

"Yeah."

Robin gently rubbed her hurt arm.

"She's a good kid. Dealt with more shit than I ever could've—than anyone I ever met, could've. She was tight with Paul. They were like brother-sister, and she took it hard when he killed himself."

"Was she there? Jimmy said.

"No," she said softly, looking down at her blood-soaked gauze.

"Where was she?"

"On the Boulevard."

"She have a witness?"

"Yeah."

"Good witness?" Jimmy said. He saw her left hand massaging the gauze.

"Sure."

"But we should still bring her in to talk, right?"

He started the car.

Casey saw the car coming towards her. Dragon said she'd cover for her. Right. What did she expect? She was nothing to her. She was nothing to anyone.

The car came closer. There were three cops inside. Who would all have their pictures in the paper tomorrow morning for arresting the street scum who killed the mayor's best friend. Case solved. All over. But for once, she wasn't going to run. She wouldn't fight or scream either. She'd let them frisk her, put the cuffs on her and take her to jail. And if she told them everything, maybe they wouldn't kill her.

Jimmy stole another look into the rear-view mirror. Robin was facing forward, but her eyes were to the side—searching. They drove towards the pillar where he saw the girl.

As he went towards her, Jimmy was suddenly standing in

front of those tanks again. And anyone stupid enough to stare down their barrels was going down. Kids. Cops. Anyone. He couldn't stop it, but he could start pulling people out of their way. Beginning now.

He stopped the car. Erin looked at him. Jimmy slipped his hand across the seat and gently touched her thigh. Barely perceptibly, Erin nodded. Jimmy turned around to Robin.

"I thought you might want to walk to the ER on your own. It's only two blocks away." He passed her his badge.

Robin quickly pushed open her door. A moment later, she stood by his window.

"Thanks, Jimmy."

"Just one more unsolved LA murder. Happens every week. Stick it on the pile."

Robin walked off, an then broke into a jog towards the pillar. Jimmy called after her. "Tell her to clear out—this offer expires at midnight."

The cops' car had started again and was heading right for Casey. She hurt in every pore of her body. But it didn't matter anymore . . .

She stepped out from behind the pillar. The car moved closer.

The cop driving looked straight at Casey. She recognized him from before. Their eyes met. He held the look—and it wasn't an angry or tough guy look, like she would have expected. It was different, the look of guy who didn't seem that bad. A look that somehow said—I understand.

The car went past her, down the exit ramp.

Casey turned to Robin, a few feet away. The pain was gone.

63

Jimmy pushed the elevator button and they rode to the sixth floor of Cedars-Sinai.

"You sure you want me to come with you?" Erin said.

He thought about it. For all he had been through, Rancher was still his son, and the day he was born was the happiest day of Jimmy's life. On the other hand, having Rancher wasn't exactly an advertisement for getting involved with him. But there wasn't another person in the world Jimmy would want with him right now. So was he sure? Yeah, he was sure.

"I'm glad you're coming."

When they reached the room, Mary was awake, but barely. An IV tube was in her arm and she was even thinner than usual. Sitting on a chair beside her, his legs tucked under him, and holding Mary's hand, was Rancher. He looked at Jimmy, surprised.

"Dad?"

Jimmy felt a rush. God, one word—*dad*. For all the bullshit and pain—he *was* his dad.

"What are you doing here?" he was completely on edge. From Mary, from the rock

"I heard Mary was here. I wanted to see how she was. How you were?"

Rancher looked at him, and then turned away. Pushed out again. Erin was a few feet back, in the doorway. Now she saw the reality of his life.

Then, Rancher turned back around. "It was bad. There was blood all over the place. Tons of blood. They had to do a whole operation on Mar', but they said she's gonna be okay. We're outta here in the morning."

"Then what?"

"Dunno."

"Look," Jimmy said, "come stay with me."

"I—we . . . We can't stop."

"You wanna try?"

Rancher lowered his head and slowly rocked in his chair. Mary looked at him.

"It's gonna be hard," Jimmy said, "unbelievably hard. But I'll help you and Mary any way I can."

Rancher looked at Mary . . . Jimmy felt a shoulder brushing his. Erin had come up behind him.

"Rancher?" Jimmy said.

Rancher turned to Jimmy and softly said, "Yeah."

"Mary?"

"If Rancher comes, I'll come," she said weakly.

Jimmy felt it in his chest. He'd seen enough to know that they might only have a couple of weeks before the Siren song of crack was too much, and he'd lose them to the street again. But with Erin in the mix too, maybe they could all tough it out and somehow, someway, win. Jimmy was ready to give everything he had to make it work. And they'd be a family. It would be a fucked-up family—with drug withdrawal, heartache, misery, and pain. But at least they'd be a family.

64

Casey stood by the Greyhound station's glass doors while Robin was at the ticket window. She looked at the magazine stand and saw the same snarling woman, watching the same snowy black and white TV. Robin had her arm sewed up and bandaged. The doctor was cute and so nice. While he worked on Robin, Casey sat to the side on a stool thinking, there's a whole world outside the street—where nice people do nice things. They help people, and get paid for it. They don't break into stores, eat from the dumpsters at Mickey-D.'s, or do dates.

Outside, as the others were getting onto the bus, Casey stood to the side. A misty rain was still falling. Up ahead, were the lights of Hollywood Boulevard. Busy as ever. Through the rain, Casey saw some kids crossing Highland. They looked like Jumper, Dog-Face and Dream. Another girl she didn't know was with them—maybe somebody new. Casey turned away.

Robin handed her the ticket, and Casey thought, maybe you don't get fucked by everybody at every chance.

"Bozeman, Montana," Robin said.

"Montana," Casey answered. She loved the sound of the word.

Casey swung a small backpack over her shoulder.

"Got everything you need?" Robin said.

"Money, orange juice, and string cheese."

"And my number?"

"And your number."

She turned and headed for the bus.

Casey wanted to look back. She was dying to look back. But she didn't. She never saw Hollywood again.

My parents, brother, and family.

The John S. Knight fellowship at Stanford University, and all former and current directors, my known and just beginnings.

My students.

And most of all—to Marina Beregkaya and Misha and Sasha Guttentag.